AWAKENING THE DARK THRONE

JESSICA ANN DISCIACCA

AWAKENING THE DARK THRONE

AWAKENING THE DARK THRONE

Copyright © 2024 by Jessica Ann Disciacca

All rights reserved. No part of this book may be used or reproduced by any means, graphic, electronic, or mechanical, including photocopying, recording, taping, or by any information storage retrieval system without the written permission of the author except in case of brief quotations embodied in critical articles and reviews.

This is a work of fiction. All of the characters, names, incidents, organizations, and dialogue in this novel are either the products of the author's imagination or are used fictitiously.

Asturian House Press

Asturian House Press books may be ordered through booksellers or by contacting: Asturian House Press, 8300 Cypresscreek Parkway, Houston, Texas 77070, or online at www.asturianhousepress.com

The views expressed in this work are solely those of the author and do not necessarily reflect the views of the publisher. Any people depicted in stock imagery provided by Adobe Stock or Getty Images are models, and such images are being used for illustrative purposes only. Certain stock images © Getty Images and © Adobe Stock.

ISBNs: 978-1-959705-18-5 (paperback), 978-1-959705-19-2 (ebook)

For those who found their power and strength in the darkest of nights

NOTE TO READER

CONTENT ADVISORY: This fantasy novel contains elements that may be unsettling for some readers, particularly those who may be sensitive to themes of violence, including sexual assault. Within the realms of this fictional world, some depictions and discussions touch upon such challenging subjects. The intention is to weave a compelling tale while being mindful of our readers' well-being. If you anticipate that encounters with these themes might be triggering or discomforting, we recommend exercising caution and considering whether to continue with the story. The fantastical nature of this narrative does not diminish the potential impact of these elements, and we prioritize the comfort and mental well-being of our readers. Thank you for embarking on this fantastical journey with us, and may your reading experience be enjoyable and mindful of your emotional boundaries.

CHAPTER 1

The smell of freshly baked bread flooded the air. My stomach tightened with hunger as I watched the baker set out the golden-brown loaves. It was almost opening time, which meant the morning rush was about to descend on the marketplace, creating the perfect amount of coverage for me to get in and out of the shop with a couple of loaves hidden under my jacket.

The town was buzzing with excitement as the summer solstice preparations were in full swing. Every family was preparing sweet cakes and candies for the celebration. The farmers gathered their harvests, making their way to the town square to sell their goods for a small profit. Colorful decorations littered the streets as children flew streamers and kites high in the air. Even though the humans didn't call the celebration 'summer solstice' due to its pagan origin, which was what this was. A celebration to honor the longest day of the year.

I always found it curious why the humans chose to continue to celebrate the holidays the alfar—or elves, as the humans liked to call them—honored. Was it to mock the pagan believers, or was it to honor them in some way? Even though our worlds were separate, the elves and the humans still were intertwined whether they liked it or not.

Three thousand years ago, the light alfar created a protective border that stretched around the land of *The Frey*, which was the territory the human race occupied. Only someone of pure alfar blood was able to cross the shield. If a human wished to enter, they must be escorted by an alfar. This prevented all the flesh-eating carnivores from wiping the whole human race off the map. As payment for their protection, the light alfar's convoy would come through the towns once a month to check on the status of the humans and collect any workers they may need.

I was a half-breed. My mother was human, and my father was an alfar. In the eight years that I knew my mother, she never talked about my father. She did her best to hide my elven features while providing for us in this harsh and unforgiving world. Eventually, life became too much for her and she passed when I was barely eight.

I quickly learned how to provide for myself by any means necessary. Stealing came naturally to me. The humans didn't have much, so I only took what I absolutely needed. I tried getting a job and working for my keep, but because of my ears and eyes, most people wouldn't even look at me—let alone give me a job. My eyes were vibrant green, almost a chartreuse color which made me stand out like a sore thumb.

Though my ears weren't as long and elegant as a full-blooded alfar, they were still tipped at the ends.

Most humans ignored me, while some threatened to cut off my ears and wear them as a souvenir or turn me in to one of the alfar courts to be disposed of. Half-breeds weren't allowed to live according to alfar law. I made sure to wear hats and scarves covering my ears wherever I went.

In every other way, I looked like a human. I was of average height and had my mother's soft black curly hair and her tan complexion. I didn't shine like the alfar did. I had a slight bend in my back, just like most working humans, and my clothes told everyone my worth, which was nothing.

Thankfully, I found a group of other cast-off children and young adults that were homeless and looking for a place of safety. There were eight of us total that lived underneath St. Paul's Church in the middle of town. A kind nun, Sister Ester, took us all in one by one and gave us protection. My family knew that I was a half-breed but didn't care. They accepted me and in return, I brought them the food and goods they needed to survive.

Our newest member, Lilian Thomas, joined us three years ago. Her mother and father both died from sickness when she was thirteen, leaving her orphaned. When Sister Ester brought her to us, she instantly became my little sister.

I remember the first time I laid eyes on her. She was so scared and scarred from what had happened to her parents. She wouldn't speak to anyone and only sang to herself for comfort. Her voice, still to this day, is the most beautiful thing I have ever heard. She had become the most important person in my world. Everything I did was for her.

Ding! The bell of the bakery door rang as customers flooded the small entryway of the shop. I moved across the street, checking if I recognized anyone in the crowd. I was in the clear. I slid into the packed shop and moved from person to person, sliding my hand in and out of their pockets without being noticed. I made my way to the front of the counter, having gathered enough coins to purchase two loaves of bread and a small jar of strawberry preserves, which were Lily's favorite. I casually pushed through the crowd and exited the bakery holding the warm bread close to my chest.

After I was clear of any onlookers, I rushed back to the church before anyone could notice their money had been lifted. Sister Ester frowned upon stealing, but she knew this was the only skill I could rely on to survive. She chose to turn a blind eye when I brought my findings home to the others.

Stealing was a crime no matter what race you were. When I was twelve, I got caught lifting an apple off a farmer's stand and was punched so hard that my nose broke. When I was fourteen, I got caught lifting a bracelet off an advisor's wife. I was publicly whipped seven times.

With each snap of the whip, I could feel my flesh break and bleed, but the officer knew I was a half-breed and would heal quickly. A bonus of my elven blood. The officer tied small shards of uylerium stone, which can injure and kill any alfar, to the end of the whip. I had never felt something more painful in my life than what I felt as the shard sliced open my back. It burned and stung all the way to my bones.

The uylerium stone had its intended effect. My skin stayed torn apart and I now sported lovely scars that stretched the length of my lower back. Though it happened five years ago, I can still feel the scars burning sometimes as if the wound were fresh and raw. The punishment was brutal to endure, but it only made me more determined to become better at my craft...which I did.

I always found it a bit odd that the humans never did turn me into the alfar courts or kill me themselves for being what I was. My mother was loved amongst the townspeople back in her day. She was a healer, like her mother before her. They delivered most of the children and tended to the weak and sick. I wondered if that was my saving grace. The people's love for my mother was what kept me from the edge of a blade.

I crossed the busy morning street, heading towards the church. All the humans looked the same. Underfed, tired, and dirty. Our town didn't look much better. Old buildings that had been standing longer than anyone alive could remember. The roofs of the buildings, if you could even call them that, had holes and patches missing. The doors and woodwork of the homes and shops were full of rot and termites. The floors inside most of the homes were just compacted dirt, occasionally covered by an old rug.

Only the town's advisors lived in finer buildings. They tried to provide the humans with a sense of purpose. They enforced laws and tried to help where they could, but with resources limited and funds even scarcer, their hands were tied. The church aided the people the most in their hardships and times of need. Something I admired the religious institution for.

I descended the stone staircase to the back of the church and opened the wooden door, stepping into the damp basement of the building. My feet glided down the narrow dark hall towards our common's areas. The rooms were small and felt cramped most of the time, but this was home. I took off my jacket and shoes before approaching the others who were most likely eagerly awaiting the breakfast I had brought.

The door opened before I could reach for the handle. Nil, the youngest of my adoptive sisters, smiled at me with a wide grin. Her long blonde hair was braided into two pigtails with colorful ribbon and flowers placed throughout. Her deep brown eyes squinted at me as she jumped up and down at the sight of bread.

"That smells yummy," she said, reaching for my arm.

"It took all the strength I had not to eat a loaf all by myself on the way home," I playfully responded, allowing her to take my hand and lead me into the room. Goose flesh instantly rose from my skin as I was wrapped with the sweet warmth of Lily's voice as she sung in the corner, brushing her hair. Lyrics in Latin filled the room making my heart swell at the beautiful melody she strung together. Uncontrollably, I felt the corners of my mouth lift into a grin as I instantly felt at peace. She turned with a bright smile on her face as she heard me enter.

"There you are," she said, running over to me. "What took you so long? I was starting to worry that something had happened to you. My mind concocted the most terrible scenarios, like what if the dark alfar had come and snatched you up?"

I laughed. "You have that little faith in my thieving abilities then?"

Once a month, the dark alfar would descend upon our little settlement, taking anyone, they deemed worthy as a sacrifice to their foul god Azeer. If you weren't found suitable to become the next human sacrifice, you ended up a slave in their castle of horrors. Our little town had a warning system of bells in place to alert us when they arrived.

"Well, I didn't say that. I just worry is all. There's a lot of people on the streets today for the celebration. Some people, who aren't from our town, may not look so kindly on you," she said, gesturing to my eyes and pointed ears.

"Don't worry. That just means that I have better coverage. Plus, that is why I wear these insufferable things," I said, pointing to the thick wool hat on my head. "You think I like sweating all day?" I pinched her cheeks.

I pulled out the strawberry preserves and handed her the small glass jar. "Here, I got you something."

She licked her lips as her eyes widened with delight. "Gen, you shouldn't have spent the money on this. You should have bought another loaf of bread, but...thank you anyways."

I smiled and nodded at her. She went to the table where Jordan, the oldest of our little gang, was rationing the bread.

Lily placed the jar down on the table. Nil and Kara's face lit up as they jumped up and down for joy.

That was Lily, always caring and sharing whatever she had with others. She was the most selfless person I had ever met. She had nothing, and yet she gave more than I had seen anyone else give, including the sisters and monks of the church. Lily wanted to become a nun just like Sister Ester. She admired the woman to a fault. She wanted to give back and help those around her in need. Even though it was never a life I would choose to live, I could honestly say Lily was going to make a wonderful nun.

The door to our little hovel flew open just as Jordan began handing out the bread. In came Conner, who was sixteen. He had a grin plastered across his freckled face. His brown eyes sparkled, and his dusty blonde hair looked like he had awoken from sleeping in the hay. We all looked at him in silence. His smile faded as he dropped his head and stared at the floor.

Jordan asked sternly, "and where have you been? You were gone before I even got up this morning."

"What, I can't go out for a walk without your permission now?" Conner asked, throwing his hands in the air.

Jordan and I were like the father and mother of our little tribe. We tried to keep them all safe and in check, but from time to time we had to bring the hammer down, especially with Conner. He was a rebellious little troublemaker and didn't care who he put in harm's way as long as he got what he wanted.

"You were with the advisor's daughter again, weren't you?" asked Jordan.

"So, what if I was?"

Jordan threw the bread knife to the table in frustration. "Dammit, Conner! Do you want to get thrown in prison, or worse?" he yelled. "You're just asking for trouble. If Advisor Harren finds out who you are, he will not hesitate to make an example of you."

Conner replied, defensively, "Danielle and I are just spending time together, that is all. Nothing to get yourself worked up over."

"Do I look stupid? You still have hay in your hair, in God's name," Jordan spat.

Lily stepped in between the two boys, trying to act as a barrier. "Conner, Jordan is just worried is all. He doesn't want to see you get hurt. Advisor Harren wouldn't react kindly if he found you and his daughter together," she said softly.

"And why is that? Because I'm a homeless, worthless, human? Because I am nothing and will never amount to anything?" yelled Conner.

"That's not what I said," Lily replied, taking step back.

"I am better than this. Better than all of you and one day I will prove it to everyone in this pathetic town." Conner stormed out of the room, slamming the door behind him. I turned to the others; their faces were long and defeated.

"Stefan, go with him. Make sure he stays out of trouble," ordered Jordan.

Stefan, who was also sixteen, nodded and left.

We all gathered around the table and ate our bread in silence. Conner was indeed smart and clever. He came from a family that had once been in the advisor's inner circle, but due to bad investments and trading deals, his father erased his family fortune and their social status along with it. Conner was only nine when his whole life was turned upside down. A year later, his mother left his father and Conner without a single goodbye. A few months after that, his father was found dead at a gambling club.

Sister Ester knew the boy and his parents from before their tragedy. She graciously took him in and tried her best to give him a sense of purpose, but Conner was never able to let the past go. He strived to regain his family's stature and make something of himself. If the odds weren't so heavily stacked against him, I would have said he had a fighting chance; but no one would ever be able to look at him and not see his father's son. No matter how smart he was or who he fell in love with, he would never be seen as anything more than a fool's offspring.

CHAPTER 2

"Just sit down and let me work," demanded Lily, pushing me into the seat in front of the small mirror in our room.

"This is a waste of time. I'm just going to have to cover it up with a hat," I said as she pulled a brush through my dirty head of thick, curly black hair.

"You will wear a scarf around those little pointed ears of yours today so people can admire my work," she said, crossing pieces of hair around one another to create delicate little braids.

"You know, for wanting to be a nun, you sure do like a lot of recognition. Are you sure that's the life you want?" I asked. I would support Lily in anything she chose, but I knew she adored children and desired a love of her own. Things she would never be able to have if she chose a life dedicated to God and God alone.

"If someone is good at something it should be admired

and complimented, no matter who they are. And yes, I am sure."

"What about Evan? He's obviously interested in you, and you seem to be entertaining the idea." She knocked me in the head with the brush, causing me to flinch. I looked back in the mirror to see a scowling Lily. I laughed, seeing her all stirred up. It didn't happen often, but when it did, I reveled in the moment.

"There's nothing going on with Evan. He's nice to me and I enjoy hearing his stories about working in the stables. That is all. You know how much I love horses," she said innocently, but I knew better.

Evan was another member of our little pack. He was eighteen and recently got a job working with horses at the town stable. He began to show interest in Lily a year ago. Though she was still young and had very little experience, she could turn on the charm faster than I had ever seen another woman do. Which made me question her desire to become a nun even more.

"He has a good income now and he would be able to provide a good life for you and a family. Won't you even consider the possibility?" I asked.

She exhaled, tying a ribbon through the woven braids she had just finished. "Why is it so hard for you to believe the church is truly where my heart lies? Is that pagan blood of yours turning you against Christ?" she asked with a small smirk.

"No, I'm just looking out for you is all. This is a big decision and I just want to make sure you won't look back one day and regret not having a family or a husband. I want you to have everything your heart desires. You can have a family and still serve God. It doesn't have to be one or the other."

Lily paused, placing her hands on either of my shoulders. "If I'm being honest, I have thought about that, a lot. Evan is a nice young man, and he could provide everything you've said. He's even suggested what you are saying to me. But... but I don't feel for him in the way I should. I don't desire him or feel like I can't live without him. He doesn't create that flame inside of me that I hear the other girls in the square talk about."

Lily looked away from my reflection in the mirror. "I've yet to experience that feeling and I'm unsure if I ever will. But one thing I do know is that I owe God my life. He has given everything to me. He gave me a new family, a safe place to call home. He gave me a purpose, and he gave me you." She hugged me from behind. "For that, I will honor him with my life."

I exhaled, nodding my head in the mirror at her. I looked at my hair as she finished, placing small flowers throughout the braid. She got a light blue scrap of fabric and wrapped it around my head, covering my ears in the process. "I almost look normal," I said sarcastically.

"You are normal, dummy," she said, pulling me from the chair. "Now let's go have some fun today and no more talk of Evan." As if he heard his name Evan's head popped out from behind the door as a grin sprawled across his sun-kissed face. I smiled at Lily.

"I won't talk about him, but it looks like you may have to," I said, gesturing to the open door.

She turned around and smiled before hiding her reaction with her hands. *Yeah, she had no interest in him, right,* I thought.

I took her hand as we all headed out towards the street together. Before we left the holy building, I said a little prayer for Conner and Stefan, hoping they would stay out of trouble.

The square was jam-packed with people. The celebration brought people into town that lived on the outskirts of our settlement. Wooden stands were set up around the square where vendors sold fruits, vegetables, soups, elixirs; anything one could think of. The only problem was people in the area were too poor to afford anything but the basics. That didn't prevent me from slipping my sticky little hands in and out of pockets, collecting a few coins on the way through the busy crowd.

We paused at the large rectangular stage that was set in the middle of the square where live music was playing. Couples and children danced in front of the musicians to the catchy beat. Nil and Kara rushed into the crowd, hand in hand, as they began to spin in circles, allowing the wind to catch their dresses with each twirl. Jordan appeared beside me; his face still heavy from his spat with Conner.

"You said the right thing today. He'll realize it in time," I said, trying to sound reassuring.

"Time is what I am concerned about. I'm worried he is going to do something stupid that will land him in jail, or worse. For heaven's sake Gen, I was not that stupid at his age. I didn't disrespect the people who cared for me. I listened and learned from them. He acts like I say these things to him because I hate him or something. Like I want to see him suffer," said Jordan.

I reached out, taking his arm in my hand. "Just give him time. He'll come to respect you, but he must make the decision on his own. Until then, all we can do is continue to try. He's smarter than we give him credit for."

"That's the problem," Jordan said, laughing under his breath.

A group of young women were looking in his direction. Though I couldn't look at him in that way, I could see the appeal he had to others. He was tall with a strong figure and beautiful blue eyes. His hair was dark brown, and his skin was the color of caramel. I nudged him, nodding towards his admirers.

"Why don't you stop worrying and go enjoy yourself," I said, smiling at him.

He looked in the girls' direction and smiled. "You sure? What about the others?"

"I can handle them. Now go, before I drag you to them myself," I said, pushing him along.

He smiled back at me, softer than before. "Thanks, Gen. Try to have some fun too."

I watched the girls giggle with excitement as he headed towards them. I shook my head, thinking of how stupid they all appeared. How desperate and clingy. All they wanted in life was a husband who would provide for them and give them children. They had no ambitions and no real talents. Nothing to rely on besides their looks. Maybe I was a little jealous if I was being honest.

I turned my attention back to Nil and Kara who were still spinning to the music. Evan and Lily were off to the side, enjoying a sweet cake and flirting with one another as if they were the only two people in the square. I stood alone in a crowd full of people, feeling like I didn't belong. I wondered if I would ever find someone who could truly love me in that way. Like a husband loves a wife. Would they care that I was half alfar? Would my ears bother them? Would the thought of starting a family with me repulse them?

I pushed the thoughts out of my head. I wasn't one of the stupid girls who only cared about marriage and children. I had ambitions. I had talents. What those ambitions and talents were, I didn't have the slightest clue, but I would find them. I was more than this town. More than my blood.

I looked over to a group of children who were sitting on the curve of the street, watching as the people ate and danced around them. Two boys and one little girl, all under the age of five. Their little faces were dirty, their hair tangled; their clothes were too small for their bodies and torn in multiple places. They were too skinny, and I could tell they weren't fed regularly. I searched for their parents, but they were nowhere to be found.

I moved through the crowd, slipping my hands in and out of the people's pockets until I had enough money, then purchased three sweet cakes. I went to the children, who looked up at me and backed away as they peered into my unique eyes. Smiling, I knelt beside them slowly and reached out my hand, offering the cakes up. Their little eyes widened as they inhaled the aroma of the dessert.

"It's okay, I bought them for you. See, one for each of you," I said gently. They took the cakes and ever so slowly each took a bite. Their bodies exhaled in relief as the food filled their bellies. The little girl looked up and smiled at me before taking her second bite. I watched with a heavy heart as they enjoyed something that they never should be denied...food.

A young woman frantically rushed over. "There you three are! Where did you run off to? Haven't I told you to stay near your father or me during the celebration?" She touched each of the children, making sure they were still in one piece before looking at the cakes and then at me. She seemed curious, as if she wanted to ask why, but didn't allow the words to escape.

"You have beautiful children," I said.

She gave me a small uncomfortable smile, looking into my eyes and then at the ribbon that covered my ears. My eyes were unique. When humans peered into them, they always questioned what I was. I was sure the rumors of the half-breed that lived among them had scattered to the nearby settlements.

"Thank you and thank you for the cakes. What do I owe you for them?" she asked hesitantly.

I shook my head. "Nothing, it was a gift," I said.

She knelt, staring at me for a moment longer before pulling the three children up off the curb. "You are too kind. Thank you again," she said, ushering them along. "We should be on our way. I hope you enjoy the celebration."

I watched as the mother and children found their father. He exhaled in relief, taking his family into his arms. My heart warmed at the sight of their affection.

I made my way back over to the others. Nil and Kara were filling their faces full of candy as they laughed and splashed each other in the fountain. Lily was trying on jewelry and headpieces at one of the vendor booths as Evan leaned against a post nearby, taking her in. Jordan had disappeared altogether.

As the night finally descended, the people of our small, innocent town became our entertainment. They were drunk off ale and whiskey as they stumbled around the broken streets of the square. They laughed freely and smiled at everyone they saw. Lily and I sat at the edge of the stage as the music slowed in tempo.

"What's it like to be drunk?" she asked me.

"I don't know. I've never taken the chance in fear of what would happen to me if I lost my wits," I said honestly.

"You deserve some fun too, you know. Why not let me watch the others and you go steal yourself a bottle of whiskey over there," she said, then clamped her hands over her mouth in shock. "I did not just encourage you to steal. That is wrong. Please don't tell Sister Ester."

I laughed, shaking my head. "Don't worry, your sinful suggestion is safe with me."

"Momentary lapse in judgment. God, please forgive

me," she said, looking up to the heavens. "You are a bad influence on me, Gen."

"Oh, that was my fault now, was it? Well, I can just leave if you'd like. Wouldn't want to corrupt you any more than I have," I said playfully.

"No, never leave. You continue to try and corrupt me, and I will continue to try and lead you to Christ."

"Deal," I said, wrapping my arm around her and squeezing her tight.

Evan made his way over to us, sitting on the other side of Lily. Across the crowd I saw Stefan emerge, looking as if someone had just killed his dog. I furrowed my brow, trying to figure out what was going on.

I turned to Lily and Evan. "Hey, will you two watch Nil and Kara?" I asked.

"Sure, what's going on?" asked Evan.

"Hopefully nothing, but if it gets too late, get them back to the church, okay?" I ordered.

"Of course," said Evan.

Lily looked at me curiously. I gave her a small reassuring smile before moving through the crowd towards Stefan. He was a wreck.

"What is it? Where is Conner?" I asked.

He exhaled deeply. "Advisor Harren caught Danielle and him together tonight during his little get-together," Stefan said in a panic. "It wasn't good, Gen. Harren went ballistic. He beat Conner to a pulp in front of all his guests and then had the guards haul him away to the cells until he could figure out his punishment. I tried to help him, I really did, but he wouldn't listen to me, and then when they took him, I couldn't get anywhere near him."

I brought my hands to his shoulders, steadying him as he swayed from side to side barely able to keep upright. "It's okay, Stefan. You did all that you could." I said, calmly. *Shit, shit, shit,* I thought. Of all nights he had to go and get caught now when there was twice the number of people and guards in town. Stupid idiot.

"What do we do?" asked Stefan.

"*We* do nothing. You've done enough for tonight. Go and enjoy the solstice and I will figure out how to get him out."

"Should I find Jordan, or tell the others?"

"No, let me worry about Conner. I want them to enjoy the celebration, which includes you. Don't worry. Like I said, I will get him out."

He nodded, walking slowly past me into the crowd of people. I thought for a moment, trying to figure out how I was going to get the stupid bastard out of jail. I frantically checked my surroundings, trying to figure out a solution, just as my eyes landed on a booth selling whiskey. I tilted my head to the side as my plan began to take form. Well, it was a celebration after all.

CHAPTER 3

Relax. Smile. Act casual. I had collected three things for my mission: a hallucinogen, alcohol, and a cloak. I held the bottle of whiskey in my hands, shaking the liquid ever so slowly, making sure the drugs had time to dissolve. Gods, if I got caught, they would turn me over to the Alfar courts for sure. Even the human's respect for my mother wouldn't be able to save me.

I made my way into the courthouse after timing the guard's shift change. I had exactly thirty seconds until two new guards rotated to the front entrance of the jailhouse. I descended the uneven stone steps into the damp and underlit prison. The building was one of the oldest structures in our town. The stone that created the foundation was broken and loose. I pulled the hood of the cloak over my hair.

Three guards sat at a wooden table, playing cards casually. They looked up as I approached, sitting taller than they had been. I wasn't plain by any means, but I was not rehearsed in the laws of seduction. I didn't know how to move my body or what to do with my face. Even when I tried, I just ended up looking like some weird chicken, strutting through the street. I smiled, trying not to overdo it.

"What do we have here?" one of the guards asked with a devilish smile.

I relaxed, trying to seem casual. "I didn't think it fair that the whole city gets to celebrate, while the men who work so hard to keep us safe are stuck down here, unable to attend the festivities," I said, trying to sound seductive.

"Is that so? You decided to bring the party to us," said another guard.

"I did," I said, placing the whiskey on the table.

The guards smiled, reaching for the bottle. One of them pulled up a chair for me to join. I took it, watching as they poured the rich golden liquid into their wooden cups. They all shot the whiskey back, then poured themselves a second helping. *This was too easy*, I thought.

After their third cup, one of the guards looked at me with pure lust lurking behind his eyes. He smiled, reaching for my leg. I remained still, praying the effects of the whiskey would kick in at any second. I bashfully grinned, trying to hide my discomfort.

"What other party treats did you bring us?" He asked with his heavy breath on my neck as his hand slid up my thigh.

"I can retrieve some sweet cakes for you if you'd like," I responded, trying to avert his attention from me.

He laughed. "I can think of something better than a sweet cake," he said, moving towards me. One of the other guards slammed another cup in front of me, breaking the guard's attention.

"Come on now, Reese. You haven't even offered the woman a drink," he said, pouring the whiskey into a glass in front of me. *Shit.*

"Oh, that's okay. I don't drink," I said, trying to seem casual.

"Well, tonight you do. Now, drink up," he said firmly. The third guard shook his head as if to try and stay awake. It was taking effect, just not as fast as I needed it to. The handsy guard began to sway in his chair as he downed another glass of liquor. "Go on girl, drink," he barked. I took the glass and slammed the liquid back, placing the empty cup on the table. My face soured as the warm liquid coated my insides. He smiled with delight.

"Thank you," I said politely. He nodded with satisfaction. I watched as all three of them fought to keep their eyes open. They slurred their words as they looked one another, trying to figure out what was happening. The first guard went down, slamming his head on the table. He passed out into a deep sleep. The second one fell. The third chair into a bucket and broom against the wall. Whiskey, looked at his comrades and then at the bottle, at me in connecting the dots together. He looked shock.

"You—" he muttered before falling back out of his chair to the floor.

I rushed to the bodies, searching for the keys. I had less time than I thought, now being intoxicated myself. I could already feel the drug working through my system. It would affect me a lot faster due to my size. I grabbed the keys and went into the cells. Conner was slumped against the wall of a cell in the front. He sat up as I approached, his face swollen, and his mouth covered in blood.

"What are you doing here?" he asked, reaching towards the iron bars.

"Getting you out, what do you think?" I snapped. I fumbled with the keys, trying to focus as my vision went blurry. I inserted the key into the lock, releasing the latch. I fell instantly to the ground as his arms reached for me.

"What is wrong? Are you okay?"

"I had to drug the whiskey I gave to the guards. They made me drink with them. I'll be unconscious any moment. We need to move now." He supported my body with his and moved up and out of the courthouse basement into the streets of the celebration. I was warm and everything spinning as I fought to keep my eyes open. My legs gave along fell to the ground. I felt Conner pull me up and out the street with him, searching for a safe place to wait

Ding! Ding! Ding! Ding! Four bells. The dark alfar had been spotted.

The crowd erupted in panic, racing to gather their children and loved ones as they sought refuge. Market stands were trampled, and food and ale poured into the street. No one cared about the sold goods. All they cared about was avoiding being captured by the dark Alfar court. Conner slid a hand under my knees and behind my back, lifting me up, just before my vision gave out completely. The last thing I remember hearing was the echoing of the bells and the screams of my townspeople.

I WOKE UP THE NEXT MORNING FEELING LIKE I HAD been worked to death. My body was limp, and my head was spinning. I pulled myself up just in time to relieve the contents of my stomach in the hay next to me. Wiping my mouth, I looked up to see Conner smiling at me from across the barn. He handed me a cup of well water and then slid down next to me.

"Thank you for coming for me," he said softly.

"You didn't leave me much of a choice. You're a stubborn bastard, you know that?"

He laughed, twirling a piece of hay in between his fingers. His smile faded as he focused on the strand of hay in his hands. "I love her, Gen. I don't know what I am going to do," he admitted.

My heart felt heavy for him. This was the first heartbreak in his young life, but it surely wouldn't be his last. I reached out, taking his hand. "You're a good man, Conner. Any woman would be lucky to have your affections. Though, I must say, you have expensive taste."

He laughed at me, reaching over to squeeze my hand. "Tell me about it. I know you don't understand, but I must find a way to redeem my family's name. I've watched, read, and studied since my father lost everything. I can be of use to the advisors if they would just give me a chance."

"I know you could, and I believe you will make something of yourself, but realistically, it won't be in this town. You need to get out of here. Start somewhere fresh and new where no one knows your family. They only know you and your talents. The Frey is large. You can go wherever you want," I said.

He exhaled in defeat. "That would mean I would have to leave Danielle."

"I want you to be happy Conner, but you won't be happy here. Even if you stay, her father will eventually marry her off to another man. Do you really want to stay and watch that?"

He shook his head. I saw the anger wash over him.

He turned to me, trying to hold himself together. "Come on, let's get back to the others. You look like you were just trampled by a horse." He pulled me to my feet.

"How about I dose you with drugs and let's see how you recover."

He laughed, holding onto me as we made our way back to the church.

The streets were quieter than yesterday. The decorations hung in disarray as remnants of food and wine littered the streets. I quickly remembered the warning bells for the dark alfar that went off in the middle of our celebration. Sadistic bastards. They couldn't let us be during the solstice? They just had to use the celebration to gather slaves for their disgusting court.

As children, we were told stories about what they would do to the humans that ended up in their court. The alfar would rape and torture those they found to be less ugly than the others. They would use humans to conduct experiments. Crossbreeding them with fairies, nymphs, and incubi, just to name a few. If a child was conceived, they would do experiments on it to see which magical traits passed from each parent. After they concluded their testing, the child would be disposed of to keep every race's line pure. I shuddered at the thought as approaching hooves drew me out of my thoughts.

A well-maintained wagon drawn by two white horses pulled up along the curb of the street across from our church. Out of a wagon sprang three young girls, all dressed in white. Their hair was freshly washed and braided away from their faces. They smiled and giggled as an older man exited behind them. *Disgusting*, I thought.

The light alfar were scheduled to come through the town this morning. The girls were going to be offered to the alfar by the man for a few silver shillings. The young idiots were surely told of the grandeur of the light court. How they would never go hungry again, and how honorable it would be to serve the elegant light alfar. Maybe one would even be taken as a lover of a noble alfar male and have a happy ending of their own. Ha, pathetic. The only thing that awaited anyone beyond the border was indentured servitude.

Conner and I looked at each other and rolled our eyes as

we made our way to the stairs of the church. My body felt heavy and weak. I fought to drag my feet along the long halls toward the commons area. Before we even reached the door, I could hear yelling and crying coming from our room. I pushed open the door to find Jordan and Evan standing in front of one another, yelling their heads off.

"Do you realize what you've done? How selfish are you?" yelled Jordan. The others were scattered around the edge of the room, huddled together, crying.

"She wouldn't listen to me. She insisted on finding Gen," said Evan.

I scanned the room, taking note of the familiar faces. One was missing. I felt my heart begin to race as my breaths became uneven and strained. I stepped towards the two boys as they turned their attention to me.

"Jordan, what's going on?" I asked, still searching for Lilian. My hands began to shake uncontrollably.

Jordan stood tall and firm and looked towards Evan with anger. "Go on. You tell her," Jordan said.

Evan looked like he was going to be sick, unable to even bring his eyes up to meet mine.

"Evan, where is Lilian?" I asked.

He took a step back.

"Where is Lilian?" I screamed, grabbing the collar of his jacket with both of my hands.

"Genevieve, I'm sorry. She wouldn't come back without you. She was out in the crowds looking for you when the bells rang. I tried dragging her with me, but she refused to leave," Evan said softly.

"So, you just left her out there all by herself?" I screamed, holding back the need to break his jaw with my fist.

"I had no choice. She wouldn't listen. I tried, but she was so worried about you. About what would happen if you got caught, being what you are."

I let go of his jacket, pushing him away from me. I took a few deep breaths, trying to calm myself.

"Have you gone out and looked for her since last night?" I asked Jordan.

"Yes, but—," Jordan stopped and shook his head.

"But what? What did you find?" I demanded.

"She was taken, Gen," said Jordan.

My heart fell into my stomach. "No, no she couldn't have been. How do you know for sure?" I asked.

"The Ranger family saw from the window in their attic. The dark alfar appeared out of nowhere and took her."

"Did...did they hurt her?" I forced myself to ask.

"They said one of them touched her head and she collapsed into his arms as if she was asleep. They disappeared into the mist with her. I looked everywhere Gen, I promise you. She's just gone."

"So, she was taken from Ring Street?" I refocused the conversation, trying to nail down the details of her capture.

"Yes."

"How many others were taken from town?"

"She was the only one. They moved into Zelsberg and Walsh before ending in Rilar this time. A total of eight were taken this month, including Lily."

I walked away from Jordan, trying to figure out how I was going to get her back. If they had hurt or tortured her, I didn't know if I could live with myself—knowing her concern for me was what had gotten her taken. I tightened my fists together as my whole body shook in fear for my sister. Feeling as if the walls were closing in around me, I flew down the hall and up the stairs into the open air of the streets. The others followed me out of the church.

"What are we going to do?" asked Kara.

"Is there a chance she could still be alive?" asked Nil.

"Of course, she's still alive. Don't talk like that!" snapped Stefan.

I focused on the busy streets around the church. The birds flying through the air. The horses' hooves stomping on the loose stone. Children playing off in the distance, dragging their brightly colored streamers through the air. I felt a hand on my shoulder.

"Gen, I'm so sorry. If I had just been there and not distracted, this would have never happened," said Jordan.

I looked across the street to see the group of young women in white awaiting the light alfar. My brow tightened as my rescue plan began to take form. I took Jordan's hand in my own and turned to face him and the others.

"I know, but now you need to take the lead with the others and keep them safe," I said to him.

His face tensed as he searched mine for answers. "What do you mean? What are you going to do? You can't cross the border. You're only half-elf," said Jordan.

"I can if I am escorted by an alfar," I responded, slowly

turning towards the three girls in white.

His eyes followed mine, stopping at the sight of them. He shook his head with vigor. "No, no, absolutely not. You cannot do this. If they find out what you are, they will kill you on sight!" Jordan snapped.

"I have no other choice. I have to get across that border and to the dark court and this is the only way."

"You're crazy! You won't survive the dark court, let alone whatever else is in those woods. And how do you plan to get free of the light alfar? What, you think they'll sympathize with you and just let you go on your merry way? They don't care about humans, Gen. We are no better than cattle to them, that is all," said Jordan.

Compared to the dark, the light alfar were the kinder elves. They didn't experiment on the humans, nor did they offer them up as sacrifices to their gods, but humans were looked at as nothing more than dogs. They cleaned the alfar's castles and tended to their royals, and their lands. Some people liked to think of the light alfar as gods and saviors, for the border of protection.

"Come on, Gen. This is a suicide mission, and you know it," added Evan.

"One I wouldn't have to be taking on if it wasn't for you!" I yelled at him.

He dropped his head in shame and took a step away from me.

I took another calming breath. "I'm sorry, I shouldn't have said that," I said.

"No, you're right. It should be me going after her, not

you," Evan said softly.

I took a long look at the six orphans who had become my family. Each was beautiful and unique in their own way. But Lily needed me.

"If something goes wrong and I don't make it, then at least I know I did everything I could to bring her back. If I don't try, I'm not going to be able to live with myself," I said.

"Please, just consider this before you do it," said Jordan. "I know what Lilian means to you. What she means to all of us, but—"

"I've made up my mind. I'm going to offer my services to the light alfar and then I am going to find Lily," I said adamantly.

Jordan took a second and then nodded.

The others looked at me with tears in their eyes, hesitant to say goodbye.

The crowds in the streets began to scatter and part as they all whispered and gawked at an oncoming convoy. I turned to see a group of light alfar riding on horseback through the town in the distance. The youngest of my family, Nil, wrapped her arms around my waist and hugged me so tight I gasped for breath.

"I love you, Gen. Please don't go," she said.

I knelt and took her face in my hands. "I will come back for you…for all of you," I said, looking up at my family one last time. I kissed Nil on the head and then hugged the rest of them, not knowing if this was the end. I turned from their teary faces and inhaled a deep breath before stepping off into the direct path of my only hope of finding Lily.

CHAPTER 4

The convoy of light alfar consisted of six males on horseback with a wagon trailing behind them. There was no mistaking an alfar, regardless of whether they were light or dark. They were magnificent creatures with flawless skin and striking features. They held themselves with grace and elegance as if their bodies had never seen a day's work. Male or female, their bodies were tall and trim.

An alfar's hair was always straight, not a wave in sight. If you were an alfar from the light court, you would have white, grey, or blonde hair. The dark alfar were distinguished by their black-as-night hair. The six males that approached were all striking in appearance. No emotion showed on their faces, yet their presence demanded attention.

Their bodies were lean with muscle showing through the thin linen shirts that adorned their pale skin. Each wore shades of brown leather pants with swords and daggers attached to a belt at their waist. Knee-high boots padded down the cobblestone street, barely making a sound.

The people of our small town scurried past the group, trying not to catch their attention. The alfar leader stopped by the older man with the three young girls. The man smiled joyously as he presented the girls to the alfar.

One alfar dismounted and headed towards them. They beamed with excitement. He checked them over, circling as if he was assessing farm animals. He touched their faces, checked their hands, and looked into their eyes for any signs of sickness. He appeared to be satisfied with their physical health. He took them by the arms and led them to the back of the wagon without a word. The alfar leader tossed the older man a pouch of coins in exchange for his new batch of slaves.

The alfar didn't have to pay him anything. They could take whomever they wished and there would be nothing any of us could do about it. The money was a way of easing the tension between the races and proving to the humans they weren't beasts like the dark alfar. No matter what price the alfar paid for you, a slave was still a slave.

The older man bowed to the passing convoy as they slowly continued forward. I clenched my fists, moving directly into the path of one of the riders. The horse halted to a stop as I stood firm, not letting it pass. The male who led the convoy turned his focus towards me from on top of his horse.

The alfar male had long blonde hair pulled back into a half ponytail with small braids intertwined throughout. He had piercing blue eyes and a face that looked as if it was made of pure marble. He was stunning and elegant. Everything I wasn't. He looked down at me, his expression seemed to be emotionless.

"Move," he said firmly.

I swallowed as I felt my body begin to tremble. "I wish to work for the light alfar," I said, with all the courage I could muster.

He looked me up and down, then smirked. "When was the last time you bathed? You smell worse than my steed." He straightened in the saddle.

"I will take whatever job you offer. Please, just give me a chance to prove myself. You can keep the two shillings. I will come willing and freely," I begged.

"You aren't worth two shillings by the look of you," he said, before turning back to signal to the one who had assessed the other girls. Horse hooves clicked softly as the leader approached. His beautiful moonlight white hair trailed down his neck past his shoulders. His eyes were yellow as the sun and his face had a slight golden tint to it. Built like a soldier, his muscles bulged through his white linen shirt.

The blue-eyed male bent down to whisper to the white-haired one, quietly enough that I couldn't make out what he was saying. The yellow-eyed alfar turned his head slowly towards me, taking note of my dirty clothes and frail form. He dismounted and approached. I trembled at his size but forced myself to stay rooted in place. He took my chin between his cold fingers and turned my face from side to side as he evaluated me.

"Open," he said, pulling my chin down. I bared my teeth as he checked for any rot or decay. I closed my mouth as we stood in silence. "Your eyes," he said with interest.

"They're a common trait on my father's side," I responded. Not actually a lie. I figured I had his eyes since my mothers were a pale brown, from what I could remember. The white-haired alfar let go of my chin and straightened in front of me.

"What talents do you have?"

"I can clean, cook, sew, tend to the fields. Whatever you need, I can do it," I said.

His eyebrow arched and his stone-cold face cracked into a small smirk, as if he could see through my blatant lie. He took two silver shillings from his pocket and placed them in my hand. I looked down at the small coins that represented the value of my life.

"I told the other male I would come for free," I stuttered.

He folded my fingers around the coins and held my hand for a brief moment. I had never been this close to an alfar before. His skin was cold, yet smooth as silk. He gestured toward my family across the street. "Give it to them, then get into the wagon," he said, before turning back to mount his horse.

I ran across the street and gave Jordan the two shillings. He took my wrist before I could run back. I turned to see his face wracked with guilt and fear.

"Good luck," Jordan whispered.

I nodded and then headed back to the wagon. The horses took off before I took a seat across from the three young girls dressed in white. They giggled and smiled at one another, not bothering to look my way.

We made five more stops, picking up other young workers from different towns and settlements before we made our way to the protective border. I peeked my head out of the wooden wagon to see the border markers coming into view. Two alfar trailed the wagon, while the other four took the lead, fanning out along the path.

There were ten of us in the wagon. The alfar had collected three additional girls like the ones from my town. They were clean and dressed in a similar fashion to one another. The other three were young men under the age of twenty. They were taken from their families against their wills. They looked nervous and afraid, unsure of what their futures held. One of the finely dressed young girls reached across the wagon and took a young boy's hand.

"Do not be afraid," she said. "We are going to a better life where we will be protected and cared for."

He pulled his hand away from hers and gave her a look of disgust. "Don't be foolish. We are going to be worked to death and treated worse than animals. You'll most likely end up under some light alfar that will only view you as a means to relieve himself every night," the young boy spat.

The girl looked shocked as her mouth fell open in disbelief. "You don't know what you're talking about. They don't treat humans like that. Not in the light court.

They will be kind to us all. We are lucky to have been chosen."

"We'll see if you'll be saying that a week from now after you've been worked to the point of exhaustion and screwed by half the court," the boy said.

"That's enough," I interrupted. "Keep your opinions to yourselves, all of you." They all looked at me with anger, but the bickering stopped.

As we approached the border, I could feel a slight humming vibrate through my bones. It was as if small shots of lightning zapped along the surface of my skin. I peeked out of the wagon but could not see a physical barrier. I watched as the alfar in the front was the first to step across the invisible fence on top of his steed. A shimmer of yellow and white light rippled as the horse split through the shield. As we approached next the male guiding our wagon laid a hand on top of our wooden carriage. A slight shimmer slid across the wood as we crossed the protective border without issue.

Immediately after we were out of The Frey, the air seemed to smell cleaner and fresher. We all peered out of the wagon at the beautiful, lush forest. Trees stretched fifty feet into the sky and their trunks were so thick around that I wondered if they had been here since the beginning of time. The late afternoon sun peeped through the dense canopies of the trees lining our path.

We continued on the dirt road for the next two hours before we finally stopped to make camp. One of the alfar warriors told us that we would reach the light alfar's kingdom, Urial, tomorrow after breakfast, but we would stay here for the night. We helped unload the wagon of supplies and food. I watched closely as one of the alfars spun his hands around in a rhythmic motion and tents and a campfire instantly appeared. We gawked at their magic. I had never seen actual magic performed. How easy life would be if I had even a sliver of their abilities? The six young girls clapped and jumped in excitement. The alfar didn't even acknowledge them.

The rest of us stood back, waiting for our marching orders like obedient dogs. One of the males gestured for us to take a seat around the fire. They handed us each a silver bowl with meat, potatoes, fresh vegetables, and a glass of wine. We looked at each other, unsure if it was real. The food smelled better than anything I had ever eaten.

The alfar sat across from us, eating in silence. The six girls looked at the rest of us, their expressions smug. We were still wary of the food and good treatment. I held the plate in my hand as my mouth watered. The smell of the food was torturous to my empty stomach.

"Is there something wrong with the food?" asked the yellow-eyed leader. He appeared in front of me, tall and stoic. I didn't even remember seeing him leave from his seat across the camp. We all looked at each other, not knowing how to respond. I bowed my head, refusing to make eye contact, hoping he would just go away. He bent down slowly, stabbed a fork into one of the potatoes on my plate, and placed it in his mouth. I looked up to find his eyes locked onto my own as he chewed quietly. "Eat," he demanded.

I took a small piece of meat and slowly placed it in my mouth. Closing my eyes, I tried to hide my satisfaction from the alfar. I swallowed the piece of meat and looked at the other three guys, nodding that it was safe. They began digging in as if they hadn't eaten for days. I looked back at the yellow-eyed alfar. His mouth curled at the corner, and he nodded at me approvingly. I turned my attention back to my plate, watching out of the corner of my eye as he took his seat across from us.

After dinner, all ten of us were piled into one tent. The alfar stayed around the fire whispering amongst themselves. My stomach was cramped from all the food I had consumed. So, this was what it was like to go to bed with a full stomach. The others fell asleep within the first thirty minutes. I dozed in and out of a light sleep. As I felt my mind slip into my subconscious, I was greeted by the familiar images that had haunted my dreams for the past three years.

Flashes of a person, a man, that I had never laid eyes on. A dark-inked design was drawn into his skin, starting from the left side of his lower neck, and extending down to his shoulder and upper arm. I never saw the man fully, only small details of his features. His smile, his hands, and ever so often I heard the faint sound of his laugh. He was always surrounded by a darkness which kept him hidden from my sight. The dream haunted me because I didn't know what to make of it. Lilian was the only one I told of it.

A few hours had passed when I was startled awake by

rustling in the nearby bushes. I popped up, moving slowly to the opening of the tent. I peeled the fabric back and took in my surroundings, steadying my breath, and listening for the sound again. The chattering of teeth, followed by the rustling of leaves, caught my attention to the left of the camp. An alfar appeared in front of me, taking me by surprise as I fell back on my bottom.

"Get back inside and stay silent," he demanded before closing the tent flap. I quietly woke the others, signaling for them not to talk. We crawled to the opening of the tent and listened.

"We just want one. That's all we are asking of you. Surely you can spare one," came a high-pitched, crackling voice.

"They aren't for sale," said one of the alfar.

"We didn't say we would buy one. We will simply let the other nine live if you give us one," said another high voice, followed by teeth chattering together.

"They're under our protection. Now be gone," demanded the yellow-eyed alfar. We heard more rustling coming from the outer edges of our campsite. One of the creatures clicked their tongue loudly.

"No, no, no. See, my friends and I are being generous, only demanding one from your harvest. As you can see, you are outnumbered. If you deny us what we are owed, most of you, if not all, will die, and then we will take all ten. But, if you give us what we ask for, then we will be on our way, and you can spend the rest of your evening knowing you prevented bloodshed. Is one pathetic human snack worth the price of the lives of you and your men, *my lord*?" The creatures chuckled.

I peeked out of the tent to see humanoid figures with sharp teeth, narrow features, and wings. They were the same height as the alfar, but leaner. Only one creature that I could recall had these features...fairies. The alfar looked at each other, debating how to handle the situation. The yellow-eyed leader looked as if he was in pain as he hung his head. The blue-eyed alfar snapped his fingers as one of the other soldiers made his way toward us. We all moved to the back of the tent, trying to get as far away from him and the creatures as possible. The girls began yelling and crying, begging not to be taken.

The alfar reached inside, taking one of the girls in white by the arm. "No, please, no! Not me, please!" she yelled, reaching for one of us to save her. I closed my eyes, trying to drown out her plea for help. I couldn't take any chances or step out of line with the alfar. I had to get to Lily. I was her only hope. Or at least, that was what I told myself.

The girl yelled and cried as they brought her to the fairy. From beyond our tent, we could hear a chorus of chattering teeth erupt at the sight of the girl. Loud, high-pitched sounds surrounded us as if they were cheering in excitement.

"Wise choice, my lord. We will accept this gift and bid you all a good night," said the fairy.

"Valor," said the yellow-eyed alfar in a deep voice. "If I ever see you again, or you try to take what is ours on this road, I will personally hunt you down and eliminate your whole hive. Are we clear?"

"Mm, we shall see about that. The dark alfar finds us quite useful from time to time. They may have something to say," said the fairy I now identified as Valor. A loud buzzing erupted around us as the swarm of fairies took off into flight. The young girl's screams faded into the night sky.

"What are they going to do with her?" asked one of the girls in white.

"Eat her, what do you think?" said an older boy.

The girls continued to cry for their friend.

We huddled together for the rest of the night. Not one of us dared to sleep, afraid of what else lurked within the trees.

The next morning, we piled into the wagon without a word. The girls in white no longer giggled and laughed. Last night was proof that their lives weren't worth a single drop of alfar blood. I kept my head down and my mouth shut, contemplating how I was going to get myself to the dark court to save my sister from a worse fate.

CHAPTER 5

The kingdom of Urial was more extravagant than I could imagine. The castle towered into the sky from the top of a mountain. Waterfalls, coming out of the top of the castle ledges poured out of each corner into a crystal-clear lake at the base of the city. There were five tall towers capped in gold. The palace was made of white and gray stone. Balconies were seen from every point. Gorgeous gardens and plants saturated the landscape with more colors than I knew existed. It was the most beautiful prison I had ever laid eyes on.

Across the surrounding territory, grain fields and orchards were scattered on the outskirts of the rolling hills and flat plains. Human workers tended the crops, working under the watchful eyes of their alfar overlords. Males and females greeted the six alfar warriors as we entered the main road. Shops, markets, and beautiful entertainment littered the perfectly paved streets. Alfar women danced barefoot throughout the alleyways as music filled the sweet-smelling air.

Fruits and vegetables were abundant lining every table. Alfar exited the shops covered in beautiful fabrics and fashions I had never seen before. A bit revealing for humans, but I guess if you looked the way they did, why cover it up? Small alfar children laughed and played in a nearby fountain as we continued to the large castle up ahead.

The wagon came to a halt at one of the palace's arched entrances. The alfar males dismounted without even looking back at the wagon. An older human woman came to the back and instructed us to follow her. We made our way through the back halls of the palace. Humans scattered the narrow corridors, rushing around as they tended to their daily work. The rooms that I could see into were plain with scant furniture. Only the basic; chairs, tables, and a few armoires for clothing.

The older woman finally stopped at the entrance of a washroom. She flagged a young human male over to her and whispered something in his ear. The man took the three boys from the wagon with him as they moved to another part of the castle.

"Everyone in the room," demanded the old woman.

We pushed into the small bathroom. There were four tubs, three sinks, and a wall of mirrors. The scent was crisp and smelled of eucalyptus. There were no windows to let in natural light and the lighting that came from the candles was dim. She set out clean yellow dresses with white lace trim for each of us.

"Are these our uniforms?" asked one of the other girls.

"No. One of you will be chosen to tend to the needs of the next king," she said, running hot water into the small tubs.

"The needs?" asked another girl hesitantly.

"Did I stutter? Yes, needs. Laundry, cleaning his room, mending his clothes, and keeping his bed warm, if he desires you, that is," she snapped.

"I—I didn't sign up for this," said one of the girls from my town. She backed away from the group. The old woman reached out her hand, aggressively wrapping her grip around the girl's forearm.

"This is your life now, girl. Adapt or die, the choice is yours. Now, you all will wash and clean yourselves thoroughly. Place the oils along your neck when you are clean and then dress and be ready in thirty minutes. The court awaits your presence." She stopped and looked at me before leaving. "And take that thing off your head," she said, looking directly at me. "They will want to see as much of you as possible. Including your hair."

I bit the side of my lip nervously. Thankfully my ears didn't stand out far from my head like most of the other alfar. The tips were noticeable, but I could hide them well enough in my thick dark curly hair. The older woman left, and we all slowly began to undress as the reality of our current situation sank in. I dipped down into the hot bath, not remembering the last time I properly washed. I cleaned every inch of myself twice, including my hair.

I dried my thick mane and dressed in the soft yellow

dress the woman laid out for us. Two of the other girls were now crying at the thought of being enslaved and raped by the future king of the light court. I focused on my goals and kept my mind on Lily. My hair sprung into curls around my face and stretched down the length of my back. The hair acted as a shield for my ears, as I knew it would. I never wore my hair down. I almost didn't even recognize myself. I was so used to putting it up in a bun to hide it under my scarves and hats.

The dress was baggy on me. I barely had any fat on my body which included my breasts. Starving will do that to a person, I guess. My skin was golden from the summer sun which made my eyes pop. Even cleaned and properly dressed, I still stuck out from the other girls. They had fairer skin, with shades of lighter hair and their figures didn't resemble a skeleton.

The door opened without warning. The older woman appeared at the threshold and signaled for us to follow her. We created a line and walked with our heads down in silence. As we made it to the upper level, the alfar we passed didn't even look at us. We were nothing more than a placeholder, not important enough for their acknowledgment.

Bowls of fresh fruit and pitchers of wine lined every table. The smell of oils and incense filled the halls. Grand arches created walk spaces between each room. Two large pillars stood on either side of each arch, reaching thirty feet into the air. The walls were lined with masterful paintings and murals, creating the most captivating views. Tapestries hung from the inner walls, and windows cut into the ceiling of the castle allowed natural light to illuminate their beautiful craftsmanship.

Statues and sculptures filled the spaces in between each doorway. Indoor fountains trickled and echoed through the vast mass of halls. Luxurious couches and seating areas were scattered throughout, allowing for social gatherings and resting places for the court. Gold and silver metals littered each surface. Gold goblets, silver plates, gold rings, gold vases. It was clear that the alfar didn't want for anything. The sun-filled each corridor as we made our way to two large golden doors. Two alfar guards stood on either side of the entrance.

The older woman turned to us. "You do not speak unless spoken to. Even then, keep your responses short. They are allowed to touch you and look wherever and however they please. Do not make direct eye contact with them. Keep your head down and your hands folded in front of you. After the future king has chosen one of you, the others will meet me back here for your work assignments." She moved out of the way.

The doors opened slowly to the throne room of the castle. Tables and chairs were placed in rows leading to the front of the room. Each surface was adorned with a golden tablecloth. Floral arrangements as large as a person were placed every six feet down the center of each table. Food displays, meat trays, and sweet treats littered the surfaces. Anything you could imagine or crave, the table provided. Doves flew overhead, as the throne room's ceiling did not exist. It was open to the outdoor elements, allowing the fresh air and sunlight to fill the room.

Members of the high houses sat eating and drinking while conversing with one another. At the head of the room was a large platform, covered in white rose petals as if it was one massive carpet. There were three thrones on top of the platform. A male, who I assumed to be the king, sat in the middle. He had long golden hair and a strong and slender face. His eyes appeared kind, though his mouth never turned up to smile. A female who resembled his age was to his left and wore a vibrant blue gown. She was tall and slender with hair as golden as sunlight. She had thin red lips and a small button nose. Her eyes were crystal blue, accentuated by her long lashes. On the king's right sat a younger female who I figured to be their daughter.

We were being auctioned off to be the princess's future husband's whore. The alfar didn't have the same values as humans when it came to marriage. Since they could live for over a thousand years, I guess the concept of monogamy didn't appeal to them. Why have just one when you could have them all?

The light court was at least discreet about their affairs. There were rumors that the dark court had monthly orgy parties, where you could have whomever, whenever, however, you'd like. They only married for formality and political matters. I had even heard one rumor that claimed the dark alfar would take slaves right in the middle of the halls in front of everyone.

We walked into the room and formed a line in front of

the thrones as we were instructed. I didn't dare look up to gaze upon the three royals, even though I was tempted by my curiosity. I had to keep my head down and keep a low profile if I would have any chance of escaping to get to Lilian. A small flutter of fear ran through my body as I tightened my eyes together, trying to remain invisible.

The chattering of the room continued as if we weren't even there. I heard footsteps behind me that treaded to the platform where the three royals sat. I briefly glanced up to see a white-haired male bowing in front of the royals. He stood and made his way over to the princess, taking her hand and kissing it formally.

The princess was stunning. She had long blonde hair and beautiful violet eyes. Her skin seemed to glow as if she had diamonds underneath the first layer. Her nose was long and pointed. Her ears peeked out from behind her hair. She had a long neck and a desirable figure. Why in heavens a male chooses to bed another female if he could have that was beyond me. One of the other girls elbowed me and broke my attention. I dropped my head back to the floor before anyone could notice.

"Lord Atros," said the king. "As promised, you may choose a human concubine to see to your needs. If you do not desire one from this collection, you may wait until next month."

"Thank you, King Lysanthier. You are most generous," said Lord Atros. His voice seemed familiar in a way, but I didn't dare look up to see if I recognized his face. The Lord made his way over to us. I was farthest from him, hoping one of the others would catch his eye before he got to me. His footsteps were slow as he examined the lot of us. He stopped occasionally, circling one of the girls before moving on.

I kept my eyes down on the floor, not daring to look at him or the other girls. A pair of black leather boots came into focus as the lord's footsteps stopped in front of me. I furrowed my brow, trying not to shake. He circled me, stopping in the back. I could feel his fingers twirl the tip of my hair at the base of my back. He made his way to my front and then stopped again. His cold hand gently lifted my chin up into the light. I pinched my eyes shut in fear, then slowly opened them to see two familiar yellow eyes looking back at me.

Lord Atros was the same male that led the group of alfar into town to collect us. My eyes widened as I looked at him in shock. His lips curled into a faint smile as if he was amused by my discomfort. I looked behind him to see the princess's curious gaze tracking his every move.

Lord Atros moved his hand slowly from my chin down my neck, stopping at the neckline of my dress. My breathing deepened as I tried not to focus on the cold contact. He saw my discomfort and removed his hand cautiously, not taking his eyes off me.

He leaned forward, bringing his lips closer to my ear. I was on high alert; afraid my true identity would be discovered. I braced myself.

"You don't really know how to cook, sew, or tend to the fields, do you?" he whispered against my hair.

I licked my lips before responding. "No, your grace," I said softly.

He chuckled. "You're a horrible liar. If you're going to stay alive here, you'll have to get better at it."

"Yes, your grace," I said, dropping my eyes back to the floor.

He backed away from me, still taking me in with his eyes.

"This one," he said, turning away from me to face the royals. The other five girls exhaled in relief. I looked at them and then back to the royals. *No, no, no, I can't be his mistress. I have to stay out of sight. I have to escape to get to Lilian. This can't be happening.* My chest began to raise and lower quickly as I held back my tears of panic.

"Interesting choice. She is... unusual, yet striking in her own way," said the king, in a monotone voice. "She is now yours. Take her away." He waved his hand.

Two guards came up next to me and took me by the arm to escort me out of the throne room.

They led me down the hall before stopping at another set of double doors and pushing them open. I walked through the threshold into what I assumed to be Lord Atros's bedchamber. The room had a large wooden bed, a sitting area with two chairs, and a couch. A wooden table sat off in the corner, a large armoire by the bathroom, and a balcony overlooked the kingdom.

The doors shut, leaving me alone in my new owner's personal chamber. I bit my bottom lip, trying to figure a way out of this. My hands fidgeted in front of me as tears uncontrollably began to fall. I collapsed on the floor, holding my face as the emotions of the past twenty-four hours came rushing out of me.

"Oh, come now, my cousin isn't that bad," came a male voice from the balcony.

I sprang to my feet, wiping away the loose tears from my cheek. A young alfar stood in front of me. He was tall and lean with white hair neatly parted down the center. He wore blue leather pants and a crisp white shirt. He had soft yellow eyes with thin lips and a strong nose.

"I'm—I'm sorry. I didn't know anyone else was in here," I said hesitantly. I kept my eyes on the floor, remembering how the old woman told me to act. The stranger came up directly in front of me and began to laugh.

"You can look at me, don't worry," he said, tauntingly.

I slowly raised my head to meet his eyes.

He was smiling as he bowed in front of me. "My name is Levos Atros. I am the cousin of Lord Gaelin Atros. I've been asked to help you find your way around here for the first couple of days."

Unsure of how to respond, I stayed silent. I could feel his eyes assessing me. He clicked his tongue.

"Do you have a name, or should I just call you pet?"

Rage slowly began to replace the fear inside of me at the title *pet*. "Genevieve Autumn," I said coldly. I was no one's pet.

"Genevieve? That's a beautiful name for a beautiful human," he said, circling me slowly. "Hmm, you're a bit thin. I can see all your bones, Genevieve."

"Starvation will do that to you," I snapped back. I shut

my mouth quickly, widening my eyes in shock at how rude the comment came out.

He stopped in front of me and smirked. "A human with an attitude. I can work with that."

"I'm so sorry. I didn't mean to offend you or speak out of turn."

"Enough with the formality. You can speak freely around me, just don't let the others know I told you that. As long as you make my cousin happy, you'll have a good life here, Genevieve."

"And... what does that exactly entail?"

He squinted his eyes in amusement. "The normal daily tasks. Cleaning, washing, and mending his linens. Serving him wine when he requests it. And of course, servicing his... physical needs."

I dropped my eyes, swallowing hard. The thought of his cold hands on my body made me sick.

Levos started laughing under his breath. "Are you rehearsed in the needs of the opposite sex?"

I shook my head no.

"Not even your own kind?" He asked, with a sarcastic tone.

"No. I still have my maidenhood," I whispered.

Levos laughed so loud I jumped back. "My cousin sure knows how to pick them. Don't worry, I will bring you some books that outline the basics of what you should be doing."

"I—I can't read," I admitted.

"Well, it looks like I have my work cut out for me then. Come, we need to get you fitted for some clothes, and then I will show you around the grounds." He extended his arm to me.

I hesitantly took it, unsure of his intentions. I ran my free hand through my hair to my ears, making sure they were still hidden. "Would it be possible to get a scarf or wrap I could wear in my hair? It's a fashion I would like to maintain," I said, trying to divert any suspicion.

"You'll have to get Gaelin's permission. He chooses how you look and what you wear from this point on, but he is a reasonable alfar. I'm sure it won't be a problem."

CHAPTER 6

I allowed Levos's brass personality and sense of humor to distract me the rest of the day. He seemed too nice to take at face value. I wondered if his kindness was some type of ploy to gain my trust. *Don't trust the alfar*, I reminded myself.

We walked the grounds where he showed me the fields that provided their food, along with their water sources. The alfar we encountered didn't bat an eye in my direction. The humans, on the other hand, glared at me with disgust, which I didn't understand.

As we moved through the city, I was in awe of the alfar's magical abilities. They could control the nature around them, growing a tree in a few minutes with just a wave of their hand. Children floated feathers around their heads in the city square, creating a snow-like effect. The alfar could also move water and commune with animals. Levos told me all about their magical abilities and how strong and powerful the light alfar were. I figured while he was in a sharing mood, I might as well try to gather information on my enemy.

"So does the light court ever have any interaction with the dark court?" I tried to ease my way into the topic.

Levos arched an eyebrow, assessing me and my boldness. "Unfortunately, yes. More lately than usual. We have a bit of a... pest problem on our lands," said Levos.

I chewed on the bottom of my lip, hesitating to push the topic further, but I was desperate. "Are the dark alfar as bad as the rumors?" I asked.

"Depends on the rumors, I suppose. We try to stay clear of them as much as possible. Though we are of the same blood, we do not view political or religious matters in the same light."

"Do they really kill humans as sacrifices to their god?"

Levos exhaled deeply. I realized I was getting close to his friendly sharing limit for the day. "It's not something we like to speak of. Their actions reflect poorly on us, but yes, those rumors are true. Thankfully, you will never have to experience their court. Now come, time to get you something to eat."

We made our way back into the palace. Levos showed me the servant's quarters and where I could get food. He waited until I ate my fill and then escorted me back to Lord Atros's bedchamber.

"Thank you for your help today," I said to Levos. "I'm sure you have better things to do with your time than babysit a human,"

"Actually, I've enjoyed this very much. Living as long as

we do, life becomes mundane. Hearing stories about how human's live... interest me."

"Well, in that case, I am sorry I am such a bore. I haven't done much with the past nineteen years of my life, except survive, I guess."

"Nonsense. That in itself is something to praise. I couldn't begin to understand your predicament. At least now you will never go hungry, and you will always have a place to lay your head as long as you keep the future king happy," He nudged me in the arm. The weight of the impending night slammed into me like a tidal wave.

"And... how am I supposed to do that?"

"Like I said, you have nothing to worry about. He is kinder than most of us when it comes to the treatment of humans. Be honest, respectful, and caring and he will treat you the same." Levos pushed open one of the doors. The moonlight filled the dark bedroom as candles flickered to life around the walls. Lord Atros stood by the balcony, leaning against the edge of the wall, looking out into the night sky.

Levos's hand pushed against my lower back, edging me into the room. I looked up at him with fear.

He smiled and leaned into my ear. "It will be okay. Deep breaths," Levos said, before shutting the door behind me.

Lord Atros turned from the balcony to face me. I took many deep breaths, holding his gaze. He was more handsome than I recalled. His jawline was strong and broad with full lips and a chin that tapered into a square. His eyes glowed in the night and his hair now fell loosely around his shoulders. The thin shirt that adorned his figure was opened down the center, revealing a sturdy, well-built chest. His biceps were large and rippled with muscles.

"Did you find my cousin amusing?" he asked.

"I..." I shook my head, trying to get control of myself. "I'm sorry, do I look at you or the floor? All of the formalities are a bit confusing."

He snickered in amusement, walking closer toward me. "In private, you look at me. In public, you look at the floor."

"Right. Your cousin was very helpful," I replied shortly.

"Did he explain what your duties consist of?"

I dropped my eyes from him, clenching my hands into fists. "Yes." Lord Atros closed the distance between us. I backed into the door. He stopped, now close enough that I could smell his scent. I turned my head, trying not to look at him. I felt his eyes roam over my face and down my neck.

"Don't worry, I'm not going to take your maidenhood. I won't touch you until you ask me to," he said softly, before walking away from me.

I exhaled a deep breath, relaxing against the door. I furrowed my brow as my mind snagged on what he said about my maidenhood.

"How did you know?" I asked boldly. Levos was with me all day. There was no time to report his findings back to his cousin.

"I can smell it on you. I've been around humans enough that I can tell the difference between the scent of a maiden and the scent of a kept woman."

"Is that why you chose me?"

He picked up a book from the table and cocked his head, not making eye contact. "Your eyes." He paused, staring down at the book as if he found it interesting. Without looking at me, he confessed, "I chose you because of your eyes." He picked up a spare blanket and pillow and placed them on the couch. "You will sleep here unless you trust me to behave myself and you'd rather sleep in my bed."

"The couch is fine, thank you," I said.

"What do I call you?"

"Genevieve, or Gen for short. And what do I call you?"

"In private, you may call me Gaelin. In public, you do not address me. When you speak of me, you call me Lord Atros." He walked over to his bed and began to take off his boots and shirt.

I laid down and turned away from him, burying my face into the pillow and pulling the covers over my body, trying to find some sense of comfort. With the wave of a hand, he snuffed the candles, and the room went dark.

The next morning when I awoke, Gaelin was already gone. I freshened up in the private bathroom before tending to his room. I made his bed, folded the blankets, and collected the dirty laundry. Before I was done, Levos barged into the room pulling a rack full of clothes behind me.

"Look what I have for you, dear Genevieve. Custom clothing made specifically for that frail body of yours. Oh, and I checked with my dear old cousin, and he said you can wear cloth headbands, but he wants your hair visible at all times," said Levos.

"I feel like I'm a well-kept mare," I said, gathering the last of the laundry.

Levos laughed as he placed the dresses in the armoire. The sound took me by surprise. "Not to be too demoralizing, but you kind of are. A well-kept mare he would like to ride."

I fought with all the resilience I had to keep my mouth shut.

"What?" He said, looking a bit disappointed. "No snarky comeback? Don't become boring on me, sweet Genevieve."

"I have nothing to say," I lied, not making eye contact with him.

He pulled at my arm until I faced him. "Remember what I told you. You can be yourself around me. I'm not a royal. Far from it, in fact. I know what you must think of all of this... all of us, but I'd like us to be friends."

"And how do I know I can trust you? Why would an alfar show any semblance of kindness to a human?"

"Because not all alfar are the same, just like not all humans are the same. Trust will take time, but please, don't censor yourself. You have a brain, so use it." I gave him a small smile. He was a fool if he thought I would ever trust him, but I could work this to my advantage. I just had to play this right.

"Well, in that case, for your information, your cousin did not ride his prized mare last night."

"I already knew that," he snickered.

"You two talk about that sort of thing?"

"No, but like I told you, Gaelin is an honorable alfar. He wouldn't have taken you unless you agreed to it."

Well, at least I had that working for me.

"Can I ask you something personal?" I said, trying to sound innocent.

He sat in one of the chairs and placed both hands behind his head. "Let the trust-building begin," he said, smiling.

"If the alfar think of us as nothing more than cattle, then why are you all so eager to have sex with us? I would assume you'd be disgusted by the thought." I sat down across from him, trying to seem eager and innocent as I batted my eyes and fiddled with my hands, appearing as if I was nervous and uncertain.

His eyebrow arched as he looked at me through slanted eyes. "You are fearless, sweet Gen. I like that about you." He exhaled, leaning back in a relaxed position. "The males especially prefer a human over another alfar when it comes to pleasure. If you haven't noticed yet, we run a bit colder than your race. The warmth that a human female offers during sex is more enjoyable than anything we could ever experience. Also, the human female's sex organ allows for intercourse without any additional lubricants, if you get my meaning."

"So, a female alfar's insides run colder and they don't produce their own...lubricant?".

"Yes. And the human females who do enjoy sex with our dreadful race are more enthusiastic during the process, which makes the whole experience more pleasurable. Female alfar enjoy sex, but they tend not to be as vocal about it."

"Couldn't they just fake it?" I asked without thinking.

He snorted, leaning forward with a smile on his face. "We would know. We can smell the hormones they release during sex. Because of our heightened senses, the sex hormone acts as a drug for both males and females. Humans tend to release theirs more frequently."

"I see." I stood up and walked back to the laundry basket.

"That's all? No more invasive or inappropriate questions?"

"Nope, I am good for now, but thank you for the insight. So, what's on the agenda for today?"

"Well, first you need to change. Put on the red dress. There's a gold headband that will go nicely with the fabric. Then we will start the washing and after lunch, you will begin your reading lessons."

"Free food, free schooling, and a handsome alfar king to screw whenever I want. What more could a girl ask for?" I said, making my way to the bathroom.

"So, you do find him attractive? He will be pleased to hear that."

I shot him a dirty look. "We're building trust, *Levos*. Which means keeping my secrets."

"Come on, give the male a little bit of hope."

I quickly changed, tying the gold headband around the tip of my ears to hide the points.

"Question," I said innocently, before appearing outside of the bathroom doorway. "What would happen if I slept with another alfar?"

His eyebrows rose and then fell as if stunned by the inquiry. "You would be killed and replaced," he said plainly.

"So, you all are free to screw whomever you want, but I can't?"

"Yes, that is the way this arrangement works. No other alfar can touch you and if they do, they will be punished. You are only Gaelin's to possess."

"And what happens if a human gets pregnant by an alfar?" I asked hesitantly.

His brow furrowed as he hesitated for a brief moment. If I didn't know better, I would have sworn I saw pain arched across his face. He stood from his chair and walked over to the door. He didn't look at me. "The children are removed before they are born. You'll be checked each month to make sure his seed doesn't take root. If it does, you will be given an elixir that will allow the babe to pass without pain."

"Does this happen often?" I asked, feeling sick to my stomach.

"Too often," he said, opening the door. "Come on, time to earn your keep."

I walked past him with the basket of clothes into the bright halls of the castle. Learning that the rumors were true —about how they disposed of half-breeds—made my situation all too real. If they had known about my mother, I would have never been born.

Did my father rape my mother? Did he love her? Are alfar even capable of love? I had so many questions that I would never have answers to. My mother never left any trace of my father for me to find. Did she run, to protect herself and her unborn child? I would have if I were her.

CHAPTER 7

After three weeks, I was nowhere closer to escaping. There were guards everywhere during the day and at night I slept in the same room as the future king, who just happened to have hearing like a bat. I couldn't even get up to use the restroom without waking him. Levos was a surprising distraction. His efforts to befriend me continued, but I remained uncertain of his motives.

Levos made the days go by quicker. He made me laugh and kept me on my toes. From a safe distance, I studied the alfar. Magic was still foreign to me. Our Christian teachings declared that their gifts were of the devil. The Christians believed that Satan wielded the alfar's magic, using it to destroy our world. But the more I saw, the more in awe I was of their talents. They were connected with nature in every sense of the meaning, including the animals that called the forests their home. The alfar could do menial tasks with their magic that made their everyday lives a little easier. How I wished I could snap my fingers and have the day's chores done in an instant.

Though the light alfar had these amazing gifts, they seemed a lazy sort of people. The members of the high houses, whom I catered to daily, relied on their human servants more than their own abilities. Even though they could run their own bathwater with a snap of their fingers, they expected their slaves to do it for them.

None of the members of the high houses fought in the military with Gaelin. The alfar of the lower classes made the sacrifices, as the nobility sat inside of the castle acting as if the world outside wasn't moving and changing. I guess they felt they were too important to get their hands dirty.

Gaelin commanded what they called the Chamber of Defense. A member from each of the high houses designated a representative to the chamber. Gaelin would inform them on pest problems or any other run-ins with creatures of different races that he encountered. They would decide on the best ways to manage the conflicts and how to best serve their kingdom.

In my short few weeks in the light court, I had begun to learn how to read basic words. The challenge was exciting and fulfilling. At night, I would stay up with a single candle, practicing my penmanship. During the day I tended to my work, making sure Gaelin's needs were satisfied. I was his slave in every way except in his bed.

After a busy day of cleaning and learning a little about the light courts political structure, I returned to the room, ready to dive under the covers and escape in between the pages of a good book. Gaelin, to my surprise, was waiting in the sitting area in front of the fireplace. On the table in front of him, lay and arrangement of food and wine. He stood, looking a bit nervous as a smile dared to creep across his face.

"I... I figured you hadn't eaten dinner. I was hoping we could share a meal together, before we retired," said Gaelin, gesturing to the table.

I placed the basket of laundry down by the door and returned his uncertain smile. "Sure," I said, trying to seem excited at the opportunity to spend time with him. "I skipped dinner anyways." I made my way over to the sofa, taking a seat beside him.

He poured me a glass of wine and filled a plate full of fresh fruit and vegetables with a variety of cheeses. I nodded in thanks, unsure of how to begin this awkward encounter.

"How are you adjusting to Urial?" He finally asked.

"It's more beautiful than I could have imagined," I replied, placing a grape into my mouth.

"Is everyone treating you well?"

"Yes," I replied shortly.

He smiled back and nodded his approval. He shifted his eyes down to the platter of food.

I stole a glance at him from underneath my eyelashes, noticing in that moment, he was just as nervous and unsure as I was. It was the most human emotion I had seen any of them express since I had been here. I felt my heart soften.

"Can you... tell me about your duties at court?" I asked, leaning in closer to him.

His eyes lit up at my effort to make conversation and I

watched as the tension from his shoulder lessened. "I am general of our military units for the light court," he said. "I train them, address any security concerns, or military advancements towards other courts."

I smiled, curling my feet underneath me as I got comfortable on the coach. For the next two hours we got to know each other. He asked questions about my life back in The Frey. I told him about my family and what I had to do to survive.

I learned that his father commanded the military of the light before he was appointed the position. The match between Gaelin and Princess Daealla, King Lysanthier's daughter, was arranged by their fathers. He did not have feelings for the princess, but that didn't change the duty he now was expected to carry out. I found it hard to believe a male couldn't look at Daealla and not have an interest, but I didn't question him on the matter.

As the hours passed, I found myself feeling more relaxed around Gaelin. He was easy to talk to and seemed to be actually listening when I spoke. I told him about my siblings, spending a few minutes on each of them as I described their personalities and shared stories about our life together. My heart swelled in pain at the thought of them. I missed my family.

I was in the middle of recalling an incident when Connor and Jordan physically got into an altercation in the middle of morning mass over God's knew what when I let out a laugh, a real laugh. I could see the two boys rolling around in between the aisles as Sister Ester chased after them with embarrassment. Gaelin let out a laugh as well. I took a deep breath, wiping the tears from my eyes as our laughter tapered off.

"Sounds like you had your hands full back at home," said Gaelin, now only inches from me.

"You have no clue. If I am being honest, this is more like a vacation compared to the havoc some of my siblings would cause back in the Frey. Conner especially," I said. My face hurt from all the smiling and laughing. I stared down at the cup of wine in my hand, remembering each of their faces as clearly as I could. I furrowed my brow, trying to will the pain of missing them away.

Gently, I felt a small tug on the end of my hair. My attention shifted to where Gaelin now spun a curl of mine around his finger slowly. I brought my eyes up to his, holding his gaze. Silently, we stared at one another as he continued to twirl my hair through his fingers. His eyes seemed to glisten in the candlelight. His face appeared so smooth and soft. It took everything I had not to reach out and brush my fingers across it just to satisfy my curiosity, but I refrained, not sure of what action to take next. A small smile that didn't reach his eyes sprawled across his face.

"Thank you," he whispered, "for appeasing me tonight. I am sure this is not the evening you had planned, but I hope I was at least equally as interesting as those characters in your books."

I chuckled under my breath, bringing my hand up to cover my face. Smiling now seemed foreign to me, but tonight, it came too naturally. "I was not disappointed," I responded.

Gaelin let go of my hair, standing slowly from the couch. "Good night, Genevieve. I hope to do this again," he said.

"That sounds nice," I replied. "And Gaelin..." Gaelin stopped, turning back to face me. "You can call me Gen."

"I'd like that."

I smiled back at him as he made his way to his bed. I curled up on the couch and pulled the blanket up to my nose. Tonight, had been a good night, I thought to myself, but a feeling like guilt quickly followed and any natural smile I had been sporting a moment ago faded. I didn't know what type of relationship Gaelin wanted out of this arrangement, but this was not the situation I would have chosen for myself. I had to be careful moving forward. I couldn't lose focus of my mission. Lily.

I LIVED MY WHOLE LIFE NOT KNOWING HOW THE alfar race who I shared one half of my genetic makeup lived. I feared them, for good reason, but that still didn't subdue my desire to know and understand them. In public, Gaelin began to look in my direction during meals and events. He would smile at me, not caring who saw. I began to notice the desire in his eyes grow throughout the weeks. Princess Daealla also noticed his consistent attention towards me. Regardless of what race you claimed, jealousy looked the same and I knew I had a target on my back.

One day during lunch, when I was on clean up duty in the kitchen, Levos came out of nowhere grinning from ear to ear. "What do you want, Levos?" I asked, scrubbing a platter caked with raspberry jelly.

"Have you ever seen a nymph?" he asked.

I stopped, taken back by the question. "Unless they're allowed across the border, that would be a no," I said matter-of-factly.

"Best follow me then," he said, strolling out of the kitchen.

I dropped the platter, drying my hands on my apron before tearing the disgusting thing off and chasing after him. "One is here?" I asked as we made our way to the great hall.

"That is correct. See, each race has their own ambassador that acts as a mouthpiece for their royals. It's an honor to be chosen as such. It shows your intelligence and merit. From what I've gathered, the nymphs have had some run-ins with some fairies and are here to ask for help. Word of advice, stay away from any nymph. They are horny little creatures, and they don't care if you are male or female, they will pounce."

"I'm beginning to think everything on this side of the border has a hyperactive libido," I said.

He laughed, nodding. "You may be right, sweet Genevieve."

We slid past the two guards posted at the throne room entrance and stood at the back of the crowd, turning our attention to the thrones. Gaelin was perched on a lower step next to Princess Daealla, listening intently to the nymphs. I moved, trying to get a better look.

Five nymph representatives stood gracefully in front of the light royals. Four females and one male. They each had beautiful flawless skin that glowed unnaturally, as if they were being lit from underneath. Two of the females had beautiful green hair, the color of a spring field. One female had white and blue hair, and the other had hair the color of stone. The male had rich brown hair that was neatly tied against the back of his neck.

They wore animal skin clothing, covering the barest amount possible. No weapons could be seen on their bodies. The stories back in The Frey said they were peaceful beings, caring only about each other and nature. They were barefoot and their ankles, wrists, and necks were littered with jewels and metal chains of all sizes and colors.

Levos leaned into me. "The two green haired ones are tree nymphs, the blue is a freshwater. The grey-haired female and the male are mountain nymphs. The water nymph's name is Haeza. She is their ambassador," said Levos.

"I thought nymphs were only female," I said quietly.

"There are males, they're just rare. I think there's something like one male to every twenty females. Aren't they lucky," he whispered, chuckling to himself.

Haeza stepped forward. "Your highness," she said in a low sensual voice, "the fairies continue to cross into our lands and take our livestock, goods, and now members of our race have begun to go missing. This can't be a coincidence."

"Do you have any eyewitnesses?" asked King Lysanthier.

"We have multiple witnesses that have reported fairies

flying overhead. We have not directly seen our members being taken by their kind, but we are not ignorant. We know how those foul beasts operate," she replied.

"There are other things happening in these woods that we are working very hard to stop, as you well know, Ambassador Haeza. We cannot retaliate against the fairies unless we have proof of their transgressions against your race. I am sorry, but I am unable to assist your queen at this time," said the king.

Haeza looked directly at the king fearlessly. "Your Highness, our territory falls under your protection. If members of our race go missing, this is a problem you must address. The fairies are not permitted to fly overhead, let alone touch down in our lands. They are restricted to the Kingdom of Doonak's territory which is where they should stay. We offered our assistance and our allegiance to your people in return for your help and protection in matters such as these. That is our agreement and that is what my queen expects," said Haeza.

With a few moments of silence, the king pondered over the conflict at hand. He finally nodded as he released a breath. "I see where you are coming from, ambassador," said the king, "I will assign a small number of guards to your territory for the next month. I will also have our ambassador pay the dark alfar court a visit to make sure they are keeping their kingdom... controlled. If these accusations have merit, we will fulfill our side of our arrangement and aid you in ridding yourselves of the threat. Is there anything else, Ambassador Haeza?"

"No, your grace."

"Good. I am glad we could come to an agreement. Lord Atros will select a group of soldiers to escort you back to your kingdom. They will remain stationed there for the next month. We would be honored if you will feast with us this evening."

"Thank you, King Lysanthier. It would be an honor," said Haeza, bowing before him.

The king waved his hand to release the court. Levos and I moved into the hall and found our way to the library. As intelligent and capable as the alfar were, no one ever seemed to use the library in this castle. It wasn't very big, but to me, it was a treasure room.

"Pretty interesting creatures, right?" asked Levos.

"Very. So, they can control nature like you all can, right?" I asked.

"Yes, but where we can control it, they can become it. They can turn into trees, fields, water, and stone. It's pretty amazing to watch. They are also sex goddesses in my opinion."

I laughed, pulling a book from a nearby shelf. "And you know this from experience? Wait, don't answer that."

"Oh, yes, I do. You think the alfar are bad? That race is savage. The only ones that can keep up with them are the incubi. Pity their races can't breed together. I'd pay to see what kind of creature came out of that union." I stiffened, thinking of my own mixed heritage.

"So, you'll be busy tonight?" I asked.

"Oh, no. Sowed my wild oats in my youth, sweet

Genevieve. Better to not get into bed with an ally. Though, I am sure the high lords are already claiming which ones they are going to take to bed tonight. It's always a treat to have something or someone new at court."

"Yuck," I said.

He laughed, and we began to study.

That night, I watched how the alfar reacted to the nymphs. Though they were allies, the alfar still treated them as if they were lesser beings. Their narcissism was insufferable. The nymphs were polite and didn't look at the humans the way the alfar did. I swore one even muttered a thank you when I filled her glass.

I got back to the room first after dinner, hurrying to put Gaelin's clean laundry away before he retired for the evening. I was quickly approaching week six of my stay in the castle. I knew with each day that passed Lilian was one step closer to death. That is, if she wasn't dead already. I pushed that thought out of my mind. She wasn't dead. She couldn't be. I had to come up with a plan to escape soon or I would have sacrificed my life for nothing.

"You ran out of dinner so fast I didn't have a chance to give you your present," said Levos, entering the room.

I jumped, startled by his unannounced visit. "Damnit Levos, you're going to give me a heart attack. Learn to knock," I snapped.

He started laughing, walking slowly towards me. "Did you not hear the word present come out of my mouth? Aren't you curious about what I got you?"

"Why would you waste your money on a lowly human? I'm not worth the coin," I said.

He smiled and held out a small rectangular box.

I took it hesitantly, wondering what hid inside. "What's the occasion?"

"No occasion. I just saw it and it reminded me of you. I figured you could use a little sparkle in your life." He gestured for me to open it. I cautiously lifted the lid. Inside was a beautiful diamond headband. The edges were made of white silk ribbon. It was the most exquisite thing I had ever held. "I thought it would be a good contrast with your hair," he added, smiling.

"Levos, I don't know what to say. I can't accept this. It's too much."

"You can and you will. Now, turn around so I can see how it looks." I took a step back, pulling away from his reach.

"I'll wear it tomorrow, I promise. I must find the right dress to compliment it," I said quickly. My free hand reaching to my ear, holding my current headband in place.

"Oh, come now, it's not going to hurt anyone if you try it on right now. Do it for me, please," he said, closing the space between us.

"I will, tomorrow. I promise."

He stopped, taking a step back. His face fell in defeat as disappointment shot through him. "You don't like it, do you?" he asked.

"Of course, I do. It is the most beautiful thing I've ever

possessed. I don't know how I am going to ever repay your kindness."

"How about you try it on for me and then we'll call it even," he said, reaching for my headband too fast for me to stop him.

"Wait, Levos, please—" he pulled the headband from my hair. I instinctually covered my ears and cowered away from him. He stood above me, silent. My chin began to quiver as tears of fear welled. I took a deep breath, straightened to look him in the eye, and dropped my hands, revealing my small, tipped ears. He took a step back with his mouth opened in shock. "Levos..."

"You're a...a half-breed?" he asked, astonished.

I nodded, unsure of what to say.

"How did you... how did they not find you?" he asked, trying to make since of my existence.

"I was born in The Frey. Most humans who cross over never leave, but my mother somehow found a way. She never talked about my father or how I came to be." There were a few moments of silence. I tried to think of something to say or something to bargain with, but I had nothing. This was it. My secret was out, and my life was going to end before I could get to Lilian. "Levos, I know I have no right to ask you for a favor, but before you turn me in, can you please do something for me? There is a young human named Lilian Thomas who was taken by the dark court six weeks ago. Can you please try to get her out? I need to know that she's going to be okay before I die. Please, Levos." Tears fell down my cheeks as I began to shake in fear.

Levos turned his attention to the floor, as if looking me in the eye was too painful. His brow furrowed as he struggled with my secret, and now my confession. He took a seat in a chair next to the fireplace. Unsure of what to do with myself, I sat down on the couch, eagerly awaiting him to respond. To say anything.

"You offered yourself into our service so you could find a way to the dark court to save your friend?" He finally replied.

"It was the only thing I could think of to get close to her. She's like my sister. She doesn't deserve that life. She deserves better. Please, I'm begging you," I dropped to my knees in front of him. I thought furiously, trying to come up with something to offer him to assure he would save Lilian.

He slowly took my chin in between his fingers, forcing me to look at him. His fingers gently brushed my hair back behind my ears, revealing the small tips.

"We all have our secrets, Gen. Your secrets are safe with me...always," he whispered.

I looked into his eyes. An overwhelming sense of relief flooded through me, and I collapsed onto his lap as I began to sob violently. "Thank you. Thank you so much," I cried.

He held me tightly and kissed the top of my head tenderly. I pulled away, wiping my eyes free of the tears. I placed my trembling hands over my face, trying to steady myself.

"Now, what are we going to do about your friend?" he asked.

"I need to find a way to the dark court in order to get her out."

"That's if she is still alive," he added. My stomach dropped even considering the possibility. "Gen, I am sorry, but you are going to have to prepare yourself for that reality. The dark court is not like the light. They dispose of humans faster than they do their own livestock."

"I know, I know, but I can't live without knowing what happened to her."

He sat against the back of the chair, as his brow furrowed in thought. "Let me think about how to find her. In the meantime, we also need to worry about Gaelin."

"How so?"

"If you haven't noticed, his affections for you are growing by the day. He is going to find out what you are, sooner or later. We may even need him if we are to rescue your friend."

"Do you think he'll turn me in?" I asked hesitantly.

"He cares for you, but he is loyal to the throne and its laws. This could go either way. I'd rather he not find out unless we are out of options. The fewer people that know your secret, the safer you will be." Levos's attention snapped to the door. "He's coming. Hurry, get your headband, and wipe your face."

We jumped to our feet. I covered my ears and took a few deep breaths, trying to appear normal. Gaelin opened the door with a smile on his face that instantly faded at the sight of Levos and me.

"Am I interrupting something?" Gaelin asked, looking between the two of us.

"Nothing at all, cousin. I found a headband that reminded me of Genevieve, and I was unable to get it to her before she rushed off to fold your underpants." Levos made his way to the door, patting Gaelin on the shoulder. "Have a nice evening you two."

Gaelin shut the door behind Levos. He was uncomfortably quiet, no doubt pondering what his cousin was doing alone in his room with his prude mistress.

I went to his bed and pulled the sheets back. He stood at the footboard as his eyes roamed over me, looking for any indication that something had happened between Levos and me. He took a deep breath in through his nose, smelling the air. I stopped what I was doing and turned my attention towards him, cocking one eyebrow and smiling mischievously.

"You can just ask me, you know," I said, walking over to face him.

"I don't like it when you're alone with another male. Even if it is my cousin," he said firmly.

"And what do you think we were doing? Carrying on an affair behind your back?" I said playfully.

"Genevieve, I am serious."

"I know you are. That is what makes this whole thing that much more entertaining. He is your cousin, Gaelin. He is loyal to you to a fault. He would never betray you."

"Then why do I smell him on you?" I rolled my eyes, placing a hand on either of his arms. He flinched at my touch. I realized that this was the first time I had initiated contact between the two of us.

"He gave me a beautiful headband that he found at the market. I gave him a hug to say thank you. That is all. He is my friend and only my friend," I said, stepping closer to him.

"Do you like gifts?" he asked.

"I don't really know. That was the first one I have ever received. I guess it all just took me by surprise." He looked away from me, chewing over the thoughts that were rolling around in his head. "Gaelin," I said, reaching my hand out slowly to his face. He closed his eyes as my hand cupped the side of his jaw. His face was cold, yet soft and somehow alluring. "I'm not that type of person."

"I couldn't blame you if you did select to be with someone of your own choosing. I took your choice away the day I chose you as my concubine. You don't deserve this."

I was taken back by his admission. Alfar didn't care how their choices affected humans. Our happiness had no weight when it came to their decisions. Maybe Levos was right. Gaelin was different. A part of me softened towards him in that moment.

"You have shown me nothing but consideration and kindness," I said softly. "You've never forced me to do anything I wasn't comfortable with and because of that, you have my respect and trust."

He turned his eyes back to my face, taking in every detail. He slowly raised his hand to my cheek, gently following my jawline down to my lips with his thumb. "Do you think you will ever want me the way I want you?" he asked.

I was taken back by the question, not sure of what the correct response was. I took a deep breath, calming myself.

"Six weeks ago, I didn't think I would ever allow you to touch me like you are right now, yet here we are. I think that in time there is a chance, yes." He smiled at me, removing his hand from my face. I pulled away from him slowly. "Is there anything else I can get for you tonight?"

He laughed under his breath. "You know what I want, Gen."

"Like I said, anything besides that?" I smiled at him, uncomfortable at his admission.

"No, I think I am good. Get ready for bed."

By the time I exited the bathroom the candles were already snuffed out and he was in bed. I tiptoed to the couch and slid under the covers. Today, I had diverted the ax and gained an ally in my search for Lilian. Levos was right about Gaelin. He wanted more and his need and desires were growing stronger by the day. I had to figure out some way to hold him off before he discovered my true identity. If he did, would his affection for me be enough to save my life?

CHAPTER 8

The next morning, I was sent out into the nearby woods to collect fresh burdock. Apparently, alfar females liked to bathe in the herb to prevent signs of aging. I laughed at the thought of an elf ever looking older than thirty, but I was not there to question their methods, only to serve. The silence of the woods was refreshing. Though most of the alfar and humans never spoke a word to me, the hustle and bustle of the city was overbearing.

I took my time, going from clearing to clearing, collecting what I needed. I ran across a patch of wild lavender and picked some for myself. The plant was rare back in The Frey, but it had always been my favorite. The scent reminded me of my mother, one of the few memories I had of her before she died.

I knelt by a fresh spring, taking a small handful of water and splashing it on my neck. The sound of metal clanking together off in the distance caught my attention. I slowly rose, looking around for any signs that would indicate danger. These woods were protected by the light alfar. Levos assured me no one else was allowed through here.

I walked slowly towards the noise, placing my basket on the ground, and picked up a large wooden stick. The sound grew louder. I could hear someone grunting and struggling in pain as metal rattled. Pushing aside a low hanging branch I saw a female humanoid caught in some type of metal trap. Her skin was white as the clouds. She had long blue hair that trailed down her back and eyes black as night. The teeth of the trap had snapped just above her knee, rendering her helpless.

She stopped moving as her eyes locked onto me. I lowered the stick to my side and walked towards her with my free hand up. Her eyes went deadly as she tried to move away from me, but the trap held her. She gasped in pain, reaching for her leg.

"I'm not going to hurt you, I promise," I said. I took another step closer.

"And why would I trust you, *elf*? Your race only cares about your own," she snapped.

"I am no elf, and I guess you're just going to have to trust me, since I'm not the one stuck in the trap." I gave her a small smile. I walked towards her with caution, trying not to make any threatening movements. Black blood oozed from her wound. I wasn't sure what type of creature she was, but I knew if I didn't get her out of the trap soon, she would die, based on the amount of blood she had already lost. That was if the being who set the trap didn't find her first.

"I'm going to help free you from the trap," I said.

"And why would you do such a selfless thing for a stranger?" she asked in a low sarcastic tone.

"Because I hope someone would do the same for me if I were in your position," I replied. I saw a moment of confusion in her eyes as she looked down at her wounded leg. "Just promise me you won't eat me after I free you."

A laugh that was deep and sensual caught in her throat. "Don't worry, your kind doesn't taste all that good, contrary to what the other creatures of this world think."

"I'll take that as assurance I'm going to walk out of this alive."

"Now little elf, I didn't say that."

I stopped what I was doing and locked my eyes onto hers.

She rolled her eyes and exhaled in frustration. "Fine, you have my word I will not harm you if you help me get out of this thing."

I wedged the stick in between the teeth of the trap, using my own body weight to pry it from her leg. She yelped as the teeth unhinged themselves from her flesh. I grunted, using all the strength I had to hold the trap open long enough for her to pull her leg free. She slid back away from the metal contraption. I let go of the tension and the metal snapped back together with force.

I stood, unsure of what to expect from the creature. I backed away towards the castle, making sure not to take my eyes off her. She stood tall, a creature of dominance. Her leg began to heal itself instantly.

She raised her head with a devious look on her face and smiled at me. "A deal is a deal, little elf. I owe you a life debt for your selfless act, something I don't give lightly. I am sure we will be seeing each other again," she said, before disappearing into thin air, leaving a blue puff of smoke in her wake.

I turned frantically around, trying to catch where she had gone, but she was gone.

I ran back to the castle and went to the library, knowing only Levos would be there. My heart was pounding so fast I thought it was going to explode. Levos saw me enter and stood from the table of books he had been poring over. He looked excited.

"I think I have it all figured out, but you're—" he stopped, taking in my current state. "Did you go for a run or something? You smell awful."

I inhaled deeply, trying to catch my breath. "What...what are those traps? Out there in the woods...supposed to catch?" I asked in between breaths.

"Yeah, about those. Do you remember that pest problem that I told you about the first time we met? Well, those are meant to catch the pests."

"And how big are these pests?"

"Big, like really big," he said, making a dramatic face.

"Levos, what is out there? What is going on?"

He exhaled, taking a seat on one of the couches. "About three years ago we noticed a surge of new creatures that kept showing up around our territory. We killed them and then studied them, but we couldn't match their origin. Around the same time the dark court contacted us with the same inquiry. We discovered that a rift or a portal kept opening around our territories, allowing creatures and beasts of all shapes and sizes to enter our world. We don't know why they're here or what they want. We never know where the rift will end up opening next, so it is hard to figure out where it all is coming from."

"And those traps are supposed to catch them?"

"Yes. They are spelled to catch a number of things since we don't understand what they are. When the trap is activated, only an alfar can release the creature it has captured. Nothing has ever gotten close to the castle, but we are still taking precautions."

I felt sick as I dropped to the couch next to him. I had just freed one of those things.

"Why do you ask?"

I was still stunned, trying to figure out what I had just unleashed into our world.

"Gen?"

"Oh, I just saw one when I was out looking for some herbs. Thought it was a bit aggressive for a fairy trap."

"Ah, well, I'd advise staying away from them from now on. Don't want you to lose a leg. Gaelin won't be too happy about that. Now, as I was saying, I think I have found a way to check up on your little friend, but you aren't going to like what you'll have to do."

My attention snapped to Levos. My heart pumped faster at the thought of Lily. "I'm listening."

"Gaelin and a group of warriors are leaving tomorrow to

go to the dark court to assist in one of their pest problems. You can ask Gaelin to inquire about your friend while he is there."

"Won't it look suspicious if he is asking about a human?"

"Yes, but he is the next king. They won't question him. But this means you have to tell him about Lilian and why you really offered yourself to the light court." I stood up, weighing the options.

"Do you think he will help?"

"I think he wants to make you happy, so yes, he will help."

I nodded, thinking of how I was going to approach the subject. "Thank you for letting me know about the dealings with the dark court. I will take it from here."

"What? You're not going to pour me a drink and invite me to stay awhile?" said Levos. I smacked him on the back of the head playfully. "Watch it now, you could lose a hand for striking an alfar. Actually, I don't know what the punishment is for a half-breed...oh wait, yes, I do. Never mind." He snickered before I smacked him again.

"Don't even play like that. This isn't a game."

He stood from the chair, taking my arms in his hands. "No, it is not, but I am glad I know your secret," he said softly, looking into my eyes.

"We should probably keep our one-on-one interaction to a minimum. Gaelin is worried about our relationship developing further," I admitted.

Levos laughed as he stepped away from me, shaking his

head in disbelief. "You've got to be kidding me. My own cousin thinks I would bed his mistress?"

"Apparently. He was even sniffing the air to make sure my maidenhood was still intact last night."

"Now I would have paid gold to see that for myself. Understandable all the same. He most likely is worried you've fallen for someone else, since you still refuse his bed. By the way, I'm very impressed you've lasted this long."

"What do you mean?"

"Most women, alfar or human, beg to be invited to his bed, yet here you are sharing a room with him and refusing him each night. That must be doing wonders for his inflated ego."

"You're not making me feel better about the situation, Levos. I am not going to be pressured into this decision."

"And I am not trying to sway you either way. On that note, I will take my leave and leave you to your scheming. Maybe if you offered to bed him as payment it would sweeten the deal," he said, moving towards the door.

I took off my shoe and threw it at his head.

He ducked, laughing as he opened the door. "Alright, alright, I get the hint. Good luck, sweet Genevieve. I will check on you tomorrow."

I sat down in a chair and worked out the details of how I was going to ask Gaelin for his help. It was just a simple inquiry. I wasn't asking him to kill anyone. He could just simply ask about her, right? I wasn't going to use sex to further my agenda with him. I wasn't that type of person, but I knew I was playing with fire. The closer I got to him, the more he wanted me and if I was being honest, it was getting harder for me to talk myself out of giving in. If I were to sleep with him, the act would guarantee my safety and survival.

That night I readied the room and waited for him to enter. I sat on the edge of the bed already in my nightgown. The white sheer fabric clung to my body, and a cotton robe covered some of my exposed skin. I wasn't going to use sex against him, but a small visual couldn't hurt. The door opened and I sprung to my feet, more alert than I had been in a long time.

"Good evening, how was your day?" I asked anxiously.

"Same as most days. We are preparing a short trip to the dark court tomorrow so I will be gone until the end of the week." He took off his weapons and placed them by the door.

I made my way over to him and began to unlatch his jacket, trying to act normal. I could feel his eyes trailing over my face. After I hung his jacket and he removed his boots, I went back to the bed and sat patiently, waiting for him to finish in the bathroom. He stopped at the threshold of the door, peering at me perched on the edge of his bed.

"I would like to discuss something with you if that is okay," I said.

He made his way over to me and sat softly on the mattress. "Of course, anything."

I took a deep breath, knowing I was putting my own life at risk. If I was going to tell him the truth it had to be all of it. If he found out I was lying about a single detail Lilian's life could be at risk, and I couldn't have that.

"I want to preface that whatever you chose to do with the information, I understand and will not fight you on the matter, as long as you promise me you will find my sister."

He straightened and furrowed his brow in confusion. "And who is your sister?"

"The family I told you about that I left back in The Frey...there is a member I purposefully left out. She is a young girl named Lilian Thomas. For three years, she has been the most important person in my life. Six weeks ago, she was taken by the dark alfar. I offered myself to your court to get close enough to find out if she is still alive. Levos told me that you were going to the dark court." I shifted on the bed uncomfortably, trying to remain strong. Gaelin continued to study me, not saying a word.

I took a deep breath and continued. "I was wondering if you could inquire about her. Just to see if she is still alive or if she is hurt or being tortured. I love her more than my own life, Gaelin. That is why I am about to tell you something that you could have me killed for."

His face went pale with shock and concern. "I would never hurt you. Inquiring about your sister is not something you would be killed over." His face filled with concern as he reached for me, but I flinched away, feeling lightheaded as the panic and fear began to sink in.

I dropped my eyes to my lap. My hands shook as I brought them to the scarf that covered my ears. "No, it's not," I said, fighting my tears. "But this is." I slowly pulled the piece of fabric away from my head, revealing my true identity. I felt him pull away. I didn't dare look at him. I kneaded the scarf in my hands, waiting for his response.

"As I said, do what you want with what you now know, but please, find Lilian and get her out if you can," I begged.

"Who else knows?" he asked coldly.

"Levos found out last night. That's what you walked in on. I didn't tell him freely; it was an accident that he saw my ears."

"And he said nothing to me."

I lifted my face, still shaking. A single tear escaped my eye and fell down my face. "Please don't punish him. He wanted to tell you, but I convinced him not to. If you're going to punish anyone it should be me."

He turned slowly towards me, taking in each ear. "Part alfar, part human. A half-breed."

"Yes," I whispered shamefully. I waited for his response. He held the fate of my life in his hands. I knew this was a risk, but somewhere, deep down inside of myself, I thought the connection we were making would be strong enough to overcome anything. At least a small part of me hoped it was.

Gaelin stood up from the bed, still refusing to look me in the face. His breathing was heavy, and his lips strained in a sharp line as his eyes flickered from side to side as if they were searching for the answer to our problem.

I stood, extending my hand out to touch his arm but he pulled away from me so suddenly I jumped back.

"Half-breeds are against the law," he said, in a tone I didn't recognize.

"I know," I whispered.

"You should never have been born." He paused, running a hand through his hair. "How are you still alive? Why did the humans not turn you in?"

My heart broke a little at his disappointment that I was not disposed of the moment my mother discovered I had been conceived. I realized that I had begun to care for Gaelin, regardless of our circumstances. It hurt like hell that he wished me dead. That he didn't seem to care enough for me to overlook my DNA.

"My village loved my mother," I finally replied, willing myself to speak. "She was a healer. I suppose as a tribute to her, they overlooked my paternal side. I don't believe my father knew about me. My mother never told me about him."

Gaelin stood silently for another moment, processing my situation. Without taking another look at me he headed for the door. I rushed after him, stopping a few feet away from him as he reaches for the doorknob.

"Gaelin!" I shouted.

He stopped, but did not turn around.

I search for something to say that would make this better. That would save my neck and get me out of this, but all I could manage to say was, "I'm sorry."

Gaelin's head tilted, but he did not turn around, nor did he say a word. He flung the door open and was gone a moment later.

I didn't sleep that night. I waited, listening for any sound of the guards coming to take me away. I had failed. I failed

Lily, my family, and myself. I was foolish to think an alfar could ever come to care for a half-bread like me.

Somewhere in the early hours of the morning I must have dozed off from sheer exhaustion. I awoke to the door latch snapping shut. I sprung to my feet, reaching for the iron poker near the fire place. I turned, ready to fight my way to my own execution when I saw Gaelin, standing at the door. No guards, no weapons in sight. He assessed me, looking at the iron poker and then to my face.

"I'll help your friend," he said without feeling.

Relief slammed through me as I lowered the poker. "Thank you," I whispered. I looked at the door and back to him, unsure of what he had decided to do with my life.

"You would sacrifice yourself for a human? Why? What makes her so important?" he hissed more assertively than I had ever seen him.

I took a few moments to clear my throat and then my head. "Because I love her. Because I am all she has," I whispered. I waited, but he didn't reply. I was tired of waiting. I needed to know what was going happen next. "Are we going to the king so he can dispose of me?"

His eyes snapped to mine. The hard, stern alfar soldier slowly melted away. His eyes filled with pain as he shook his head.

"No, you're not going anywhere. And no one else is to know of this," he said, taking a step towards me.

Uncontrollable tears began to run down my face. My breath shuttered as I tried to hold my emotions back. I gasped for a breath to help calm me. "I don't understand," I was able to get out. "Why?"

In another breath, he was in front of me, staring down at me with those beautiful golden eyes. "This," he said gesturing between himself and me. "I have never experienced anything like this before in my long and lonely life. I have been with both alfar and human females, but I have never longed to know someone, to be near someone like I do you."

I smiled and a laughter erupted from deep inside of me. I felt relief and even happiness to know that he didn't want me dead. He wanted me to live.

"Gen," Gaelin said, in a serious tone, reaching down and taking my hands into his. "This game that you are playing. This position you are now in is dangerous. And by me not saying anything, I am going against my vow. Against everything I am." I could see the conflict in his eyes. I reached up taking his face in my hands.

"I am so sorry that I have put you in this position," I said, and honestly meant it.

"This isn't your fault. You did not ask for any of this and you can't control who your parents are. And if I am being honest, I find you absolutely perfect, just the way you are. I wouldn't change a thing about you, including these," he said with a smile as he gently stroked the edge of my ears.

A smile erupted across my face as my body eased into his. I felt peace, for the first time since I could remember. I also felt safe. He watched me, running his fingers through my hair and exploring my face with small grazes and strokes. Something inside of my chest swelled as I took him in. Every path his fingers explored left a warmth across my skin I had never experienced before. I wanted this moment to last. I wanted to stay here, with him, just like this.

"May I...may I kiss you?" I asked nervously.

His eyes dropped from my gaze as if ashamed. "I'm not going to force you to bed me so that I will keep your secret," he said, beginning to pull away.

I tightened my grip on him. "I know that. I would like to kiss you because... because I want to."

He peered down at me, still unsure of my motives. I moved in closer to him, running my fingertips along his lips. I could feel his warm breath against my skin. I stretched up on my tiptoes and softly brushed my lips against his, testing the waters.

His arms latched around my waist, preventing me from pulling away. We gently glided our lips across one another. The taste of him electrified every nerve in my body. I let out a moan of satisfaction. He pressed me against the wall taking my mouth harder as his tongue thrusted in and out with each passing. His body sealed me to the surface as his hands roamed over the thin fabric of my nightgown.

He pulled away, breathing in deeply from the passion we had just shared. I couldn't help but smile up at him. He let out a small laugh before pulling me away from the wall. He kissed me again softly, stopping only to admire my face.

"See, I told you I wanted to," I said playfully. He grinned

fully, his smile stretching to his eyes. So, this is what Gaelin looked like truly happy.

"Did you sleep last night?" He asked, not taking his hands from me.

"An hour or so," I admitted.

He took my hand and lead me to the bed. My heart fluttered as excitement and nervousness slammed through me at the same time. I hesitated, stopping in the middle of the room as Gaelin tried to pull me forward. He turned back towards me, noting the hesitation on my face. A mischievous smile crept across his face as he looked from me to the bed and back again.

"We're going to sleep. Nothing more," he said, reassuring me.

I let out an awkward giggle as oxygen returned to my lungs again. "Oh," I replied, still planted in the middle of the room.

Gaelin arched his eyebrow and moved slowly towards me. "Unless," he said in a deep sultry voice, "you had something else in mind."

I froze, looking up at him. His sensual smile turned playful, followed by a laugh. I pushed him back, shaking my head.

"My emotions can't take any more uncertainty," I admitted. His laughter continued as he reached for me. I let out another laugh of relief, allowing him to pull my body into his. I relaxed my head against his strong and toned chest, relishing in our contact.

"We're just going to sleep. I promise," he whispered. I felt his lips brush against the top of my head.

"I can't, I have too many chores to do," I admitted, already feeling the exhaustion settling in my bones.

"I leave for the dark court soon, and I want to spend the next few hours with you. So, therefore, I am relieving you of some of the chores until I see that you are well rested," he said, pulling away and leading us to the bed. I smiled at the sight of a bed. A real bed.

I slid in between the soft, crisp sheets as Gaelin pulled them over my body. He went around the other side and crawled into the bed, taking off his shoes and belt. We turned towards each other, staring at one another in complete contentment for a few moments until he reached his arms around my waist and pulled me into him. His fingers tangled through my hair in a calm caressing motion. Though every nerve in my body was heightened from being this close to him and from the passionate kiss we had shared, exhaustion took over, forcing me into a deep sleep.

CHAPTER 9

I awoke to an empty bed. I rolled onto my back and smiled, grazing my fingers across my lips, remembering how his mouth felt pressed against mine. Was I falling for him? No, I couldn't be. I wasn't going to be stuck here as his sex slave. Though, I wondered what type of lover he was. Was he gentle and soft, or hard and selfish?

My inside lit up at the thought of our bodies pressed against each other. I closed my eyes, stretching myself along the bed, playing different fantasies through my head of how it would feel to be consumed by him. Maybe I could just have him once before I took Lilian back to the Frey.

"Sleeping in the bed now, are we?" Levos stood at the door.

I popped up, grabbing the covers around me. "Why can't you figure out how to knock?"

"Why would I? I find you in the most interesting

situations when you think no one is watching." He closed the door, came over to the bed and laid down next to me. "So, last night was a success? I'm assuming so since you still have that pretty, little head of yours."

I grabbed a pillow and hit him in the face.

He laughed, swatting me away.

"I told him everything," I confessed. "Though it was hit and miss for a second, he agreed to help with Lilian, and he doesn't care that I am a half-breed." I grinned, uncontrollably.

"Oh, sweetheart. Are you falling for him?" Levos smiled at me.

"I...I don't want to talk about that." I got out of the bed and headed to the armoire. Levos grabbed me around my waist, turning me to face him.

"Oh no you don't. Why were you in his bed, hmm?"

"We just slept next to each other, that is all. And I may have kissed him. And I also may have liked it. A little too much," I confessed.

Levos laughed, shaking his head. "Well, it looks like life has turned in your favor, sweet Genevieve."

I smiled at him, bracing against the wall. "Levos, I can't fall for him. What life is this? I would only be his mistress. Only something he would use for pleasure. He would still have to sleep with Princess Daealla to conceive an heir, and if he got bored of me, he could throw me away, or take another. I would be trapped, unable to have a family of my own or a new lover." I paused, taking a moment to focus myself. "This wasn't part of the plan. This wasn't supposed to happen."

"This sounds like something you should be talking to Gaelin about, sweetheart, not me. For what it's worth, you would be safe and cared for here. That's more than you could say if you were still in The Frey."

I nodded, knowing he was right. I chewed on my bottom lip trying to force my thoughts away from Gaelin. "Talk to me about something to distract me for now. Tell me about the dark court. I want to know everything," I said, moving to the bathroom to change.

"With Gaelin gone, we do have time to get you up to date on the courts. Alright, where to begin? I guess it begins with the gods. Freyr is the alfar's creator. Originally, he arrived in the kingdom of Asgard as a hostage, but he soon became a friend with the gods and then shortly after one of them. He looked down upon our mortal race and found us beautiful and honorable. We treated our world with love and respect. We tended to the fields and saw every creature and living thing as something to be cherished and protected. Freyr and Frigga granted us the gift of immortality, and the gift of nature and magic to continue to bring beauty into the world.

"This lasted for centuries. We would often have interactions with the Norse gods and goddesses. Our powers began to grow, and with time no longer an obstacle, we brought in the Golden Age. We crafted magnificent architecture, art, music, inventions. Everyone lived peacefully, no matter what race you were. We thrived, and in a way, became God-like.

"When the humans' Christian god exiled Lucifer and a third of his angels from heaven, that is when everything changed. The demons ravaged our world, killing, possessing, eating, and laying waste to everyone and everything. The alfar weren't warriors. We had never had to fight. We were farmers and philosophers. We weren't ready for what was to come.

"Since the demons were celestial beings, nothing we had killed them. We could cut them down, dismember them, burn them, and yet they would still come back. They descended on this world like it was their very own buffet for the taking. Not wanting to get their hands dirty, the Norse gods broke the Bifrost gate, severing our physical connection between the two worlds.

"We were on our own and we were desperate. After decades of war our most revered general, Maleki Drezmore, refused to continue the endless cycle of bloodshed. We had lost three-fourths of our population and the other races had given up fighting altogether. He hated the Norse gods for turning their backs on us in our time of need, so he turned to other sources of power. He found a fire god named Azeer and made a deal to save our people.

"In order to save our race and our world, Maleki agreed to Azeer's terms. The god wanted an eternity of worship from our kind. He wanted us to turn away from Odin and the other gods, and worship him in their stead. He demanded human, virgin, and innocent sacrifices to be brought before altars built in his honor. He also demanded that Maleki and his whole infantry be the first to kneel and sacrifice their lives to broker the deal. In exchange, he would give our people a weapon that would rid us not only of the demonic threat that plagued our lands, but any celestial being that dared threaten us again.

"Without consulting the other leaders of our people, Maleki took the deal. He and his infantry knelt before Azeer and took their own lives. Three days later, Maleki and his infantry awoke unexpectedly. They thought their sacrifice was final, but Azeer had other plans. The infantry now possessed abilities, unlike anything we had ever seen. They could manipulate the mind, cause pain without even touching you, shield themselves from attacks. They could break bones with a single snap of their fingers or cause someone to do their bidding with a single smile.

"Maleki's gift was the dark flame. He could destroy any celestial being. The flame is described as the most beautiful and cleansing form of magic anyone has ever experienced. Maleki and his infantry swept over the land with their new gifts, sending the demons scattering to the ends of the universe. When our world was once again safe, Maleki told our leaders of the bargain he had struck with Azeer. They refused to honor the deal and would not turn away from Freyr and Frigga.

"Rage overtook Maleki and his infantry. They saw the others' refusal to comply as a sign of disrespect for their sacrifice. Their powers and abilities continued to grow in force and number. When Azeer demanded his payment in sacrifices, the elders of our community forbid Maleki and the others to continue with the rituals. They were forced from our lands and that is when they formed the Kingdom of Doonak.

"Maleki took the throne, creating the dark court. They performed the required sacrifices and honored Azeer as the savior of our world. The dark power that Maleki and the others consumed began to change them not only physically, but morally. We heard rumors of rape, brutality, and torture being conducted at the court. When we tried to intervene, they closed their gates to us and no longer allowed communication between the two courts."

I was sprawled on the couch, in awe of the history that belonged to a part of me. When he paused, I sat up, still eager for more. "So, why don't you just kill them all and end their lines?" I asked bluntly.

Levos laughed at me as if I were a child. "Oh, sweet Genevieve. If only it were that simple. Yes, the dark alfar make up a very small percentage of our population. I believe it's something like one of them to ten of us, but their powers are not to be underestimated. They are strong and clever little beasts. They also train everyone in their kingdom as if they are warriors. Though we have a greater population, the high houses do not entertain the idea of battle. They are content to live their sophisticated lives behind these walls while others do the fighting for them. The dark alfar know we have the numbers, so they want every member of their court to be prepared if we ever did decide to attack."

"So what? You just sit on your hands and let them kill innocents?" I demanded.

"We don't agree with their way of life, but we must choose our battles. Each race is responsible for its own people. Though we try to protect the meek, we cannot be everywhere all the time. We cannot control what other races eat or how they choose to find pleasure or even what god they chose to worship. We are not all powerful."

"And what about the dark flame? Does the king of Doonak have this ability?" I asked.

"No, thank the heavens. Maleki was the only one that ever possessed that gift. King Drezmore possesses the power of paralysis shock."

"And what does that exactly do?"

"It mutes all power from being used. He can also paralyze your body. Causing your heart to stop, preventing you from moving. He can even stop you from breathing."

"Well, that doesn't sound pleasant."

Levos laughed, standing up from his chair. "No, it doesn't and thankfully, we will never have to experience his power. The light and dark court have only recently been on some level of good terms these past few years, because of the little pests trolling our lands. Personally, I would love to have gone with Gaelin to see the court firsthand. I'm not essential, so I get to stay here and babysit Gaelin's mare."

"Ha, ha. Why would you want to go there anyway? Sounds horrifying and disgusting."

"Maybe some parts, but I was told they have what they

call Jestu twice a month. I wouldn't mind getting an invite to that."

"Are you going to make me ask what a 'Jestu' is?"

"Just did. Jestu is like a sexual exploration of sorts. The whole court partakes. You're allowed to have anyone and anything regardless of race."

"Disgusting," I said.

"Oh, come on, it doesn't sound that bad. Plus, they don't have all the rules and formalities the light court does. Don't get me wrong, I would never want to live there, but a visit may be nice."

"I may have to disown you as a friend for saying that."

He placed his hand across his chest. "Aw, Gen, am I officially your friend?"

"You were promoted and demoted all on the same day. Only you could pull that off," I moved to the door. "So, what am I to do when Gaelin is away?"

Levos rushed to my side as we walked down the halls of the palace. "Oh, right. I forgot to tell you. Princess Daealla would like a private audience with you in...ah, ten minutes."

I stopped dead in my tracks. "What? Why?"

"Just the messenger, sweetheart." He laughed, making his way past me. "But do be a doll and fill me in on all of the details after dinner." He left me in the hall alone.

I made my way to Princess Daealla's room, trying to figure out why she would want to meet with me, especially when Gaelin was away. Alfar males were known to take mistresses. She had to be used to this. It was normal in her culture.

I stepped up to her door and knocked lightly. A guard appeared, peering down at me. I dropped my eyes to the floor, remembering proper etiquette.

"Princess Daealla has requested my presence," I said.

The guard stepped aside, allowing me to pass. I didn't dare look up once I was inside.

"You may leave us, Termos," said Daealla. I heard the door slam behind me. Daealla approached me slowly, circling as if I were her prey. "You may look up."

I cautiously lifted my head to see the grandeur of her chamber. It was twice the size of Gaelin's and full of gold furnishings. Paintings lined the walls along with statues and musical instruments. A young male stood by the window, eating a piece of fruit. He was tall and lanky with golden blonde hair. He had vibrant blue eyes and a slender nose that pointed at the end.

"Do you find everything to your liking?" Princess Daealla asked.

"Your chambers are amazing, Your Highness. I've never seen such beauty in one room." I hoped I sounded meek. My eyes snagged on the young male before I returned my gaze to the floor.

"I'm sure it is quite the step up from that church basement back in The Frey," she said, moving to a table. She poured herself a glass of wine, motioning her hand through the air towards the young male. "That is Filo. He is none of your concern," she said in a dismissive tone.

I wondered how much she really knew about me or could dig up. Was her random comparison to the church basement and this palace a threat? Step out of line, and she will destroy anyone and anything that I held dear?

"Yes, it is. What can I do for you, Your Highness?" She walked back over to me, her eyes assessing each inch of my person.

"How are you and my future king getting along? Are you...satisfying his needs?"

I swallowed hard. I didn't think this interaction could get more uncomfortable, but I was wrong. "I provide the necessary services that are required of my position, Your Grace."

She took my chin with one of her long cold fingers and lifted my face to hers. She was so beautiful it was unsettling. "Why did he choose you, I wonder? Of all the humans he could have had, he chose one that looks so opposite of his future wife. Does he talk about me with you?"

I looked back to the floor, shaking my head. "No, Your Grace."

She straightened. "From this point on, anytime he utters my name you will report it to me directly. I need to make sure this alliance between his family and mine is solidified. That, of course, means an heir," she said with a bite in her tone.

"Of course, Your Highness."

She waited for a moment, before finally dismissing me without another word.

I turned to the door.

"Oh, and human," she said before I could leave. "If he continues to disrespect me in my own court and look at you with desire while in my presence, you will be the one to pay for his actions."

I waited to make sure she was finished before leaving the room.

THAT NIGHT, I BUSIED MYSELF WITH LAUNDRY AND cleaning, not wanting to ponder on Daealla's threat or Gaelin's current situation. I could only imagine what disgusting things he was being forced to witness in the court of horrors. I carried the heavy basket of wet laundry out to the courtyard to hang the garments in the night air to dry. Breathing deeply, I expected to smell fresh rain and flowers, but instead, something foul and heavy tainted my senses. It smelled of rotting flesh and decay. I looked around but saw nothing out of place.

A scream erupted from inside the main hall, a floor above me. I rushed into the castle, wondering what had happened. The servants were cowering against the walls in the hallways, too afraid to move. I ran up the stairs to the great hall to see hordes of decaying humanoid figures ransacking the place. They attacked anyone that they encountered and gathered as much gold and silver as they could carry.

One turned himself into a bear four times its normal size before biting a guard's head clean off. I froze in shock, unable to comprehend what I was seeing. The guards used their magic to fight back. A ripple of air flooded the passage, slamming the bear into the wall. Vines reached from the floor, wrapping themselves around some attackers' necks and tightened until they left the creatures without heads.

The guards unsheathed their swords that hung from their waists and swung their blades as the monsters met them with their own weapons. Metal clashed, filling the great hall with a vibration. The undead appeared to be intelligent and skilled fighters, able to keep up with the guards trying to fend them off. One turned to look at me as the screaming continued. I backed away slowly, trying to avoid its gaze. I looked around the hall for a weapon, but there was nothing. I was defenseless.

The creature strolled over to me casually, scrutinizing me up and down. My body froze in fear. Though my mind was screaming for me to run, my limbs were useless. Its skin was pale gray, and the smell was unbearable. Part of its jaw was visible through the decaying flesh hanging loosely from its eye. Its body was missing skin, exposing its kneecaps, shoulder blades, and elbows. The hair that remained on its head was thin and matted with blood.

An arm curled around me from behind and the creature went flying back into the air. I turned to see Levos. After he placed me safely against the interior wall Levos unsheathed his sword and walked fearlessly towards the creature. The monster stood up, meeting Levos's broad stroke of his sword with its own. Levos pushed the creature away, extending his hand into the air, pulling rock from the wall down towards his opponent. The creature dove out of the way, forced to the ground, and Levos took the advantage. As the creature began to morph into a bear, he cut its head clean from its body mid-transition. I relaxed against the wall, watching as the last of the undead were put down.

"What are you doing up here?" Levos asked. "Are you okay?"

"I'm fine. I guess my curiosity got the best of me," I replied, studying the creatures from afar. Though I was terrified, my interest was piqued. Missing limbs, rotted skin; what were these things, and why did they appear more dead than alive? My heart was racing as I tried to calm my nerves. Was I going to have to get used to random creatures popping in unannounced?

"Your curiosity is going to get you killed, sweet Genevieve. Word of advice: when you hear screaming, run away, not towards it."

"I'll try to keep that in mind. What are they?" I asked.

"Draugr. They're undead. Nasty little things that usually keep to themselves. Their lands lie in the dark court's territory. They can shapeshift, grow in size, travel through stone, and have great strength."

"Why did they attack the castle? Surely, they knew they would be cut down."

He shrugged. "The pests rolled through their land a few days back, taking their treasures and destroying their crypts. I guess they were desperate enough to come here looking for handouts." Levos took me by the arm. "Come on, let's get you to bed. Gaelin will deal with them when he returns."

I laid in bed that night trying to get the image of the draugr out of my mind. The smell of their rotting flesh still hung in the air. If those things were desperate enough to attack the castle, the monsters coming from the rift must be making quite an impact. The thought made me weary. I needed to get to Lily and then somehow get us both back behind the protective border before a war broke out.

CHAPTER 10

At the end of the week the court assembled in the throne room to welcome Gaelin's entourage back to the light court. I stood off to the side, trying to be invisible. The large doors opened and Gaelin and his men walked in with dominance and strength, demanding the attention of the room. He and the others knelt before King Lysanthier, waiting to be acknowledged.

"Rise, Lord Atros," said the king. "What report do you have from the Kingdom of Doonak?"

Gaelin stood to his feet. "A beast the size of five men terrorized their lands," reported Gaelin. "Taking their livestock, murdering anything that it came in contact with. It had large fangs that dripped with poison and a hide of armor." The court gasped in shock. "We hunted and eliminated it as instructed. We lost two from the light court and one from the dark. As agreed, the dark court will conduct their research, then send the remains to our kingdom for our own discovery," reported Gaelin.

"Very good, Lord Atros. We are glad to see you and your men in good health. The fallen will be honored this evening and we will have a feast to commemorate their sacrifice. Until then, welcome home." The king waved his hand, releasing the court.

I rushed past the crowd, heading straight for Gaelin's bedchamber. It was over thirty minutes before he finally entered. I was pacing with anticipation, barely able to contain myself. He closed the door, dropping his sword in its usual place. He looked at me and gave me a small, tired smile.

"Lilian? Did you find her? Is she still alive?" I blurted out.

He nodded and stepped closer towards me. "She is alive, and surprisingly doing well in her current situation."

"What? How? What do you mean?"

He sat down on the edge of the bed, taking off his shoes. He winced in pain at the action. "She sings," he replied. "You didn't tell me she sings."

"What does that have to do with anything?" I demanded.

"They're keeping her for entertainment. Apparently, the court likes the way she sounds."

I exhaled, feeling relief rush over me like a cold wind. I sat on the bed next to him, reeling from the news that my sister was alive. "Is she...is she being harmed?"

"Not that I could assess."

I laughed, not knowing how else to react. Gaelin's eyes

were heavy. "Thank you, so much," I said, taking his hand in mine.

He smiled tiredly at me with a nod.

"And how are you? Are you hurt?" I asked.

He exhaled and pulled his jacket away from his side. Blood seeped through his shirt from bandages that wrapped a wound on his left side. I stood instantly, rushing for freshwater and cloth.

"Why didn't you say something when you first came in?" I exclaimed.

He chuckled. "You didn't really give me the opportunity."

"I'm so sorry. Here, let me change those for you," I said, kneeling in front of him. He painfully removed his shirt from his torso. I unwrapped the saturated bandage from his skin, revealing a gash about four inches across his side. "Do you have a healer or something that will quicken the healing process?"

He gestured to a dresser. "There's a balm over there. It will help ease the pain while it heals. It should be gone by tomorrow morning." I retrieved the balm and cleaned his wound gently. I felt his eyes on me, never straying. As I finished wrapping his side, his fingers trailed through the curls in my hair.

I remained kneeling and raised my hand to his bare chest, gently grazing the back of my knuckles over the skin. His hand trailed down the back of my neck, leaving goosebumps in its path. He cupped the side of my face as his traced thumb over my lips. I leaned into his touch, savoring the moment.

I met his beautiful golden gaze. Desire had replaced the pain and exhaustion in his eyes. I placed my hands on either of his knees, sliding them slowly up his strong muscular thighs. He took in a sharp breath as I rose over him. I softly straddled my legs around him, lowering myself onto him. I held his face in my hands, committing every detail to memory.

He had given me what I so desperately desired —the knowledge that my sister was safe. He had kept my secret. He knew what I was and yet he still wanted me. And I wanted him. gods, did I want him. I slowly pressed my lips to his face, kissing down each side before ending at his full lips. His grip on my hips tightened as our kiss deepened. My hand slid down his chest to his bandage. Remembering that he was hurt, I pulled away, feeling selfish.

"I'm sorry. We can wait until you're healed. I don't want to cause you any more pain," I said.

He laughed under his breath. "Pain is not what you'll cause me, Gen. I can promise you that. If you are willing, I see no reason to wait."

I smiled down at him, slowly pushing him back onto the bed. He unbuttoned the back of my dress, sliding it over my shoulders, revealing my bare chest. He took all of me in. Studying the curves of my breasts and the flat surface of my stomach. He flipped me underneath him, ripping the rest of the dress clean off. He eagerly undid the latch on his pants, sliding them to the floor.

We scooted up towards the head of the bed. Without removing his lips from mine, he pulled at the small band of my underwear, tearing them off my body. As we lay against each other completely naked, he slid his cold hand down my neck to my chest, studying my body as if it was the most desirable thing he had ever seen. His fingers circled around my navel before moving to my thighs.

I arched my back at the sensation that each touch left on me. My body burned for him more than I had imagined. I closed my eyes as he explored every inch of me. I felt his nose softly graze against mine, bringing my focus back to him. I opened my eyes to see his face smiling back at me. He gently pushed the hair away from my face, then leaned down slowly, closing his eyes, and kissed me again.

His other hand parted my thighs. I inhaled nervously, allowing my legs to fall to the sides. He slid gently on top of me, and I felt the soft skin of his abdomen press against me as my body cradled his. I could feel the hardness of him between my legs, waiting for the right moment. He pulled away from our kiss, peering deep into my eyes. He slowly pressed the tip of his hard length against my pelvis, opening the center of me to receive him.

I gasped as my body warmed and tensed. He watched my face, studying my reaction. He continued to push inside of me until I felt like I was going to burst. I wrapped my hands around his arms, squeezing to relieve the tension. Gaelin slowly pulled back as he began kissing my neck and chest softly.

I took another deep breath as he pushed himself back

into my body. This time, as he filled me completely, I moaned with satisfaction. My body relaxed under his as my hands began to glide over every muscle in his back. He quickened his pace, and my body became putty in his arms. I took his face, bringing his lips to mine, needing to taste him.

He moaned as he wrapped his arms around my waist, continuing to join our bodies as one. I could feel myself tightening around him as my insides throbbed with pleasure. My body felt like it was on fire in the best way possible. Suddenly, I felt my insides clamp down on him as my body shook from the most incredible sensation I had ever experienced. Gaelin pushed one last time to the very depth of me before he let out a roar of his own.

We were both panting, unable to catch our breath. He looked down at me with sated eyes and smiled widely before kissing my lips tenderly. He pushed himself off to the side as we both lay in silence. My face was frozen in a smile. I tried to move my legs, but they felt limp and heavy.

Gaelin turned to look at me. He sat up on his elbow, casually trailing his fingers between my breasts, down my abdomen, to the bundle of nerves in between my legs. I closed my eyes and moaned from the contact. His finger circled the soft tissue, sending floods of pleasure throughout my entire body. I could feel my heart begin to race as the heat and pressure from within me rose back up with fervency.

A release slammed through me as my back arched up toward the ceiling. I could feel my nipples harden and my breasts swell as the sensation devoured me. My insides contracted with each slow swirl of his fingers until my body collapsed back to the mattress, spent. The smile returned to my face as I turned towards Gaelin, pulling my legs into my stomach. He looked at me with tenderness as he skimmed my flush cheeks with the back of his knuckles.

"You felt so—"

"Human?" I interrupted.

He smirked, leaning in to kiss me on my head. "In the best way," he responded. "How was it for you?"

I sat up on my forearms. "Levos says your sense of smell can answer that question," I said playfully.

"I think we need to limit your time with Levos, but yes, a certain pheromone is released if the partner is enjoying themselves."

"And did I release any certain pheromone?"

He smiled, bringing his arm behind his head. "Yes, multiple times."

"Well, there's your answer, Lord Atros."

"Your scent was remarkable," he said, looking up at the ceiling.

"What do you mean?"

"Each person has their own fragrance, almost like a flower. You smelt of lavender and sandalwood. I've never experienced the two scents before like that. When they released it hit me like a massive force. I lost all control, which is why the session wasn't as long as I would have liked," he admitted.

I laughed. "It was perfect, Gaelin. Every part of it was perfect," I said, lying next to him.

"May I have you again?" he asked softly.

I looked at him in shock. "You mean you can already go again? Doesn't it take time to recover... after?"

"Maybe for humans, but not for alfar," he said, placing his body over mine.

"I'm beginning to like the alfar more and more every day," I said.

"And I like you more with every taste," he whispered, silencing me with his mouth as he pushed himself back inside of my aching body. I inhaled at the motion, basking in the power and masculinity of his body.

CHAPTER 11

The next few days I did nothing but roll around in the sheets with Gaelin. The laundry piled up, the room was a disaster, and none of my other chores were being done, but I didn't care. I had found a small slice of heaven in this nightmare I had descended into, and I was going to hold onto that lifeline with every ounce of strength I had left.

At night when we had exhausted ourselves, I would drift into a relaxed state. Even though I lay next to the most perfect male I had ever seen, when I closed my eyes, I saw the images of the strange dark figure. His black marking along the side of his left shoulder and arm. The symbols I knew nothing about. His vibrant smile beneath his full lush lips. His strong jaw and shapely chin. I willed myself to stop seeing the stranger, but my brain never got the message.

After a week of being laid up in bed, we finally emerged from our sanctuary. I immediately tended the laundry since neither of us had much to wear that was clean. My body ached and throbbed from the extra activity of the past few days, but I smiled at each discomfort, knowing the reward was well worth the aftermath.

Levos eventually found me as he always did. He demanded details, but I kept the private parts to myself. It was expected of me to attend dinner each night during the weeks after, for whatever reason I still didn't understand. I stood along the walls of the hall with the other humans, heads down and hands folded in front of us. I could feel Gaelin's eyes on me along with that of his betrothed. I didn't dare look up, remembering her threat.

The more time I spent getting to know Gaelin, I found myself growing jealous of his impending nuptials. He seemed to truly care for me, and against my own convictions I had fallen for him. I didn't know how to approach the topic or what his reaction would be, but I had to know the answers to my questions, even if they would destroy my heart. Levos encouraged me to speak freely with him. He said that Gaelin had never given me any reason not to trust him and he was right.

We had been physically together for three weeks. My jealousy and uncertainties were eating away at me so I decided I would risk the answers and just ask. After dinner one evening, I got back to the room to find Gaelin already waiting for me, lounging lazily on the bed, half undressed. Gods was he a sight. I smiled, closing the door gently. He beamed up at me and slid a small box across the bed.

"For me?" I asked nervously.

"I remembered you saying something about liking presents."

"This would be the second present I have ever received so the verdict is still out." I walked over to the bed and sat on the edge, peering down at the small box. "You didn't have to get me anything. Really."

"I wanted to. I saw it and thought of you."

I smiled widely, happy to know he thought of me when we were apart. I picked up the small box and took the top off. Inside was a beautiful silver necklace. The pendant was in the shape of a star and had nine points. Each point had a small diamond at the tip. In the center was a beautiful green gem. It was the most exquisite thing I had ever laid eyes on.

"Gaelin—"

"A star because you love watching them at night when you think I am asleep. The green gem is for your eyes. My favorite part of you." He softly drew the back of his hand down my face.

"It is so beautiful; I don't know what to say. Thank you isn't enough."

"It is, and you're welcome." He sat up, taking the necklace from the box. He gently moved my hair to the side and slid the cold pendant around my neck, latching it in the back. My heart swelled, but I pushed the feeling down, trying not to get ahead of myself.

"Why don't you ever say anything when I am out on the balcony at night if you're awake?" I asked.

"I like watching you. The way you move. The way you let your guard down and look up into the sky, knowing no one is watching. I wish you could be like that more often. Carefree and able to be who you truly are."

I smiled at him, reaching for the necklace. My face fell at the thought of this not being real. He was keeping his mistress happy. That was all.

"Is something wrong?"

"Am—am I allowed to wear my gift outside of this room?" I asked, easing my way into the subject of our unconventional arrangement.

"Of course, you are. You can wear anything I give you," he said, rubbing his fingers along my arm.

I took a deep breath in, preparing for the uncomfortable encounter. "Gaelin, I don't mean to ruin this moment, but... what happens when you and Princess Daealla are officially married? What becomes of me?"

He pulled back, seeming taken off guard by the question. "Things remain the same as they are now. I will have to lay with her a few nights a month when she is fertile, but the other nights I will be here, with you."

My heart cracked, imagining his body enjoying another female. "And...will you take others if you desire?"

His brow furrowed.

"Have you taken others since you've been with me?"

"Gen, where is this all coming from?"

"Please, just answer the questions. I don't know how this all works. I'm just trying to understand my future here and what becomes of me after this."

His eyes dropped from mine. He was uncomfortable as I was.

"Am I not supposed to ask these questions?"

"No, of course, you can ask. You know you can ask or tell me anything. I just wasn't expecting this tonight." He straightened. "When I first chose you and I realized you didn't want me in that way, I took a few others in the first weeks of your stay here. When I began to know you and desire you more intimately that behavior stopped. I haven't been with anyone since you. I don't plan on taking another into my bed, but if that time comes, I promise to be honest with you. No matter where you and I end up going, I will always make sure you are safe and well cared for."

"And...if I get pregnant?" I asked, knowing the answer.

He grimaced. "I can't have children with anyone except for my wife. You know this, Gen. It is our society's way, and I can't change that."

I nodded, feeling the sting from hearing the words come out of his mouth. "So, I will never be a mother." The word mother felt heavy as it rolled across my tongue.

"Is that something you wanted?"

"I don't know. I never really thought about it. Before you, I never really thought of having a person to love or becoming a mother. It wasn't important to me because I didn't know I could feel this way for another. Yes, on some level I was lonely and desired a connection or some type of comradery, but I thought I would have time to decide." We were silent for a few moments, not knowing what to say next.

"I know the humans and alfar have a different formality about relationships and marriages, but I want you to know that I do care about you. More than I thought I would. More than I thought I could," he said, turning my face to his.

I looked into his eyes, feeling devastated at the thought of not being with him. "I know it's not my place, but I don't want to share you, Gaelin. Not even with her." A small tear escaped my eye.

He caught it with his thumb, scooting closer to me. "I don't want to be with her. You know I want to be here with you. When we are in here, nothing and no one out there matters. I am yours and you are mine."

"How can you say that? I can't even look at you outside of this room. I am nothing but your whore."

"Don't say that. You are not my whore. You never were and you never will be. Gen, I didn't expect any of this. To feel the way I do for you. To care about you so deeply. Being with another sickens me and hurting you makes it even worse. I want to give you everything that your heart desires and I wish I could, but our world doesn't allow me to do that."

I dropped my face from his hand, knowing that the pain was only going to intensify as time continued. "I'm sorry for bringing this up. I'm just still not sure how to feel. I've spent my whole life watching humans fall in love, raise families, and dying at each other's sides. Having mistresses or sharing partners is looked down upon in The Frey. This is all foreign to me and my emotions are getting the better of me."

He took my hand. "I've never been in love before and I've rarely seen it, but believe me when I say, I've never felt for another what I feel for you. You're a light in every sense of the word. I want to make you happy to the best of my abilities if you will allow me the chance. I know I can't give you the life you deserve, but I promise the life I will give you will be full of happiness."

I smiled. Nothing I could say would change our situation. Better to hold onto the small moments of heaven in this hell. I took his face in my hands and kissed him gently. This was my life. This was who I was and all I was ever going to be unless I found a way to escape. I would have to learn to share him. I would have to learn to look the other way if he chose another to warm his bed. I would have to learn how to survive, but most importantly, I would have to learn how to shield myself from falling in love with him.

An alfar who could offer me nothing but fleeting moments of happiness. Play the game and survive. Just until I could escape. But leaving would mean letting him go.

I pushed him back onto the bed, straddling him as I unbuttoned my dress. He watched my every movement. As the dress slid down my body, leaving me naked and exposed, he ran his hand down my neck to my chest, touching the small star pendant. I leaned into him, taking his mouth as I removed the last article of clothing from his body. That night I distracted myself in ecstasy, not dwelling on what I couldn't have, but focusing on what I did.

I AWOKE VIOLENTLY FROM A DREAM, SWEATING and panting, out of breath. I looked over at Gaelin; still sound asleep. I crawled out of bed and leaned against the balcony, allowing the night breeze to cool the moisture that covered my skin. I closed my eyes, reliving the images that flashed through my head. Dark soldiers in the light court's throne room. Violence and manipulation. War and death.

I tried to sift out the memories of the dream to make a clear image appear. I could see Gaelin's face, tense with worry. A darker-haired male approached him, smiling with satisfaction as if he was taunting Gaelin. I felt the tension between Gaelin and myself as if something was coming between us, but what, I could not see. A banquet or celebration was being held in the throne room. Food and wine lined every table. I could see dark alfar soldiers eating with the light. As I focused on the event, my hand suddenly cramped with pain. I pulled it against my body and took a few deep breaths, trying to keep quiet.

I didn't know what was happening or why I would have a dream like that, but something about it felt real and familiar. Gods, I wished I could talk to Lily. She could always help me sort through the mess that was my own head. I took one more look up at the stars before crawling back into bed. I closed my eyes, willing myself to have a peaceful sleep, but I couldn't shake the feeling that something or someone was coming.

I didn't get much sleep for the rest of the night. I got up before Gaelin and started on my chores for the day. I was able to escape during lunch, using the excuse that I needed to find herbs for Gaelin to get away from the hustle and bustle of the court. I found a field of lavender and laid down among the familiar scent. Images of my mother began to play from my memory.

Her kind and loving smile. The creases around her eyes as she laughed while I danced for her. The way her kiss felt on my forehead. The sound of her voice as she sang me to sleep. I missed her so much. I wanted her to appear to me now more than I had in the past eleven years. She had gone through this and survived, but how? I cried softly until my body tired, and I fell asleep amid the comforting purple blossoms.

Something rough scratched along my lower cheek. The strong nudge jolted me awake, and I could feel hot breath as something panted against my skin. I slowly realized I was no longer alone in the lavender field. I opened my eyes slowly to see a scaled muzzle with two large nostrils hovering over me.

I scooted out from underneath it cautiously. The creature backed away from me and I saw the yellow and black of its slitted eyes, like a reptile's. Its body was full of scales ranging in color from green to red, to purple. The creature's toes were long with clawed hooks for nails. Sharp, needle-like teeth hung down out of its mouth.

It never took its eyes off me as it tilted its head in curiosity. I slowly got to my feet, realizing I very well could be dead at any moment. The creature began to stomp its feet as two massive wings sprang from either side of its back. Its tail whipped at the ground, sending the grass and lavender plants into the air. It was some type of small dragon.

I dropped back to the ground and curled into a protective position. I was barely able to breathe. I could still feel its shimmering eyes on me, studying me. A few moments went by before it moved closer to me, its warm breath on the back of my neck. It slowly bent down its scaled rough snout to my head and nudged me again. When I didn't respond, it repeated the motion, letting out a small whine.

I couldn't stay here and wait for it to get hungry. Against my own body's protest, I lifted my head, shaking every inch that I rose. I sat back on my knees, making eye contact with the dragon. It looked at me for a moment and then brought its head gently to mine. I closed my eyes, waiting for the teeth to snap my head off, but instead, it nuzzled against me like a dog. I tried steadying my breath as it pulled away from me. Still shaking, I took a chance and stretched out my arm as it lowered its head to my hand, taking in my touch.

The scales were rough and ridged, yet smooth in certain areas. Realizing I wasn't going to be its dinner, I stood and took a step closer. I ran my hands across its neck, studying the magnificent creature I had only ever heard tales of. Two horns protruded from its head, black as night. As I peered into its eyes, a loud whistle sounded from afar. The dragon snapped its head up, backing away from me before flaring its wings to take off. I fell to the ground from the massive force of wind. The beast soared into the sky.

I got to my feet without a second thought and took off back to the palace. I ran through the halls, trying to find Gaelin or Levos to tell them what I had just seen. Both the alfar and the humans seemed to be on edge, which was out of norm, but I didn't care. I had to tell someone what had just happened. I rounded the corner towards Gaelin's chambers and was caught by Levos's strong arms. He slammed me against the wall without warning.

"Where have you been? We've been looking everywhere for you?" he snapped.

"You will never believe what just happened," I said, panting for breath.

"It will have to wait. The dark court has arrived unannounced. Everyone is meeting in the throne room. You're with me." He pulled me from the wall, and we walked towards danger.

"What? Why are they here?" I asked, feeling a small chill of fear radiate down my spine. Images of my dream the night before began to reply in my mind.

"Apparently there was a large horde of beasts that came through the rift yesterday. They've been tracking them since they left their lands, and the horde has now set up camp along our kingdom's borders. The horde is led by a general we've had encounters with before. He goes by the name of Otar. We think Otar is controlling the rift, or at least what comes out of it."

"Is Otar an alfar?"

"Oh, no. He looks like a demon. His skin is black as coal. He has sharp yellow teeth and bat-like ears with yellow eyes. He's a smart creature though. Something that is able to scheme and think independently. The royals are hoping that if we eliminate Otar the rift will close."

"So, the dark court is here to help then?" I asked.

"We shall see. There are a lot of them, so stay close to me and don't go anywhere alone until they leave. The castle isn't safe while they are here."

We entered the throne room and slid into the crowd. I tried to move to the wall the other humans were standing along, but Levos locked his arm in mine and shook his head, keeping me close.

The king, queen, and princess sat on their thrones with Gaelin perched at Daealla's side. He looked at me and nodded. I didn't respond. Both large golden doors in the back of the room flung open without warning and a group of dark-haired warriors, both male and female, entered the throne room. The light alfar tensed as the dark court entered like they owned the place. They walked with confidence and pride as if they were the most powerful beings in the world. From what Levos had told me, they very well could be. Their faces were unnervingly beautiful, if not more so, than those of the light court.

The group was being led by a man who could have been Lucifer himself. He was devastatingly handsome and elegant. His jaw was broad and strong. His eyes were silver, the color of liquid mercury. His powerful back veered to form a V at his waist. He wore all black: a floor-length jacket that hugged every part of his body perfectly with satin trim tracing the collar, a buttoned shirt that lay open at the top to reveal his chest, tight-fitting pants, and boots that came to his knees.

The rest of his followers were dressed more practically, in black leather. Some of the females wore revealing tops and dresses. Their hair was styled in all different fashions. A few members of the group winked at some of the light alfar members as they passed by. Most, kept their eyes forward, fixated on the royals at the front of the room.

As I watched the beautiful dark alfar pass us by, my breath caught in my lungs as something familiar caught my eye. A few of the dark alfar members had black markings on different regions of their bodies like the one carried by the man in my dreams. I forced my eyes to the floor before I was caught looking. My mind was in shambles. The connection to what I saw in my dreams and the dark court was uncanny.

The leader stopped in front of King Lysanthier and simply nodded. No bow, no curtsy, just a nod. I couldn't help but smile at the insult. Suddenly, I had a sense of déjà vu. The dark figures, the throne room, the tension, all of it. I shook my head to dislodge the thought. No, that was impossible.

"Ambassador Lyklor, we weren't expecting you. A letter would have sufficed," said King Lysanthier.

"When our fellow brethren are in danger, we come to the rescue. Isn't that what our little treaty agreed upon?" said the ambassador. His voice was deep and smooth like a shot of whiskey coating your insides. It sent a chill through my body that I couldn't explain. Levos pulled me closer.

King Lysanthier looked at the ambassador with disgust.

"We appreciate the assistance in eliminating the threat at our borders. Since we have only just discovered the position of the horde, we will need time to prepare for an attack. Lord Atros will take charge of the situation. You will relinquish control of your infantry to him for this mission."

Ambassador Lyklor smiled, revealing a perfect set of white teeth. His canines were longer than normal with sharp points at the end. "While I do respect that we are in your territory," said Lyklor, "my infantry will only defer to me. But I will be happy to share what I've learned about the enemy along with helping Lord Atros defeat our mutual threat. When shall we begin planning? I think we would all agree the sooner the better."

"Immediately," said Gaelin coldly.

Lyklor turned slowly to meet Gaelin's gaze. "Excellent. And in the meantime, what are the living arrangements for my court?" Lyklor looked around the room at the alfar and then at the humans lining the wall. His gaze tracked to the front row where Levos and I stood arm in arm. I could feel his eyes lock onto me only for a moment before he returned his attention to the king.

"We will have rooms ready for you by the end of the day," answered King Lysanthier. "Until then, you are our guests. I feel the need to remind you that our laws are not like the ones you are accustomed to abiding by. If any action is taken that breaks them, your kind will be punished accordingly."

"We can behave ourselves, *light king*. None of your confinements will be broken by *our* kind while we are under your roof. Though, I must say, you seem to have quite an excessive number of humans. It seems to me we need to revisit our original arrangement," said Lyklor.

The king tensed. "I'm sure if your kind refrained from offering up human sacrifices to your insufferable god our courts would have the same number of humans," he said.

Lyklor laughed, shaking his head. "Perception isn't always reality...king. Gaelin, shall we?"

Gaelin tensed, stepping off the platform. He walked past Levos and I, taking another look at me before leaving the throne room.

Lyklor tracked Gaelin's attention towards me as if studying our connection. The ambassador grinned at me in a way that made my blood run cold. I dropped my eyes, moving slightly behind Levos. Lyklor and his court followed Gaelin out. A sense of relief swept through the light court, as if the air had been let back into the room.

CHAPTER 12

"So, what did you think of the sinful dark court?" asked Levos, plopping down onto Gaelin's bed.

"Dark, rebellious, scary, and intimidating...yet beautiful," I said, lying next to him.

He laughed at me. "Now do you understand my fascination with getting a peek behind their evil curtain?"

"Uh, no. There is nothing that would possess me to want to go to the dark court. Maybe if there was a way to get Lily out, but I would still be scared as hell to step foot in their little court of horrors."

"Each to their own, I guess."

"Can I ask you something?" I said hesitantly.

"Stop asking if you can ask. Just ask!" he snapped playfully, pinching me in the arm.

"Is there a chance that I could have...powers like you all do?"

Levos looked at me curiously, chewing over the

question. "Most alfar show signs of their gifts before their fifth year of life. If you had our gifts there'd be no question about it, sweet Genevieve."

I exhaled disappointedly. *It was just a dream, Gen. Just a dream.*

"Who is Ambassador Lyklor? Is he King Drezmore's son?" I asked.

"Ha," he scoffed. "No. King Drezmore doesn't have an heir yet. Erendrial Lyklor is a conniving fox who shouldn't be trusted by any means. He came from nothing. His parents were lower class. From what our spies have told us, they died before he turned eleven. Somehow, he found favor with a family who had money. He got a proper education and then slowly ascended to the table of the king. He is smart, devious, and will do anything to get what he wants."

"And what does he want?"

"Power, station, the crown…who knows? Not our court, not our problem."

"If he becomes king, won't it be your problem then?" I asked, pushing him for more information.

He looked at me and smiled as if I were a child. "Erendrial Lyklor will never be king. The dark court would never allow a lower-class bastard to sit on their throne. King Drezmore will eventually have an heir. It's just a matter of time. For now, stay away from Erendrial. He's the very image of what the dark court stands for."

I smiled at him and nodded in compliance. "He's the very description of Lucifer Morningstar if you ask me."

"The fallen angel? You've got to be kidding me. Don't become smitten with him, sweet Gen."

"I'm not smitten. I am just saying. He is—"

"Devious, malicious, deadly, yet surprisingly hard not to stare at. Yeah, I know. You aren't the first female here to think so," he said, winking at me.

"I didn't say that."

Levos shook his head and settled back into a pillow. I continued to fold the laundry as my mind fixated on the dark court. There was so much I still wanted to know, to learn. Now that they were here, maybe an opportunity would present itself to get me closer to Lily.

Levos had gone by the time Gaelin came back to his chambers to change before dinner. He was tenser than usual. I drew him a hot bath and filled it with lavender. He came up behind me and wrapped his arms around my waist, burying his face into the crook of my neck.

"Will you join me?" he asked.

I smiled, turning to face him. "If that is where you wish me to be, then that is where I shall be," I said, kissing his lips softly.

"It is. I need you," he said as he tore at my dress, slamming me into the bed like I weighed nothing. My dress ripped down the seams, falling into pieces. He unfastened his belt buckle and slammed into me with force. I let out a loud moan from the instant pleasure that rushed through my body. He took me on his bed harder than he ever had before. He engulfed my mouth with his, devouring every part of my body that he encountered.

He let out a deep groan, slowing as he came to a finish. He leaned against me panting and out of breath. I trailed my fingers along his back. He pulled away and looked into my eyes. I gave him a small smile, unsure of where his head was.

"I'm sorry, I shouldn't have taken you like that," he said.

I laughed, wrapping my arms around him. "It's okay. I enjoyed it a little rough."

He smiled back, lifting off me, then taking up my naked body and carrying me to the bathroom. He set me into the deep bath water and stepped in himself. I got the sponge and began to clean his flawless skin. His muscles were tense from the day's negotiations. I scrubbed my fingers through his hair as the soap foamed.

"I'm here if you want to talk about it," I whispered.

He looked back at me with his golden eyes, arching one eyebrow. He let out a long exhale as he leaned back against the other side of the tub across from me. "The dark court is unreasonable and selfish. I hate working with them no matter what the threat is," he admitted.

"Planning didn't go as you expected?"

"It went as I expected…long, unfruitful, and pointless. They are in our territory and yet expect to claim Otar's body when he falls, since they brought the impending attack to our attention. That is not the terms we agreed upon, yet Lyklor somehow has spun his web of deception, making it sound as if the treaty favors his claim."

"Is that his power…deception?"

"Ha, you would think the way he operates. No, he can inflict pain with a single look. He also can manipulate his pheromones to affect others in a way that favors his ambitions. The deceptions, scheming, and negotiation are all something he, unfortunately, taught himself. And though I hate to admit it out loud, he is good at it...too good."

I slid across the bath, crawling onto his lap, pressing the fullness of my naked chest against him. "He may be a fox, but you are the hunter. You will catch the fox and skin him alive. Never forget that no matter how hard he tries to undermine you. The battlefield is your court, not his."

He cupped my bottom with his hands, rubbing himself against me as he peered into my eyes with a smile. "Our conversation last night. I didn't like talking like that with you. I know I hurt you and I'm sorry," he said, kissing my chin.

"As you said, it's the way of the world and I have to learn to adapt," I whispered, dropping my head as my heart throbbed in pain. He caressed my face with his hand, pressing his forehead against mine.

"I love you, Genevieve," he said slowly.

I pulled away, looking at him with confusion and shock. "What?"

"I love you and I am sorry I forced this life upon you. I know you wanted something different, someone different, but—"

I took his face and kissed him passionately, sliding myself onto him until I felt his hardness hit the top of my insides. I arched back, enjoying the feeling of being filled by this male. *Take the small pieces of heaven where you can, Gen,* I thought. He pulled my mouth back to his as the rhythm of our motion splashed the water out of the tub onto the floor.

"I love you, Gaelin," I said in between pants. He smiled, still holding me close to him.

I GOT DRESSED JUST IN TIME FOR THE KNOCK THAT came at the door. Expecting it to be Levos, I rushed over, swinging the door open freely with a smile on my face. Erendrial Lyklor stood on the other side of the threshold. My face dropped to the floor as my eyes averted his. I stepped back, remembering my place.

"May I help you, Ambassador Lyklor?" I asked.

"Don't worry, you can look at me, I won't tell," he whispered, leaning into my ear as he passed into the room. A sharp shuttering feeling crawled up my spine from being this close to him. I couldn't decide if it was fear or curiosity. Gaelin came from the bathroom, back straight and shoulders broad in a defensive stance.

"What is the meaning of this visit?" said Gaelin.

I closed the door, moving off to the side of the room.

"Sorry, was I interrupting?" Erendrial said, inhaling deeply. "Sure does smell like it." He turned and winked at me.

"Your purpose, Lyklor?" demanded Gaelin.

"Ah, yes. I think I've come up with a solution to our little Otar problem."

"It couldn't wait until our next meeting?" Gaelin asked, continuing to dress.

"Call me nosy, but I wanted to see how the other half lived," Erendrial said, acting as if he was assessing the room. "Anyways, I propose that we both have our own teams of people examine the body together. We choose a secure, neutral location for the examination to take place. This way, anything the other team finds will be noted and we both can understand what creature Otar is just in case he isn't the one controlling the rift."

Gaelin stood for a moment, contemplating. He nodded slowly, with a stern face. "I will bring it to the king tomorrow and report back when a decision is made."

"Excellent. See, that wasn't so difficult, was it? This is the beginning of a beautiful relationship, Lord Atros," Erendrial smiled smugly. He turned back to me and then made eye contact with Gaelin. "Is she a favorite or are you in a sharing mood? Since we're friends now and all."

Gaelin growled, his hands clenching into fists. "She is my concubine. No one else touches her; especially not filth like you"

Erendrial clicked his tongue before turning back to Gaelin. "And they call us selfish. I will see you at dinner, Gaelin." He moved to the door without another word and left.

I relaxed, moving through the room, trying to distract myself from the dark court's presence.

Gaelin took my arm and pulled me into him. "He will

not touch you; I promise." He kissed me on the head before leaving for dinner.

Ten minutes later I followed him into the throne room, taking my place against the wall. The dark court sat among the light, laughing, and eating their fill of food and wine. They acted as if they weren't among enemies but friends. I didn't know if it was a way to mess with their opponent's minds or their legitimate perception of reality. The light alfar looked at them as if they were gunk on the bottom of their shoes.

Dinner felt like it dragged on longer than most nights. I rushed off to the kitchen to help with cleanup before heading back towards Gaelin's chamber. The halls were quiet, even more so than usual. I guessed the light alfar didn't want to have any unexpected run in with the dark court members. I thought back to my dream, trying to catalog the similarities of the day's events. Not everything in my dream had happened, but there were too many coincidences to simply look past as if it meant nothing.

If I did have magic, there was no way of ever finding out without outing myself. If that happened, I wouldn't have a head attached to my shoulders to understand my magic anyways. I turned down the main hall past the throne room. Crews were still inside, cleaning up after the feast. I entered, not wanting to go back to Gaelin's chamber yet.

"Do you need an extra pair of hands?" I asked the other human servants inside.

They looked at me and laughed mockingly. "Go crawl back into your lord's bed, whore. You're no longer one of us.

You're a disgrace to our race," a man said, spitting on the floor in front of me.

My smile fell as I backed away slowly from the group. The embarrassment and shame I felt when they looked at me was like a dagger to the gut. I didn't choose this, but I could no longer say I didn't enjoy it.

Gaelin had told me he loved me, and I had said it in return. Did I love him? I cared for him, but how could I ever truly love someone who kept me as a glorified pet? Our relationship could never be real. At least not in the way I needed. My job was simple. Keep him happy and keep myself safe while still trying to figure out how to get Lily out of that nightmare.

I went to the linen pantry at the end of the hall to gather fresh towels and herbs. As I exited, shutting the door behind me, I knocked into a cold broad figure. I looked up to see Erendrial Lyklor looking down at me with his striking, devilish grin. He slid one hand into his jacket, holding his position in front of me. I was blocked between him and the door behind me. I swallowed heavily, debating if I should scream or not. I dropped my eyes, playing like passive prey.

"What can I do for you, Ambassador Lyklor?" I asked softly.

He huffed in amusement. "First of all, never ask a male that question, you won't like the answer or the results you'll get from it. Second, my name is Erendrial, you may call me Eren if that is easier. Third, didn't I tell you, you could look at me? I won't report you, I promise," he said sarcastically.

"And why should I trust you?" I snapped a bit too aggressively.

"A female with some fire...I like it. And honestly, you shouldn't, but I will say you can if it makes you feel better."

I ground my teeth together in annoyance. "Unless you need a clean towel, I really should be getting back to Lord Atros's chambers."

"Ah, right, so he can fuck you until his ego is sated."

My eyes snapped up to him as I felt my heart slam against my chest in anger.

"Is that fury I see behind those eyes of yours, little one? It's a good look on you."

I pushed past him, trying with all my might to hold back my tongue.

"Aren't you going to ask me how she is?" Erendrial said in a low tone.

I stopped dead in my tracks, turning back to him slowly. My breath quickened. *Act like you don't care*, I thought. *Put on a mask, don't let him see.* "And who should I be asking after?" I said, with my head higher than it should have been.

He smiled, walking to me casually. "Adorable Lilian Thomas of course. She's the one you had your master asking after during his last visit, was she not?"

My heart dropped into my stomach. How did he know? Damn, he was clever, but what was he after?

"You're not going to ask?" He said, shrugging as if it was nothing of importance. "Well, I will do you the courtesy of telling you anyway. She is doing well. She is regularly fed. We let her out to play with the other humans and bathe her occasionally when the stench starts to linger. Her little body is well cared for. Well sought after by the male alfar, I should say."

"Do not—" I yelled, taking a step towards him, but stopping myself before I could sign my own death warrant.

He cocked his head in a predatory way with that devious smile stretched on his face. "Ah, so you do have some bite to you after all. I just have to strike the right chord." His silver eyes roamed over my face for a brief moment. He leaned in, placing his lips close to my ear. "She has taken a lover, you know. Very seductive, the little human is." He circled me as I stood grounded to the floor. I could feel my blood begin to boil. "His name is Zerrial. They fuck day and night. She's quite the squealer, that one."

"Stop talking about her like that," I said, gritting my teeth.

He was taunting me, that was all. He was trying to get a rise out of me, and it was working.

He stopped in front of me with an eyebrow arched in amusement. "What? You don't like the word fuck, is that it? Isn't that what your master does to you whenever he feels like it?"

"No. It's not—" I stopped myself, realizing he was goading me.

"It's not what? Like that between the two of you? Would you rather I say making love? Isn't that what humans call it? Sorry to be the bearer of bad news little one, but an alfar can't experience love. We live too long, and we care too little. Believe whatever you need to, to get yourself through the encounters, but he does not love you...he can't."

I closed my eyes in an attempt to shut him out, holding the towels tightly against my chest, trying to calm myself. I heard him huff a small laugh before he walked around me down the hall. His words replayed through my head, then I heard his footsteps stop.

"Oh, and by the way," he said, turning halfway back to me. "You have his eyes." The corner of his mouth turned up.

My head went into a frenzy trying to make sense of his comment. "Whose? Whose eyes do I have?" I said too quickly.

He gloated at me over his shoulder. "Your father's." Then he was gone.

My heart skipped a beat. No, he didn't know my father. This was a trick. He couldn't. He was a conniving fox, after nothing more than his own elevation.

I shook off the comment as best as I could, but he had gotten to me in more ways than one. He knew my weakness, Lilian. He knew too much about my relationship with Gaelin, and now he was dangling my father in front of me? Which would infer that he knew I was a half-breed. I made my way back to Gaelin's chambers, trying to act normal. To my surprise, Gaelin was already asleep, which honestly, I was thankful for. I sat on the balcony and looked up at the stars, trying to come up with my own defenses against the ambassador of horrors.

CHAPTER 13

After hours of contemplating ways to kill Ambassador Lyklor, I finally came to the realization that in my current situation I was powerless to do anything. If I was even seen speaking with him, the other alfar would assume I was being unfaithful to Gaelin and have me killed. The alfar's senses were too adept to use poisons. I would never be able to get close enough to kill him. I was powerless and I hated it.

That night I dreamt of Lyklor. I saw flashes of him and a light alfar who looked vaguely familiar speaking in the corner of the castle. I couldn't make out what they were saying, but I recognized the alfar's face. He was a young representative of one of the high houses. I had seen him at dinner and speaking with the king and also in Princess Daealla's room the day she had summoned for me. I watched as the two of them conspired and plotted against Gaelin. This light alfar had joined forces with Lyklor and the ambassador was using his naivety to his advantage. I jolted awake with the new information.

This had to be a power, not just a coincidence. Gaelin was already up, getting ready for the day. I dressed quickly, eager to seek out the alfar I had seen in my premonition. Gaelin came to kiss me on my head before collecting his jacket.

"What's on the agenda for today?" I asked.

"More arguments with the dark representatives. Trying to keep my own people on my side in the process," he said, sounding irritated.

"Why wouldn't your people back you?" I asked.

"As I said, Lyklor is very convincing. Either he has someone on our side working with him or my court has very little faith in me, which doesn't reflect well on the crown."

That was all the confirmation I needed to be certain I wasn't going crazy. My premonition was of Erendrial's inside informant, it had to be. But how was I going to oust him? Gods forbid if I was wrong, they would take my head for interfering. I had to plan this one out on my own before I brought it to Gaelin. I didn't want to add more stress to his plate. Plus, if this was just another dream, I didn't want to seem like a desperate fool. I had to confirm this for myself first.

"You have nothing to worry about. The alfar love you," I said.

He leaned in to kiss me on the mouth with a small smile. "Only the alfar?" he asked playfully.

I smiled, trying to hide my discomfort. Looking back at

that moment, I may have said those three little words too hastily.

"Stay in crowds today or find Levos and stay with him. I will see you at dinner."

"Of course," I said, gathering the laundry and heading out of his chambers.

I dropped the clothing at the wash station and headed towards the debriefing room I knew Gaelin and the others would be in. The members of the council were out in the halls, huddled in small groups, talking amongst themselves. I stationed myself near a large cupboard, pretending to dust the monstrosity as I scoped out the players, searching for the face in my vision.

Filo turned the corner with two other alfar males trailing him. A pair of hands settled on top of my shoulders and startled me. I turned to see Levos staring back at me.

"What are you doing up here and why are you dusting this hunk of crap?"

"Chores and all. Who is that?" I asked, gesturing to the blonde man.

"Uh, that is Lord Filo Uytum, son of Lord Freg Uytum. Why do you ask?"

"Just trying to learn about the court is all," I turned to leave the hall.

Levos caught up to me with one long stride. "You've been here for almost four months, and you are just now asking questions about the houses? Sweet Genevieve, do us both a favor and never enter into politics. Do you take me as a fool? What was that inquiry about?" Levos asked.

Erendrial Lyklor and five of his court members turned the corner heading straight towards us. His eyes locked on mine, and he grinned. I glared at him before dropping my eyes to the floor. As he passed by, I heard a faint laugh deep in his throat.

Levos looked from me to Lyklor and then back to me. "And what in the heavens was that about?"

"Nothing, you're just seeing things, Levos."

"Uh, no sweetheart. You better start talking, or we are going to have an altercation and fair warning, you will lose."

I turned to him, pulling us out of the way of oncoming traffic. "Don't ask me how, but I think Lord Filo is working with Lyklor as his inside man. That is why Gaelin is having so many problems trying to persuade the other light members to his side. Because Filo is working against him and using his influence to do Lyklor's bidding."

Levos looked shocked, trying to process the accusation. "Alright, I am going to pretend I don't want to know how you got this information. Gen, do you realize what you are saying? If this information is wrong, you will be signing your own death warrant. Not even Gaelin will be able to save you. On top of all that, Filo is a favorite of Princess Daealla. They have an... interesting relationship if you get my meaning."

"I know. That's why I was doing a bit of snooping before I said anything."

"But if you're right, the king will execute Filo on the spot. If he truly is a traitor, we need to eliminate the spy before any more of our information is leaked to the dark court."

"Does that mean you'll help me?" I asked eagerly.

"You know I have nothing better to do, why not? Let's just try not to get ourselves killed. Now, about the Lyklor situation back in the hall there?"

I rolled my eyes. "He approached me last night and gave me an update on Lily. Don't ask me why or how he knew about my connection to her, because I really have no clue. He's a clever bastard, I'll give him that."

"He must be trying to gain favor with you to get to Gaelin somehow. Did you tell Gaelin?"

"No, he was asleep when I got back to the room. Plus, I think he would flip if he knew he talked to me alone."

"You're right about that. And please don't make me remind you what happens if anyone else sees you two alone together. I'd rather not have to find a new best friend."

I couldn't stop myself from grinning. "Awe, a human, your best friend? I am touched."

"You're not completely human so there's that, but that's not the point. Don't be stupid. Stay away from him. He's after something." Levos stood for a moment in silence, thinking to himself.

I thought back to the comment about my father. I wanted to tell him, but I couldn't. Not yet. Not when I didn't even know if it was true or not.

"If Filo did make a deal with the dark court," said Levos, "there would be a contract. He isn't stupid. He wouldn't trust them out of the kindness of his heart. A blood bond would have been made, which means there must be a paper contract hidden somewhere in his chambers. We'll have to find a way to get in. Maybe at dinner I'd have time, but I'd need a distraction. Something that would hold everyone's attention."

I thought for a moment of a way I could help the plan. I was limited, but I still had a card to play. Alfar loved nothing more than to see humans in pain, right?

"What is the punishment for looking at Gaelin in public in Princess Daealla's presence?" I asked.

Levos cocked his head to the side, probably trying to figure out if I was serious.

I walked into the throne room for dinner and took my normal place against the wall, keeping my head down and eyes to the floor. The lords and ladies of the light court entered, followed by our dark alfar guests. Erendrial sat at the table closest to the royals. He faced the wall of humans but didn't glance at any of us. The royals came in last, including Gaelin.

Pitchers and food trays were brought out for us to serve the alfar. I took a ceramic jug of wine and held it close to my chest. My breath trembled and my heart raced. As soon as everyone took their seats, we were signaled to begin making our rounds. The alfar chattered among themselves quietly, making small talk as their dinner and wine were placed in front of them.

I moved to the royal table even though that wasn't the table I had been assigned to serve. I pushed past the other human girl who was headed their way and began filling the king's goblet first. I moved to the queen and then Princess Daealla. She stared directly at me with the fire of jealousy I had come to recognize behind her eyes. I took a deep breath and moved to Gaelin's goblet.

My hand was trembling as I felt his eyes on me. I allowed the wine to trickle from my pitcher to his cup. I felt sick, but this had to be done. I slowly raised my head to his, locking our eyes across the table. His eyes widened in terror as he searched my face to figure out what in the hell I was doing. I locked my eyes on him, pulling the pitcher away from his glass. My head was held high, my shoulders were taunt, and my back was straight.

Gaelin angrily mouthed for me to bow my head, but I did no such thing. Princess Daealla turned to me slowly, baffled by my direct insult. I saw a small smile stretch across her lips. Gaelin tensed, dropping his head in panic.

"Father," said Daealla proudly to the king, "it looks like we are going to have another form of entertainment this evening." I waited a moment, long enough in hopes that the king would notice me before finally releasing my gaze, allowing it to fall to the ground.

"Lord Atros, your concubine knows the expectations of her station, does she not?" asked King Lysanthier.

Gaelin glanced up to me, still scowling. "She does," he muttered.

"Well then, it looks like we are going to have to reprimand her for her direct disobedience and disrespect.

Guards, please restrain Lord Atros's mistress," barked the king.

Daealla leaned over to her father, whispering something into his ear. He nodded as she took her leave from the table. Two guards grabbed each of my arms, turning me to face the court. The king stood from his seat as the room quieted.

"Tonight, we will have a demonstration of what happens when you disobey even the simplest law. No matter your station, no matter your responsibilities, humans are not and will never be our equal." He turned to the wall where the humans stood in a line. "Your race is beneath us. You are here only to serve us as we command it. This human has dared to disrespect the future queen of the light. For that, she will be punished."

I looked around the room. No one seemed to care that I was about to be punished for a simple glance. Some of the light alfar even smiled and gawked at me as if I deserved what was coming. I looked to the dark alfar. Erendrial and his companions sat stone-faced and gave no reaction to the situation.

Filo appeared from the back of the room carrying an iron hammer. I inhaled deeply, anticipating the pain I was about to endure. The king sat as the other two guards turned me back to face Gaelin. One of them pulled my left hand from my side, spreading my fingers across the white tablecloth directly in front of Gaelin. I was shaking in terror, trying to pull back only out of instinct, but I was trapped.

Filo brought the hammer to the table, hovering it over

my left hand. "This is going to hurt," Filo whispered in my ear.

I looked up at him and saw his sadistic smile. I focused on it, knowing he was the reason I was in this position. I looked to Gaelin, expecting him to do something, anything, but he just sat there with his face turned away from me as his whole body tensed. How could someone watch the person they claimed to love suffer? A small tear escaped my eye as I bent my head, no longer able to look at him.

Filo brought the hammer into the air, then barreled it down until it crashed into my hand. I screamed in immense agony as I heard the bones in my hand crack and break. He brought the hammer up a second, then a third time, flattening my hand until I could no longer move a single finger. My screams seemed to land on deaf ears. No one came to help me. No one moved a single inch to stop what was happening to me.

Filo finally stepped away from the table. The others let go of me as I fell helplessly to the floor, cradling my limp, numb hand. I looked at the tablecloth, now covered in my blood. Gaelin refused to look at me. I was trembling as I peered down at my bloodied and bruised hand. I could see spurs of bone poking out from the skin. My nails were shattered, and my wrist bent in an unnatural way.

My vision blurred from the shock and tears as I curled my legs under myself, trying to conjure whatever dignity I had left to stand on my own. I heard footsteps coming from behind me and turned to see Princess Daealla walking towards me with a wrought-iron poker in her hand. The tip had a vibrant red glow. She grabbed the right side of my dress, ripping the fabric to reveal my chest before jabbing the red-hot poker into my skin right underneath my collar bone.

I opened my mouth to scream in pain, but nothing came out. She pushed deeper, allowing my skin to blister from the heat of the metal. She bent down slowly, placing her lips near my ear.

"Now, every time he looks at you, every time he touches you, he will think of me," whispered Daealla. She withdrew the poker from my chest.

I could feel my skin ripping and tearing as parts of my melted flesh went with the iron poker. I doubled over, feeling sick to my stomach. Tears saturated my face as I forced myself to remain conscious.

"You are dismissed," said King Lysanthier.

I slowly got to my feet, cradling my hand to my chest. I didn't dare look at the other alfar. Some of them laughed quietly to themselves as I passed their tables, heading for the exit. I barely made it back to Gaelin's chambers. I closed the door behind me, sliding down the wall, unsure of what to do now. Hopefully, my sacrifice wasn't in vain.

Ten minutes passed before Levos entered the room holding a yellow scroll. I was still shaking from the trauma of my punishment. He took one look at me, and his face fell. He rushed to me, taking my warm face in his hands. I began to cry again as I looked at my hand, trying to figure out how my bones would ever heal.

"Gen, sweetheart, look at me. You're going to be okay.

Remember, you will heal. This is only momentary. Your hand will be fine," he said.

"You need...you need to find a piece of ulyrium," I forced out.

"What? Why?" he asked.

I pulled my ripped dress to the side, revealing my brand. His eyes widened as he looked at my burnt flesh. "I need you to go over the brand with a ulyrium stone, or it will fade, and they will find out what I am," I said.

"Gen, I can't. I can't hurt you in that way," he said, holding onto me.

"You have to. To save my life. Please, Levos," I whispered. He his eyes darkened in pain as he nodded, leaving the room.

He returned with a small ulyrium dagger. The stone was a mix of red and orange swirled together to create a fluid design. He held the dagger over a flame, heating the stone, then gently placed a rolled piece of cloth in my mouth before removing the edge of my torn dress. I pressed my head against the wall, breathing deeply. I nodded for him to begin.

The smell of my burning flesh was all I could focus on. This branding was slower and much more painful. I yelled through the cloth as my whole body shook. It took everything I had to stay seated and not move away from the dagger. Levos steadied me with his other hand as he traced over the already fading mark.

Just as he finished the last lines of the design, the door flew open and Gaelin stepped into the room, his face horrified. He charged at his cousin, picking Levos up by his shirt and slamming him into the wall next to me. My vision was still blurry as I fought to stay awake.

"What in the god's names are you doing?" Gaelin yelled.

"Cousin, I had to. If the mark faded and they saw, then they would know what she is. It had to be done. I didn't want to. Believe me." Levos said heavy-heartedly.

Gaelin let him down slowly as they both turned their attention to me.

I looked directly at Levos, not able to stomach the sight of Gaelin. "Was it worth it? Is it what we thought?" I whispered.

"You were right and now we have the proof," Levos said, picking up the piece of yellow parchment.

I smiled, knowing I could at least destroy one evil in my life.

"What are you two talking about? Tell me, now," Gaelin growled.

I tried to get up but was too weak. Gaelin reached for me but stopped hesitantly when I turned away from his touch. Levos made his way over to me, helping me stand to my feet. I looked between the two of them, still having trouble breathing.

"You tell him. I'd like to bathe. If you permit me to, that is," I said sharply to Gaelin.

His eyes filled with pain, and he turned away from me. I walked into the bathroom and closed the door. The water burned my brand and my broken hand. The adrenaline was beginning to wear off and my nerves were screaming in pain. I could feel the wounds of my hand beginning to mend, but

I didn't know how long it would take to fully heal. I would have to fake the injury for some time, acting as if I was healing at a normal human rate.

I curled my legs into my chest, still cradling my hand. I was shaking, replaying the punishment over in my head. Tears poured from my eyes as I sobbed heavily, letting it all go. I brought my fingers to my chest, hesitant to touch the raised raw skin. The brand was oozing as the skin began to turn different shades of green and purple. *It's just a body, Gen*, I thought. *It's only skin. This doesn't define you.*

The door of the bathroom opened slowly. Gaelin stepped inside, keeping his eyes to the floor. I curled my knees as high as I could into my chest, trying to cover myself. He walked over to me and knelt beside the tub. He couldn't look at me.

"Why didn't you come to me? Why didn't you just tell me what you had discovered? This all could have been avoided," he said softly.

"There wasn't time, and would you really have believed me? You would have wanted to know how I found the information, and that is something I can't explain to you because I don't even understand it fully myself," I said.

"I would have at least listened to what you had to say."

"And what, taken the word of a half-breed over one of your own? Filo is the one that has been turning your own people against you. He is the one that has been working with the dark alfar and now you have the proof you need to take back control of the council."

"Why? Why involve yourself in this at all?"

I stopped, biting my lip as I thought of Lilian. "Ambassador Lyklor, he approached me yesterday evening... alone."

Galen looked at my face finally, trying to connect the dots.

"He knows about my affections for Lilian and that you asked about her when you were in his court. He was testing me, trying to get a rise out of me by pushing my buttons and he succeeded. I figure he's priming me to influence you for whatever he has up his sleeve, but he's a threat to Lilian and to you, so I wanted him gone. I discovered his connection with Filo and moved as quickly as I could to eliminate the threat."

"This isn't your fight, Gen."

"No, it's not, but he has my sister locked in his house of horror. He told me things about her that I can't even repeat out loud. I'm powerless, unable to save her, so I struck the only way I knew how. I saw an opportunity and I took it."

Gaelin reached for my shoulder, but I recoiled away from him.

"Please, don't push me away. Let me help," he whispered.

"Like you helped at dinner," I spat out. I looked at him for the first time with disgust. He pulled his hand from me, gripping the edge of the large tub. "How could you just sit there and do nothing? How could you watch as my blood splattered across your table? As the sounds of my bones breaking and my screams of pain filled the air. How can you sit there and say you love me, yet you did nothing?"

"I couldn't have done a thing, you know this. You knew the laws and you used them to create a distraction for Levos. How is this my fault?" he said.

I took a breath, calming my head and my temper. "You're right, I did choose this. I knew what I was doing and what had to be done. The point is that you sat there without emotion and watched as they mutilated me. You sat there and you heard me cry out in pain and you did nothing to even try to prevent this from happening. Outside of these walls, I am nothing more than another human body bag that can be used and abused and then thrown to the wolves if it would please the other alfar."

"That is not true. You know how I feel about you. You know I love you."

"Do you, Gaelin? Are you even capable of love?"

His face went somber.

"If Ambassador Lyklor wanted to take me from you, would you even lift a finger to prevent it?"

"Of course, I would. You are bound to me. You are mine," he said angrily.

"Yes, I am your property, but I am also the property of the king. If the king allowed Lyklor to take me there'd be nothing you could do, is there? Because I am just another disposable human, here for your pleasure and your convenience." I held my head as small tears ran down my face.

"You mean more to me than you know," he whispered.

A few moments passed before I cleared my throat enough to speak again. "What does the brand mean?" I asked, indicating the mark on my chest. He hung his head in shame.

"It's the sigil for house Lysanthier."

I nodded, realizing how clever that little bitch was.

After my bath, Gaelin tended to my hand. Because of my alfar blood we couldn't call in a healer to quicken the healing process. He reassured me that it would heal in a few days. I curled into bed, facing the balcony. He kissed me gently on the top of my head before turning out the lights. My hand wasn't the only thing that had been completely shattered. Filo might as well have taken the hammer to my heart and any hope that Gaelin could truly love me.

CHAPTER 14

Gaelin was gone by the time I woke up the next morning. The table on the balcony was covered in fresh fruit and breakfast foods for me. I walked into the sunshine and took a seat in front of the feast. If it weren't for the events from last night, I would have thought this to be romantic, but I knew it was a symptom of his ever-growing guilt. I ate in peace before dressing for my big day.

My hand still throbbed and ached something terrible. The mark on my chest was even worse thanks to the ulyrium blade. I bandaged my injuries and headed out to find Levos. He was tucked away in one of the service halls making out with a human slave I didn't recognize. I cleared my throat, trying to be subtle. He turned with a growl of aggravation. Once he saw it was me, he calmed, motioning for the young girl to be on her way.

I had almost allowed myself to forget that he was an alfar. He was kind to me, but he used humans just as much as the others. My heart broke a little seeing him for who he really was. He walked over to me with a smile on his face. I tried to regain my composure, but I failed miserably.

"Hey, you're not looking too well. Should I walk you back to your rooms?" he asked, taking my shoulders in his arms.

I shook my head, refocusing. "What's happening with Filo?"

He smiled his charming grin at me with a little laugh. "You will be happy to know that Gaelin brought the contract to the king this morning. There's going to be a gathering in a few minutes to confront Filo and the dark alfar."

"And you weren't going to tell me? I deserve to be there, to see this," I snapped.

He took a step back, seeming surprised by my aggression. "We just figured you'd want to sleep while you heal."

"Stop assuming what I want and just ask. For heaven's sake, I know I am a worthless slave, but I'm still capable of thinking for myself."

"Gen, where is all of this coming from? I don't find you worthless and I am certain you can think for yourself. You made that very clear with the Filo situation."

I rolled my eyes, trying to keep my composure in check. *Play the game, dammit.* "Sorry, I'm just in pain and tired. Can we head to the meeting now?" I walked past him towards the main hall.

Levos followed behind me without uttering a single word. When we got to the door, crowds of alfar were waiting to be invited inside by the king. A few smirked at me as I entered. Erendrial and the rest of his company approached the door, walking with pride and power.

Erendrial looked at me, raising an eyebrow as if to ask why I was present. I smiled at him. holding my head high. He stopped and gave me a curious look of amusement before returning to his group.

"How're your injuries by the way?" asked Levos.

"They hurt and I can't bear to look at my hand, but I will be fine. Thanks for asking," I said flatly.

He exhaled in frustration. "What did you want to tell me by the way?" he asked.

"What?"

"The day the dark alfar got here. You came into the castle out of breath and excited. You said I wouldn't believe what had just happened to you. What happened?" I thought back to the dragon-like beast.

"I ran into a dragon, or at least a smaller version of one, in a lavender field."

"A ragamor you mean. The dark alfar travel on their backs. They are unable to mist into the court thanks to our runes, so they must have ridden their ragamor beasts to get here."

"So, it's not a dragon?"

"A smaller version of one, I suppose. It can't breathe fire, but they are extremely strong and deadly. No one has seen an actual dragon for years. The ragamor were created by the same dark magic that runs through the veins of the dark alfar. That's why they can control them."

"And what is misting and runes?"

"Misting is another little gift from their disgusting god. They can dematerialize their physical form, turning into a black mist and traveling to a destination of their choosing. The runes are magic symbols that we put on the entrances of our kingdom so they can't mist in unannounced whenever they feel like it."

"Good to know," I said, realizing the massive bear I was poking.

"The ragamor are beautiful creatures, though deadly. You should feel lucky that you only saw it flying by. If you had a closer encounter, you might not be standing here."

I swallowed hard, remembering the feeling of the armored scales that I traced my fingers across. The way the creature nuzzled me as if I was its owner. *Don't say another word, Gen.*

"Yes, lucky," I responded.

The large doors of the meeting hall opened, revealing the king and Gaelin inside of the room. The alfar began to funnel inside, taking their seats around a large rectangular table.

"I have a little present for you," Levos said, leaning into my ear.

"You know how much I love presents," I replied, sarcastically.

"I had Gaelin place my chair directly across the table from Erendrial. You will be standing behind me so you will have a front-row seat to his devastation."

I genuinely smiled at him, excited for the takedown to begin. "My favorite gift yet."

He laughed, leading me to the chair.

As everyone settled in, I stood behind Levos steeling glances at Erendrial when I could without being detected. The king signaled for the room's attention as the doors closed us inside.

"Thank you all for attending. I will get directly to the point. Today's meeting will not consist of strategies for our attack against Otar and his forces, as previously discussed. After recent developments, I have decided that we will move forward with Lord Atros's plan for the attack without any disagreement from anyone at this table, including our dark alfar guests," said King Lysanthier.

"Pardon me *king*," said Erendrial, "but this was to be a mutual arrangement when it came to the attack and how we should move forward with Otar and his remains. Lord Atros and I have come to an agreement that benefits both kingdoms and our desires to understand this enemy better."

"There will be no more negotiations. If Otar's body falls on our land then it is ours, and only ours, as stated in the treaty. All infantries will defer to Lord Atros for instruction from this point on," said the king.

Erendrial leaned into the table, perhaps trying to work out where his negotiations had faltered. "We have complied with all your requests. This was to be a mutually beneficial arrangement," said Lyklor.

"Yes, it was. Until a most interesting discovery has come to light, revealing your court's true nature." The alfar looked to one another, trying to decipher what they all had missed. "It has come to our attention that members of the dark court have been conspiring with my own subjects in order to gain influence and inside information regarding our private affairs."

The light alfar gasped, looking at each other as if to accuse one another. I kept my eyes on Erendrial, gleaming at his undoing. He stared at the table, as if trying to piece it all together. His head rose as his attention locked onto my broken hand and then to my eyes. He leaned back in his chair, lacing his fingers together in front of him, still holding my eyes with his. I didn't back down.

"Lord Atros has brought to my attention a blood contract that was forged between the dark court and a member of our own, Lord Filo Uytum," the king continued. Filo looked panicked as the table turned to stare. "The contract allows safe passage for Lord Uytum to enter the Kingdom of Doonak. It promises marriage to a dark alfar of high standing and access to any resources the dark court has in return for compliance and full disclosure of any information pertaining to the inner workings of the light court." The room quieted.

Erendrial's eyes were still on me as he spoke. "And when was this contract discovered?" asked Erendrial.

"It was discovered in Lord Uytum's private chambers, during our dinner banquet last night" replied the king.

Erendrial smiled. "Clever girl," he said softly.

"Excuse me, Ambassador Lyklor?" said the king.

Erendrial's eyes finally left mine, returning his attention

to the king. He knew it was me. That this was all me. I reveled in that knowledge, yet something inside of me shook with fear.

"May I see the contract please," asked Erendrial. A guard approached him with a yellow piece of parchment. He took a moment to look it over before handing it back. "I can assure you that I have never laid eyes on this contract. If there was an arrangement made with Lord Uytum and someone within my court, this is the first I am hearing of it. I have had no direct contact with Lord Uytum besides the interactions that have occurred in this room." He was calm and smooth when it came to public speaking. If I didn't know how deceptive he was, I might have believed him just now.

The king waited a few moments before responding. "Since there is no specific name on the blood contract, Lord Uytum, would you like to use your last moments to speak the name of your accomplice?" Filo looked terrified. He didn't look at any of the dark alfar. I could only imagine he feared their punishment far more than anything the light alfar could do to him.

"I made the deal unaware of who I was communicating with. They never revealed their name or face. I have failed you, my King, and for that I beg your forgiveness," said Filo.

The king looked unmoved. He flicked his first finger to signal to the guards. Two alfar approached either side of Filo. "You will have to face your fate for your treachery in whatever afterlife you end up, Lord Uytum," said the king. One of the guards unsheathed a ulyrium sword, swinging the blade at Filo's neck. With a hard thump, his head fell to the floor. I couldn't help but jump.

Blood pooled at the base of the chair as his headless body slumped against the table. My mouth fell open. I had never actually seen someone beheaded before. I turned from the sight, meeting Erendrial's eyes. He tilted his head as if to ask, 'satisfied?' I gave him a small smile, trying to hide my discomfort.

"Ambassador Lyklor, as you can see, we no longer trust your judgment in this matter. Please be comforted that Lord Atros is our most trusted general. He will lead us to victory," said the king, standing from his seat. The other alfar stood in respect. "Please enjoy our hospitality before the battle commences two days from now. If any other foul play is discovered, you and your members will be dealt with accordingly."

The king left while the other alfar stood around, still in shock at the betrayal. One of their own had made a deal to leave their court to work with the dark alfar. I waited by the wall behind Levos, keeping my head bowed and my eyes to the floor. He spoke to the other alfar as if he were just as surprised as they. Erendrial left the hall without saying a word to anyone. I smiled. *Take joy in the little things, Gen.*

CHAPTER 15

Levos didn't leave my side for the rest of the day. He watched me curiously as I completed my chores in silence. Honestly, it was best that I kept my mouth shut. I was afraid of what might slip out if I got started.

I watched the other humans around me clean, cook, and tend to the alfar's needs. I felt like I had been in a blindfold until this point. I was so focused on finding Lilian and my hopeless relationship with Gaelin that I missed the suffering that passed me in the halls every day. No wonder why they hated me. I was living the high life in comparison to what they had to deal with each day.

A young girl was cleaning the terrace outside one of the dining rooms. I noticed an alfar male watching her from the other side of the room. The girl acted like she didn't notice his gaze, but I could tell she was fully aware of his intentions based on the straightness of her spine. The male finally approached her casually. He whispered something into her ear briefly before making his exit. The girl's whole body went stiff. Her eyes dropped to the floor as she placed the duster down and followed him out of the room a few moments later.

In the fields, if the human boys didn't work hard and fast enough, they would be whipped and beaten for slowing down the harvest. The female alfar took human lovers in their bed, but it wasn't so excessive like it was with their counterparts. I stood on the edge of a field and watched as the boys labored for what seemed like forever without a single break. They looked tired and hungry. Their skin was tanned and blistered from the sun.

Every other thought in my head evaporated. I must have been standing there for a while because when I looked around for Levos, he was gone. I couldn't just watch and do nothing, but what could I do to help them? I looked around and found a few pitchers of water and a cup leftover from the alfar's lunch.

I took the cup and pitcher and made my way into the field. I went to the first young man and filled the glass with water and handed it to him. He looked at me with confusion and terror, then around to see if his overseer was watching.

"Drink, hurry," I demanded.

He took the glass and threw it back. Streams of water poured from the sides of his mouth. He handed me the glass and considered me for a moment before nodding a thank you. I made my way to the next worker, offering what little reprieve I could. Once the pitcher was empty, I refilled it and went back into the field.

I had filled over twenty glasses of water before an alfar guard finally noticed me. He walked with authority over to where a young boy, no older than fifteen was standing alongside me. He looked at me and then to the boy.

"What is the meaning of this?" The guard said in a deep voice. The boy didn't move his eyes from the ground.

"I was offering water to the workers," I said.

"And who told you to do this?" The guard asked.

"No one. I saw how hard the men were working and thought to offer them refreshment." The guard looked from me to the boy.

"I did not authorize a water break and you did not ask permission. Disobedience of any kind carries a punishment. Three lashes," said the guard. The boy began to tremble. The guard unraveled his leather whip and took a step back. I began to panic. Without thinking I stepped in front of the boy.

"This was my fault. I will take his punishment," I yelled, standing firmly in between the boy and the guard. The men in the field stopped working and turned to see what the commotion was about. The guard looked at me with annoyance. I saw a small flicker of a smile flash across his face as his eyes swept up and down my body.

"You will take the three lashes for the boy?" The guard asked.

"Yes."

The guard smiled, stepping towards me. He forcefully flung me around to face away from him. He undid the teeth of the clasps in the back of my dress to reveal my bare back. I held my arms around my chest to prevent the dress from falling. The guard pushed me to the ground. I sat up on my knees, preparing myself for the sting of the whip.

The first snap came as a surprise. I felt the blood fall from the opened skin. I winced, but I did not yell. I wouldn't give him the satisfaction. The second one came faster and harder. Then the third. I staggered to my feet, turning to face him so my back was out of his sight. I had to make sure that he didn't see the wounds already beginning to heal. I held onto the front of my dress with my eyes to the ground.

"May I go?" I asked the guard.

He didn't even respond, only turned, and walked away. The young boy I had taken the lashings for came up behind me, fastening the latches of my dress closed. I knew it was ruined. The blood was still warm and sticky on my skin. The boy gripped my arm tightly as a few tears escaped my face.

"Why?" He asked. I looked into the young boy's eyes. They were deep brown with flecks of gold throughout. I smiled softly before taking my leave without another word. I walked through the field back to the path up to the castle. I saw a dark figure looming against one of the arches up ahead. I shielded my eyes from the sun and realized it was Erendrial, watching me intently. I rolled my eyes, hoping he would leave me be, but I wasn't so lucky.

"If I didn't know better," he started, "I would be inclined to believe you enjoy pain. As much as you throw yourself directly into its path, that is." He kept pace with me.

I tried to ignore him, walking faster through the crowds

of humans in the lower halls. They took one look at Erendrial and parted like the Red Sea.

"Oh, come now, the silent treatment, really? That little smart mouth of yours has nothing to snap back at me? Please, say something. I do so enjoy our tiffs," he said, stepping in front of me. Dipping his eyes down, trying to capture my line of sight. I looked firmly at the doorway behind him.

"What can I do for you, Ambassador Lyklor?" I said, too tired and beaten to argue.

He raised an eyebrow, which I was learning was a normal reaction for him. "What did I tell you about asking an alfar male that question? And my name is Eren. I expect you to call me that from now on. I have a feeling we are going to be fast friends," he said slowly, reaching out to the collar of my dress that covered my brand.

I stepped back out of his reach.

He laughed, closing the space between us once more.

"Genevieve sweetheart, there you are," said Levos, walking hastily towards us.

Erendrial didn't even flinch at his voice. His eyes were locked onto my face, searching for something, but I didn't know what.

I felt Levos gently take my good arm, pulling me out of the path of the dark alfar. "Lord Atros has been looking for you. Return to his chambers immediately." Levos stared down Erendrial until he finally took a step away, allowing me to pass.

I walked casually away as if nothing had happened. My

back still stung from the lashes. My hand was throbbing, and the damn brand still felt like it was on fire. A few alfar turned and stared at me as I walked down the main hall to Gaelin's chambers. I got to the room, expecting to see Gaelin, but it was empty.

I went over to the balcony, peering down at the beautiful kingdom that was created and maintained by slavery. The breeze was cooler this high up. I took a deep breath in, savoring the clean air. Footsteps approached behind me. I recognized Levos's staggered walk.

"Why is the back of your dress covered in blood?" he asked, in a hesitant voice.

"I gave a young boy a glass of water. For that, I was beaten," I said.

"Gen, you have to stop taking these risks. You already have a target on your back after last night. If you aren't careful, they will figure out what you are and then that will be the end of you, for good."

"Would that be such a bad thing?" I asked, turning to look into his eyes. "What purpose does my life have? What value? I get to sit up here and watch as other humans are raped, beaten, starved, sold, and killed, because we don't follow your stupid, ridiculous laws. How can I ever be happy, knowing that my people suffer while I sit up here doing nothing?" I said firmly.

"We are your people too," he said slowly.

I laughed. "The humans in my town knew what I was, yet they never made a move to turn me in or kill me for it. Yes, they were cruel in other ways, but I wasn't just something to be disposed of. The alfar would behead me without question. I didn't ask for this. I don't want this, but this is what I am. I am stuck between two races, two sets of rules that will never allow me to live a normal life."

He turned me to face him. His eyes were stern and his face tense. "Look at me. You have people here who care about you. Who want to see you happy."

"Is that what you were doing this morning? Making that human girl happy?" I said sharply.

He let go of my arms and ran his hand across his face, then spoke slowly "Her name is Madison," he stopped, taking in a deep break. Something about him softened at the mention of her name. "She's been here for over a year. She works in the kitchen. She has two brothers back in her village," moving to the edge of the bed, he took a seat. I watched as something like pain stretched across his angelic face. "Her mother died when she was young and she was raised by her father." He paused for a few moments, before continuing. "Her favorite cake flavor is lemon. Her favorite scent is peonies. She likes music. She wanted to be a dancer before she was taken, and she is actually very good at it.".

"You...you care for her?" I asked.

His eyes finally found mine again. "Very much. I do my best to protect her from the others, but my influence only goes so far and when I fail, I have to find a way to live with myself."

Crap, now I looked like the emotionless idiot. I took a seat next to him on the bed as everything about Levos began to make sense. His kindness towards me. His loyalty. His protective nature. It was all because of her. Because of Madison.

"That is why... that I why you've helped me?" I whispered. "Why you didn't turn me in. Because you're in love with a human."

Levos nodded.

"Levos, I am so sorry for assuming. I just—"

"You just thought that all alfar are the same? That we aren't capable of feeling true emotions? Especially towards a human?" He laughed, turning away from me. "Have I not proven myself to you enough by now? Has Gaelin not proven his love for you?"

"Don't bring him into this. That is a different situation altogether."

"How? I fail Madison every time another alfar takes her into his bed. Every time someone of high-class spits on her, smacks her, looks down at her; and no matter how much I want to stand in the way of them and the pain they cause her, I can't. I would be killed for going against my own, as you saw happen today. Gaelin is in the same situation, Gen. We do not agree with the system, but we can't change it. There are few of us and masses of them. This is the world we live in. We have to learn to adapt and unfortunately, to look the other way."

I held my head down. Even though I knew some of what he was saying was true, it didn't change the searing desire inside of me to burn this whole city to the ground.

"I am sorry for the way I treated you," I said, trying to defuse the situation.

"You don't have to be sorry. You have every right to feel the way you do, but never forget I am your friend, and I will always be looking out for you, as best as I can." He took my hand in his. "Now, let's get you cleaned up. I'd rather not have to explain to my cousin why you got yourself beaten yet again."

I took a bath, washing the blood from my skin. Levos had a clean gown set out for me when I finished. He rewrapped my hand and changed the bandage on my brand. The lashes on my back were already closed. They would be gone by evening so Gaelin would never know what happened. Levos was gentle with me. He brushed my hair, braiding it into a thick line that trailed down my back. I placed the headband around my ears, covering my secret.

"So, what are we going to do about Erendrial? He clearly has something in mind for you," said Levos.

I laughed, thinking about how messy my life had become. "He asked me to call him Eren."

"That seems a bit personal."

"He also demands that I look at him in his presence. He doesn't seem to care if we are in public or in private. He is an odd character that is for sure. Oh, and he knows it was me that spoiled his little plan with Filo."

"He is extremely intelligent. He didn't rise to where he is by sheer luck. Now that he knows, he will be gunning for you, so you need to be careful. You can't be alone, not for a moment." Levos finished my hair, moving to face me.

"I wasn't alone today. I was in a group of people, yet he didn't seem to care. I don't know if he is trying to get me killed or if he just likes taunting me, but he isn't playing by any limitations or rules that I can tell. I don't know how to get rid of him."

"Well, thankfully he will either be dead or on his way back to the dark court in two days. Ideally the former, but here's to hopeful wishing." I laughed at Levos and stood to stretch before we headed to dinner.

I kept my head down during the meal, not even looking at the other humans. An older human girl came to stand next to me by the wall, waiting to serve the alfar. I could tell she was trying to get my attention, but I didn't respond. I was in too much pain to endure any other injuries today.

"Thank you," she whispered.

I furrowed my brow, trying to figure out what she was talking about.

"The boy you took the beating for today. That was my younger brother, Marty."

I exhaled, nodding at her.

"My name is Felicity by the way. You're Genevieve, right?"

I gave her another silent nod.

"Your kindness is unexpected. Especially because of the position you hold."

"I didn't choose this, just like you didn't choose to be here," I snapped at her.

"You're right, you didn't. I will make sure to tell the others about the kindness you showed my brother. Hopefully, that will make them ease up on you a bit. It's the least I can do. Thank you again," she said before taking a tray and moving into the crowd.

After the meal concluded, I left the dining hall before anyone could say another word to me. I got ready for bed and crawled under the cool crisp sheets, hoping to avoid an uncomfortable conversation with Gaelin. He came into the room an hour later and pulled a chair up to my side of the bed. I kept my eyes closed as he gently moved the loose curls from my face.

I opened my eyes slowly, looking at his face in the dim light. His white hair glistened in the candlelight. His yellow eyes looked tired and heavy. He pulled his hand away from me, dropping his eyes to the floor. We had left things unfinished the night before, but I didn't know what to say to him.

"I've been thinking about how to make things right with you all day. I can't seem to come up with a solution that will give you everything you deserve, but I think I have found a way to give you a part of the life you desire," he said.

I sat up from the bed, looking at him intently. "What are you talking about?" I whispered.

He brought his eyes to mine and exhaled. "When I marry Daealla, I won't be crowned king right away. In our society, if the female is the rightful heir, she remains in control and holds the majority of power until an heir is conceived. Once an heir is born, her husband is officially crowned king, diverting the power to him. After I give Daealla an heir, I will never touch her again, you have my word.

"I will then lift the law that condemns half-breeds to death. It will take time, but it can be done. I have Levos looking into the details and logistics of it as we speak. Once that is done you will not have to fear being found out. Then, in time if you still wish to have children, we can. They would have no claim to the throne, but they would be ours and we could be together."

"You would do all of this...for me?" I asked, reeling from the thought of a free and safe life.

"I am limited, but at least I can give you something to live for," he whispered.

I stared out at the balcony, not yet ready to look at him, trying to sift through everything he was offering. I cared for Gaelin, but I didn't know if I loved him. Too much had happened. Though what he was offering was better than my current predicament, I would still be his mistress. I would still be a slave. I knew he was trying and for that, I did admire him. He was working with what he had. I knew the other alfar would rally against his proposal to remove the death order on half-breeds, but if he wasn't certain it could be done, he wouldn't have brought this to me.

Could I be happy with him? Even a small fraction of happiness was better than my current state. And children? Would they be in danger? Would he love them the way I always dreamed a father should love his children? But I would get the chance to be a mother. I would get a chance to raise a child with the love and nurturing my mother showed me. A small smile escaped at the thought.

"Does this make you happy?" He asked.

I turned to him, feeling a sense of warmth at the sight. "Thank you," I said.

"I know it doesn't make up for what happened last night. But it made me realize I never want to feel powerless in a position like that again."

"I shouldn't have been so hard on you. I knew what was going to happen and I knew you'd be unable to do anything about it. I don't know why I expected a different outcome," I said.

"Because human spouses protect each other. They fight for one another. Am I correct?"

I looked at him and nodded. "I guess I am still getting used to this new life and the way things actually are."

He reached out, taking my hand in his softly. "I want to be able to protect you. To make you feel safe."

I knew he meant well, and he may have actually believed what he was saying. He did care about me. At least, however much he was capable or allowed to care about me. I pulled him out of the chair, bringing him closer to the bed.

Whatever protection he could offer, I had to take it. I had to continue to play the game. I had to keep my feelings in check and my head clear. I would find a way out of here, but until then, I had to keep Gaelin happy. I had to make sure he trusted me. I could take small moments of happiness from this arrangement to keep myself going, even if they were all illusions of the life, I wished I could have.

"Thank you, for showing me how much you care," I whispered, pressing my forehead against his.

He exhaled, letting the stress go from his body. His other

hand swept through my hair. "How are your injuries?" he asked.

"Hand is feeling much better. The brand still burns. I can't even bring myself to look at it," I admitted.

"What did she whisper to you when she branded you," he asked uncomfortably.

I pulled away, still able to hear her voice in my head. "She wanted to make sure that every time you looked at me. That every time you touched me, you'd be forced to think of her."

He pulled me in closer to him until our eyes were locked together. "Not one single time have I thought of her when I've been with you. No mark is going to change that. I promise you," he said with a soft smile.

I smiled back, slowly lifting my lips to his. He kissed me, unsure of if I truly wanted this. I pulled back, brushing my good hand against his face.

"We don't—"

"I want to," I said. "Just be a little gentle with me. Injuries and all," I smiled up at him.

He moved his lips back onto mine. I had to do this. I had to play the game. *It was only flesh, Gen. This doesn't define who you are.* I closed my eyes tight as he eased me back onto the mattress.

He was gentle with me. Taking extra time to make sure that my needs were met. I found it astonishing that even though my brain and heart weren't in the act, my body still reacted to the sensations of another. After he had finished, he laid next to me without a word. In that moment I had realized he never held me after sex. I found it a bit odd, but I wasn't about to ask. I never asked for it and he never initiated it.

As I closed my eyes, images of the strange dark figure drifted through my head. I took comfort in the familiar visions. The dark swirls that outlined his shoulder and arm. His entrancing smile. The sound of his laugh that sparked some sense of joy inside of me I had never known before. I fell asleep with the images of one man behind my eyes and the body of another next to me.

CHAPTER 16

The next morning, I went on a walk to clear my head. My hand had healed but it had to remain covered, so I appeared to be human. The only thing that remained was my brand below my collar bone.

I went to the lavender fields, my favorite place in the kingdom. Here, I could unburden myself of courtly matters. Here, I could think clearer. I could breathe without worrying if I was going to be struck down for doing so. Here, I could feel my mother. The fragrance was hers.

My fingers traced the soft petals of the plants, taking in the vibrant shades of purples and green. I brought my healed hand to the pendant Gaelin had given me. The green in the stone was truly the same shade as my eyes. Even though he had given it to me, the pendant was now mine. It was a reminder that no matter where I was, there was freedom to be found in the smallest moments.

Suddenly, a high-pitched scream came from the woods

behind the field. I jumped to my feet; my attention fixed on the thick clustering of trees. Another scream came, followed by sobbing and cries for help. I took off without thinking, running straight towards the pleas.

I pushed past the thick foliage, the low branches, and thorny bushes. The scream came again, forcing me to pick up my pace. I could think of nothing but the pain I heard in the victim's plea for help. Barreling through the thick coverage, I stumbled into a clearing—and froze in horror as I peered up at the source who was just moments ago crying for help.

A human woman was strung up in the trees by her arms, completely naked. Her skin was slashed to ribbons. Her eyes were covered in blood that streamed down her face like tears. Her back had been torn open and her ribs pulled backwards and out to resemble wings. Her breasts were gone, and her genitals were unrecognizable.

I began shaking as I felt bile rise in my esophagus. I fell to the ground, my stomach emptying at the mortifying sight I had just beheld. I gasped for air and tears of fear saturated my face. From behind me, buzzing cut through the air. Loud crunches of leaves followed. I was no longer alone.

I turned slowly to see five fairies standing in front of me in an arc. I was so screwed. Lean, muscular bodies covered in pale white skin, slightly tinted with a blue hue. Their noses were sharp, their ears pointed, and their long faces came to a rounded point at the chin. Long lashes lined large, almond-shaped eyes. Their thin lips didn't conceal their sharp pointed teeth.

I fell back onto my heels, searching for a weapon or anything for that matter to protect myself with. Their wings were magnificent. Long and powerful, and as the sun poured through the canopy of the trees, they seemed to change colors like a rainbow. Iridescent at times, with flickers of color trickling through them like a wave.

A female walked slowly towards me, tilting her head to study me. I gradually stood to my feet before them.

"Well, well, well. What do we have here?" Her voice, high pitched, yet sophisticated in some way. She examined me up with her electric orange eyes.

"Another snack?" a male asked.

"How lucky are we?"

"Two in one day." The fairies surrounded me, leaving me no option for escape. They licked their lips as the all too familiar chattering of teeth erupted from the group. They closed in, herding me like an innocent lamb. I looked up at the girl hanging from the trees, wondering if I would soon be hanging next to her, filleted into an angel.

One of the fairies came from behind me, digging their sharp teeth into my shoulder blade. It shook its head as its teeth locked into my skin. I yelled out in pain as another took a quick bite out of my leg.

"Enough!" said the female in charge as she circled me, sniffing the air. The two fairies let go and I stood panting in pain. She faced me and smiled with those sharp, deadly teeth. "What are you? You don't smell human, but you aren't alfar either."

I stood silently.

"Kill her and let's get back. We can't stay here much longer," said another female. The one in front of me stepped closer, dragging her sharp nail along my cheek. Blood spilled from my face. I watched her bring her finger to her mouth as my blood dripped onto her tongue. Her eyes closed as she moaned with pleasure.

"Oh yes, you are delicious. Whatever you are, I am going to enjoy you very much. Yes, I am," she said, wrapping her long fingers around my arm. She pulled me into her, still smiling. Suddenly, her eyes snapped up to look behind me as her body tensed. The other four fairies drew weapons, waiting to strike at whatever was coming from the tree line. I pressed my eyes shut as hard as I could. How could this get any worse? Leaves crunched behind me, but I didn't dare open my eyes.

"Now, I am not from these parts," came a familiar voice from behind me, "but I am certain fairies are not allowed to step foot on the light court's territory. Am I mistaken?"

I turned my head to see Erendrial and five other dark alfar beside him. The female that held me chuckled, relaxing a bit at the sight of him.

"Ambassador Lyklor, nice to see you again. We were just passing through. No harm done. We will take our leave now," she said, pulling at my arm to follow her.

"I wouldn't call that no harm done," Erendrial said, nodding to the girl strung up in the trees.

The female exhaled in frustration, turning back to face him. "Blasphemy to their Christian god. If they love angels so much, why not become one?" The female fairy chucked, shaking her head from side to side with a wicked smile. "It is our gift to the light court and their Norse gods. I'm sure Azeer would appreciate our artwork."

Erendrial began to laugh mockingly under his breath and folded his hands behind his back. His long dark coat fluttered in the wind as he hung his head low, walking towards us. "Cerci, please do not assume that you can begin to understand what our god does and does not enjoy. The matter remains that you are on light court territory, uninvited. You took one of their pigs and hung them up in the trees and have the audacity to call it art. How is that pig going to serve her alfar lords now?"

The female fairy trembled slightly as Erendrial approached. I noticed her face go somber "Doesn't matter to me. They can just go get another to replace her. These humans produce faster than rodents. Shouldn't be a problem since you all can cross the border whenever you please," she snapped.

He smiled at her, now with only a foot between them. He looked down at her possibly assessing what to do next. Then, he smiled and nodded his head. "You're right. She is of no importance. Off you go before a light guard finds the lot of you. It would be such a shame to see that pretty head of yours removed from your body," he said.

She smiled and bowed her head to him. I looked at him, begging for help with my eyes, but I couldn't find the word. He didn't even glance in my direction.

"Thank you, ambassador. You are one of my favorites, yes you are. We will be on our way. I look forward to our next meeting," she said, pulling me roughly back to her group of flesh-eating savages.

"Leave the human, Cerci," I heard Erendrial say behind me. The fairy stopped, stiffening every muscle in her body. She turned around slowly as possessiveness and rage flickered through her eyes.

"She is mine. I found her so I get to keep her," she hissed.

Erendrial stood calm, not even a flicker of panic or worry. "Actually, she is Gaelin Atros's. The future king of the light if you were unaware. Now, how do you think he is going to react when he finds out you stole and ate his favorite plaything?"

"The future king is your problem, not mine. I want her, I take her," she said, digging her nails into my bicep.

I felt warm pools of blood well underneath her nails. She sniffed the air with one long inhale. She looked down at me with a hunger I had never seen in any living thing's eyes before. Her teeth bared from behind her thin lips as she brought the saturated nails to her mouth, licking my blood from them. "She is delicious. Do you know what she is?"

"A human," replied Erendrial coldly.

Cerci's teeth chattered together as she cocked her head like a reptile. "No, no, no. I have never tasted a human this delicious before. She doesn't smell of it, nor does she taste of it. I will take her and that is final."

Erendrial walked casually towards her, hands still behind his back. He stopped only when he was inches from her face. He slowly bent his head down to her, his face now stone cold like something out of a nightmare. "Cerci darling, please do not force me to kill your comrades and then string you up like the Christian girl. You already have wings, I don't see why you need a second pair," he whispered coldly.

Cerci growled, baring her teeth at him. She looked behind him at the other alfar warriors casually waiting for their command. She threw me to the ground, standing powerfully against Erendrial. "I will remember this, Lyklor," she said, shooting straight up into the air.

Her companions followed suit, clearly not wishing to spend another minute in the dark alfars' presence.

I scampered back away from Erendrial and the others, unsure if I had just escaped one hell to be trapped in another. Erendrial looked at me with that unfeeling smile he wore as a mask to hide his wickedness. He walked over to me and extended his hand to assist me to my feet. I pushed myself up on my own, standing with my head tall. He smirked at my feeble attempt to show strength.

"What? No, thank you. Do they not teach manners in *The Frey*? We'll have to remedy that. Come, let's get you back to your master," said Erendrial as he turned back to the others.

"He's not my master," I barked.

The other alfar began to laugh under their breath.

Erendrial turned around to face me. "What is he then? Your friend, companion, lover? Surely not your protector. The banquet dinner made that very evident to everyone who had the pleasure of watching you be mutilated for a simple look."

I felt the rage building inside of me. I hated this bantering. If he was going to torture me or kill me, just get on with it.

"What are you going to do with me?" I asked through my teeth.

"What am I going to do with you or what do I want to do with you? Two very different questions, two very different outcomes, little one," he said.

I rolled my eyes, tensing my fists together.

"I am going to escort you back to the castle. When I am sure you are safe, I will leave you in the care of your...hmm, not master. What about, mounter, rider, penetrator?" The other alfar were laughing loudly at this point. "Fucker, yes. He shall now be known as Gaelin the fucker. What a valiant king he will be," said Erendrial

I pushed past him, heading back to the castle. The others looked at me with amusement. Gods, I hated him. Erendrial appeared at my side, poised and elegant as always.

"Did I push too far?" he asked.

"I'd like to walk back on my own," I said, trying to quicken my pace.

"You may walk back, but not alone. You tend to find yourself in trouble when you're left to your own devices."

"Why do you care? You should have left me back there. One less human to care about, right?"

His tongue clicked sharply as if a warning signal. "You're right. It would have been one less human to worry about. If you were human that is."

I felt my lungs collapse on themselves as if someone was

suffocating me. I didn't dare look at him. He couldn't know. How could he have known? He wasn't a mind reader...or was he? He did say he knew my father.

"I'm human," I responded shortly.

"Whatever you say, little Genevieve."

We walked for a few moments in silence. My mind kept replaying the images of the human girl through my memory. All the blood and skin, just hanging there. The way her ribs were pulled apart. How her breasts were cut clean off. I felt the bile rising in my stomach again I turned just in time to puke in a nearby bush.

I pulled myself up slowly, feeling dizzy and cold. Erendrial held out a handkerchief. It was black and silk, just like the trim of his jacket. "Go on, take it," he said.

I did, using it to wipe my mouth. I shoved it in the pocket of my dress as we started back towards the castle. I couldn't help but think of Lilian. "Is that what you do to humans for entertainment? Back at the dark court?" I asked.

He smiled. "Would you believe me if I said no?"

"No," I replied coldly.

"Then why ask?" I didn't respond. He nodded. "Ah, Lilian. You are afraid the same fate awaits her."

Dammit, he was a mind reader. What the hell?

He laughed again. "As I said, Lilian Thomas is safe and contrary to popular belief, we do not treat our humans like that. Why waste a perfectly good warm body in that manner?"

I rolled my eyes. "So, you don't sacrifice them to Azeer?" I asked.

"I didn't say that, but that little display of 'artwork' you saw back there is only practiced by the fairies."

A chill of disgust ran up my spine. I thought back to the young girl Gaelin and the others gave the fairies when they were transporting us from The Frey. I wondered if she met the same torturous fate. Her skin torn apart and eaten as she watched. I couldn't imagine that type of pain

"Thank you," I whispered.

"You're welcome. Let's keep our little outing from your ma—Gaelin for now. I am on thin ice since someone spoiled my perfectly executed plan and I don't need him looking at me any harder than he already is." He walked past me as we entered the city arches. The dark alfar followed him, not looking back in my direction.

I made my way to the room, changing my outfit and washing the blood from my skin. This was becoming a habit. When I exited the bathroom, Gaelin and Levos were standing at the table looking at a map. I walked over to them, taking note of their tense faces.

"They have to be coming from the south," said Gaelin. "That is where our scouts last saw them. They wouldn't have time to move everyone without tipping us off. We attack tomorrow. We'll have the dark alfar take to the sky, creating a cover for our ground troops to move in. If we attack from the east and west, we will have them pinned with no hope of escape."

"I agree," replied Levos. "That is the best plan. I am just hesitant about our enemies' abilities. The dark alfar have had little interaction with them. We don't know what they are capable of. I don't want to be surprised."

"I agree, but we can't let this opportunity to kill Otar escape us. This may be our only chance."

I moved to Gaelin's side, looking at the map spread out on the table. He wrapped his arm around my waist and kissed me on my head softly. I smiled up at him, returning my focus to the map.

I took note of all the different colored markers representing different infantries and attack teams. I looked at the southern border of the kingdom where Gaelin expected the attack to come from. My eyes slowly trailed up the map to the northern wall behind the castle. The room began to spin as my vision got hazy and spotted. Electric shocks zapped at the nerves in my back up my neck and then into my brain. I felt myself falling slowly. Gaelin caught me before I could hit the floor.

A vision of a battle commenced behind my fluttering eyelids. Light armies rushed to the southern border, but once they arrived, their enemy was gone. Ragamor flew overhead, searching for a threat, but there was none. Confused and angered, the troops return home only to be greeted with the castle overrun by massive wolf-like creatures on their hind legs. Body parts littered the halls. Blood stained every wall and every rug. The humans were ripped to pieces.

In the throne room, the king, queen, and princess hung from the ceiling with long red ulyrium spears piercing their hearts. A black-skinned figure sat upon the throne. His yellow eyes glistened and blood dripped from his claws. He wore the king's crown. I saw Gaelin and Erendrial along with both light and dark warriors enter the hall. As soon as the room was full, massive explosions overtook the city. Each detonation propelled pieces of ulyrium through the air, cutting the army down. Then, everything went black.

CHAPTER 17

My eyes fluttered open, feeling like they were weighted. My head was pounding as if I had been hit by something hard. I tried to sit up—I was in Gaelin's bed, I realized—but I was too weak. I felt like I had been to battle and back. Levos and Gaelin rushed to my side. They checked my eyes, tilting my face from side to side. I could see that they were speaking, but I was only able to make out muffled sounds. Suddenly, my ears recovered, and their voices boomed against my eardrums.

"Are you okay? What happened to you?" asked Levos.

I grimaced at the loud projection of his voice.

"Just give her a minute. Let her fully wake up," said Gaelin. He handed me a glass of water. I sipped it slowly as the memories of my vision came flooding back more clearly. I looked at the map on the table and then at Gaelin.

"The enemy isn't coming from the south," I blurted,

needing to tell him everything I remembered before it escaped me. He looked at me, confused.

"What?" he asked.

"They will come from the north. They will take the city while you seek them out in the south. They will kill the royals and everyone who is left inside the walls. When you return, they will kill you as well. It's a trap, Gaelin," I said frantically.

He pulled back. "Gen, you hit your head pretty hard. Maybe you need to rest a bit longer before you try to get up," he said.

"Please, listen to me. I know this sounds crazy, but I saw it. I saw everything," I said.

"What do you mean, you saw?" Levos asked.

I bit the side of my lip, not wanting to sound like a fool. "I think I have powers, like other alfar. I think I have visions," I said slowly.

Gaelin huffed with amusement.

"Gen, we've been over this," said Levos. "If you had powers, they would have shown themselves when you were young. Plus, we don't have that type of gift at court."

"What if I am not part light alfar? What if I am dark?" I asked, feeling sick at the possibility.

Both their faces went stern.

"Don't talk like that," snapped Gaelin. "You hit your head. That is all."

"Gaelin, please, just send out the scout one more time. They can be back before dinner. What is it going to hurt to make sure? Please," I begged.

He looked at me for a long moment and then nodded. "Levos, send out two scouts immediately," said Gaeln.

I exhaled in relief and fell back to the pillow, as Levos left the room. Gaelin sat by my side on the edge of the bed.

"Would it be a horrible thing if I was part dark alfar? Would it change anything?" I asked.

He leaned down kissing my lips tenderly. "You'd still be you. That's all I care about. Now get some sleep. I will come to wake you before dinner."

I STOOD IN FRONT OF THE MIRROR IN THE bathroom, glaring at the bandage that covered the brand. I had to look at it. It was a part of me whether I wanted it there or not. I could carve it out of my skin, but knowing Daealla, she'd just mark me somewhere else out of spite. I pulled the small square of cloth away from my skin.

Underneath, inside a raised circle, was a beautiful winding tree. Its limbs stretched to the edges of the circle. It was actually kind of pretty, in a way, but it's meaning still bothered me. I was branded by the light court for the rest of my life. No matter where I went or what I did, people would know they had owned me. I was branded just like a heifer.

Gaelin came in, seeming shocked to see me out of bed. I turned to him, anxious for a report.

"Have the scouts checked in?" I asked.

"Yes. The threat still lies at the southern border. They saw it with their own eyes," said Gaelin.

I braced myself against the sink, sure of what I had seen. Something wasn't right. This must have been a trick. It felt so real. Just like when I saw the dark court arrive. When I felt the pain in my hand. Those visions had all come to pass.

Though, I had never had a vision while I was awake. I had always been asleep when they came, but this one was clear as day. No room for misinterpretation. I went to Gaelin, throwing my arms around him. I had to make him trust me. I had to make him understand.

"Gaelin, I know I am asking a lot, but you need to trust me. I've had these visions before and the events in them have come to pass. This was more clear and more real than any I've had. If you don't listen to me, we are all going to die. Please trust me, please," I begged.

He gently pulled my arms from his neck, taking a step away. "I do trust you, and I've done as you've asked, but the threat is still to the south. If you do indeed have these gifts, you are new to them. You may not understand what you're seeing, or you may be misinterpreting them. Relying on your gift at this point is too great of a risk."

"I don't want to see you die, Gaelin. Please trust me. I would have never said a thing to you if I wasn't sure," I said.

He exhaled, standing in the doorway of his room. "I'm sorry, but I need to go with the source that is most accurate. My orders remain the same. I will be late tonight after dinner is over, so don't wait up," he said, then shut the door, leaving me alone in the room.

I spent the entire dinner trying to figure out a way to make them believe me. Though I wouldn't mind a few specific alfar dying terrible deaths, there were humans here. Innocent humans that didn't deserve to be mixed up in a war they could never win.

The dark alfar left dinner early. Gaelin was going to be away most of the night preparing for the upcoming battle. I drifted back to the room, feeling hopeless.

Gods, I hated being so weak and powerless. In The Frey, it wasn't too bad. At least I could still outsmart most of the humans. But here, I was surrounded by magic, powers, and years of conniving and scheming. Though, I had outsmarted the smartest male in the room, so there was that.

I stopped dead in my tracks. That was it. Erendrial was the key. He knew what I was. There was a chance I could convince him that my vision was true and not some symptom of a concussion as Gaelin thought.

I veered off towards the guest chambers. King Lysanthier had put the dark alfar guests as far away from his subjects as possible. I had to make sure I wasn't seen. If anyone saw me entering or leaving another alfar's chambers, I would be killed. But if I didn't take the risk, we were all going to be dead tomorrow anyway. There would be no victory without risk.

I kept my head down. Surprisingly, the guest wing was like a ghost town. I guessed everyone feared them enough to keep their distance. I took a deep breath in and knocked three times on the door I knew to be Erendrial's.

"Come in," he said in a deep, rich voice.

I opened the door and slid into the room, quickly shutting it before anyone else could see me. I turned to find

Erendrial seated up against the headboard. He was shirtless, only wearing a pair of black silk pants. A blonde human girl was draped across him, naked as he twirled his fingers through her hair. Another human girl was dancing at the foot of the bed, completely naked.

I turned my face quickly, not wanting them to see me, but it was too late. They both got up, reaching for their clothes, never once taking their eyes from me. This was it. I was dead. I heard Erendrial laugh as he got out of the bed.

"I was expecting dessert. Not what I ordered, but I can definitely make do with you," Erendrial said seductively.

I kept my face turned away from the two girls as they frantically dressed. Erendrial stood in front of me looking from them to me and then smiled. "Don't worry, I will take care of them," he said, moving in their direction.

"Wait," I said, reaching out to grab his arm. He looked down at my hand on his forearm and arched a brow. I pulled my touch from him instantly. "Don't hurt them. Please," I begged.

He shook his head in disbelief, holding my stare. He walked over to them, taking their faces in his hands. They were still bare from the waist up. I noted bite marks and bruises on their skin. Some around their breasts, others around their neck. Their skin was still flushed from the dalliance I had obviously interrupted.

Erendrial relaxed and exhaled slowly, looking at both girls. He rubbed the sides of their faces with his thumbs. The two women relaxed against his touch. Their eyes looked back at him lazily. One of them bit her lip as if she were being turned on all over again.

"You will not remember anyone in this room but me. You both will go back to your beds and only remember the incredible night we shared together. You never saw another woman in the room with us. Understood?" Erendrial asked.

They both nodded heavily. They finished getting dressed and then left the room without even looking at me.

"How did you..." I asked, shocked by what I was seeing.

"Pheromone manipulation. They will never remember you were here."

"Is that how you got them to sleep with you in the first place? Manipulating them so you could bite and beat them to your liking?" I said with disgust.

He turned to face me. His eyes were dark and heavy. A shiver of fear ran up my spine. I had somehow managed to forget how deadly he was. I bit my lip, lowering my head in a submissive reaction. He stalked over to me, like an apex predator about to assert his dominance.

"Just to be clear, I have never had to manipulate a female of any race to lay with me. I only give them what they ask for. Bite marks and all. Believe it or not, some females like it a bit rough in bed. Not that you would understand. I am sure Gaelin treats you as if you could break at any moment."

"I'm sorry. It isn't my place to question your actions," I said quietly.

He huffed. "Why are you here at this hour?" He asked, moving across the room to a table where he poured two glasses of wine.

I lifted my head, preparing to begin my plea for help when my eyes locked on a black inked marking that covered his left shoulder. Starting from the base of his neck, it covered the length of his cuff and moved down to his arm. It swirled in a pattern so familiar I could have drawn it from memory. I searched for other details that were familiar. His smile, yes, his smile. It was the same. The same full soft lips. The same elongated canine teeth. The same shade of white. His chin even had the same dimple in it that I had admired so many times.

No, no, NO! How could this be? Why had I been dreaming of *him* for the past two years? My angel wasn't an angel at all. He was a demon sent to torture me.

Erendrial walked slowly over to me, offering me wine. I focused on those all too familiar hands. The long strong fingers. The veins that ran under his skin. The shape of his fingernails. All of it. He had three rings on his hand, just like I had seen for so many years.

I took the glass and gulped it down before locking my eyes on the tattoo on his left shoulder. He turned his head to his marking and then back to me slowly. He tilted his head up and almost posed, putting his strong, flawless body on display for me. I pulled my eyes back to the ground, not wanting to spend another moment in this room with him.

"See something you like?" he asked playfully, taking a sip of his wine before moving to a chair next to the table. "Come sit," he demanded.

I did as I was told, trying my best not to look at the damn marking, but I had to know. I had to know what it meant. I had wondered for so long. "Your...marking. On your shoulder. What is it?" I asked, not making eye contact.

He refilled my glass before placing his own on the table and leaned back into his chair. "Genevieve, if we are going to have a conversation. I expect you to be able to look at me. You came here on your own, without an invitation and interrupted a very rewarding evening that I wasn't quite done enjoying. The least you can do is look at me while we talk."

I slowly brought my eyes to his. My whole body was tense. I crossed my arms and legs, wanting to fold in on myself, but this was the smallest I was going to get. What in the hell was I thinking? Coming here, locking myself in a room with someone—something—as dangerous as him.

"Very good. Now, you were inquiring about my marking. It's called an imprint. When a male in the dark court turns eight it appears on our body in a random place. Each marking is unique to the male alfar. When an alfar takes a wife, she takes the imprint on herself the day of the wedding. Some magical connection or whatnot. It ties the two together as a visual representation of their union."

"Like a wedding ring?" I asked.

He laughed to himself. "A bit like that I guess, except you can't take it off and get a new one whenever you want."

"Why don't the light alfar have them?"

"It started when my kind made the deal with Azeer. We think it's some dark magic connecting all of us."

I paused, trying to note all the differences between the two courts. "And where is your wife?" I asked.

His face scrunched together as he flashed a genuine smile. It was the same. Every line, every tooth. The way his cheeks formed into dimples from the motion. The way his creases outlined his lips.

"I have no wife and never will."

"Why?" I asked.

"A wife doesn't suit my aspirations in life, I suppose. Plus, a female would want children and I can't stand them, so there is that. Genevieve, did you come here to get to know me on a more personal level, or is there something you need from me?"

I took a sip of wine and looked at him, trying to calm myself. "I need your help."

"Already filled my quota of helping you for the day," he playfully said.

"Well, now it's my turn to return the favor and save your life," I said confidently.

He perked an eyebrow and tilted his head down. "I'm listening."

"Gaelin believes the attack will come from the south border, but he is wrong. He is going to send the whole army south, but the enemy won't be there. While he is busy searching for them, they will attack the northern wall. They will succeed and take the castle, killing everyone inside. When the army returns, Otar will be in the throne room. He will kill everyone, including you," I said.

Erendrial's face remained emotionless, difficult to read. He leaned over his knees rubbing his face with his hand. His neatly trimmed black hair was tousled, and locks fell across his forehead.

"Why tell me this? Why not Gaelin?" he finally asked, calmly.

"I did, but he doesn't believe me. To his defense, he sent out two scouts to make sure the threat was still at the south border. They reported that they were, but something isn't right. The enemy I saw were large wolf-like creatures. They tore everything to shreds. That...thing, which I presume was Otar, has some power that I don't think any of you have seen yet. I think he's using that to make it appear like the enemy is in the south, when in reality, they're waiting for you all to leave so they can attack the wall."

"And how do you know this?"

I chewed on my lip. Even though I was almost certain he knew what I was, I wasn't going to make the mistake of telling him out loud. "I can't tell you. I know I am asking a lot, but I figured with the ragamor you brought, you could send out your own scouts to the north to see if I am right. The canopies of the forest will provide them good coverage, but from the air you should be able to spot them if they are there."

He nodded his head as if considering my suggestion. "Anything else I should know about?"

"They have ulyrium spears and some type of explosive devices. They're full of ulyrium. He has enough to wipe out the whole army."

"Unexpected, but clever, nonetheless. Makes things a bit more inconvenient."

I waited a few moments in silence, allowing him to think. "Also, I don't believe Otar is the reason for the rift."

He looked at me curiously. "And why not? He has been the most powerful being we've seen yet. He is the only one capable of controlling the beasts that come through the rift."

"When I saw all this happening, Otar was in the throne room when you, Gaelin, and the others entered. He detonated the bombs to kill you while in the same room, sacrificing himself in the process. What power-hungry leader in any race have you ever heard of willingly would choose to kill himself just as he conquers his foe?"

He leaned back, smiling at me as he took another sip of wine. "If what you say is true, why should I not leave tomorrow morning before the battle commences. Sounds to me like this information, if accurate, will eliminate both of my king's enemies in a few hours," he said tauntingly.

I paused, weighing the outcomes. "Because, if Otar isn't the most powerful thing to come out of the rift, you will need all the help you can get, including the light alfar. If they aren't here, the border to The Frey collapses, which would allow anything to get inside. There go your human sacrifices, your slave labor, and your endless supply of warm bodies. Territory wars will commence from the other races trying to take control of the land. Countless fae lives will be lost battling over a piece of land while the things from the rift keep coming. They will look to attack the dark court first, taking out their biggest competition. Though you are powerful, you don't have the numbers to cover that much land. You can't fight two wars at once and win," I said confidently.

He laughed and shook his head. "Very impressive. It is nice to have a conversation with someone who isn't so… simple-minded."

I smiled, dropping my eyes to the floor.

"Ah, never look at the floor. You reveal your weakness to your opponent."

"Why do you care?" I asked.

He shrugged. "I enjoy a project occasionally. Especially one who is clever enough to out-wit me at my own game." He tilted his head. Trying to read me. "I presume whatever little talent you used to discover the battle plan you also used to root out Filo?"

"I don't know what you're talking about."

"You're smart not to trust me. No hard feelings," he said, standing to his feet. He extended his hand to me. I hesitantly took it, pulling myself up from the table. "Where is Gaelin now?"

"Preparing for tomorrow's battle I presume. He told me not to wait up."

Erendrial smirked. "I think it is time for you to be on your way."

"Does that mean you believe me?" I asked desperately.

He looked down into my eyes. The silver of his iris's swirled around his dark pupils. "You'll have to wait until tomorrow for that answer." He smiled, gesturing to the door. He pulled it open, checking the hall first. "Good night, Genevieve."

I stopped, taking another look at him, cataloging all the familiar features I had memorized. He nodded to the hall. I took my leave, moving quickly to put as much distance between myself and his room. I had done all I could to save this stubborn, miserable race. I just hope it was enough.

CHAPTER 18

I didn't even hear Gaelin come to bed that night and by the time I woke up, he was gone. I moved around the room, trying to distract myself with laundry and cleaning. If Erendrial didn't believe what I told him, I could try to get as many humans and children as possible out of the castle before Otar attacked. That was my next move. I had to get them ready just in case things went south.

I dropped the basket of clothing to the ground and was moving to the door when Gaelin and Levos came barging through. Gaelin slammed the door, eyes deadlocked on me. It was very clear that he was pissed. Levos looked worried behind him, pacing back and forth.

"What did you tell him?" yelled Gaelin.

"What?" I asked, taking a step away from him.

"Erendrial. You went to him, didn't you? You told him about your vision."

I began to tremble, not knowing what had transpired in the past few hours. "Yes, I did," I admitted.

"Why, Gen? Why go to him? Of all alfar? He is dangerous and deadly. He hates me and all light alfar and yet you went to him and told him something that he can now use against you. You have placed your life in his hands. He would have figured out that you are half alfar by now. Do you realize what you've done?"

"I'm sorry. I didn't see another choice. You weren't listening and I am certain of what I saw. If I have to sacrifice my life to save everyone in this forsaken place, then it was worth the risk!" I yelled.

Gaelin strode towards me with an anger I had never seen in him before. He raised his hand as if he were about to strike me. Levos stepped in between us.

"Gaelin, you need to calm down. What's done is done. You need to prepare yourself for the battle," said Levos softly.

Gaelin lowered his hand, still locked onto my eyes. "You've sealed your own fate. He will use your identity against me, and I won't allow it. You will have to clean this mess up yourself."

"I was trying to save your life!" I yelled.

"You didn't trust me. Instead, you went to him for help. Our enemy," said Gaelin. He took one more look at me before turning to leave the room.

Levos held onto me, preventing me from following. I was so mad I wanted to hit something. How dare he get mad at me for using the only resources I had available. This was his fault, not mine. Levos turned to me, holding my shoulders.

"His pride is hurt, Gen. You were right. Otar is using some type of illusion that allowed us to see his forces in the south, when in reality, he was preparing to attack the northern wall."

"Then why is he so angry with me?"

"Erendrial came in during this morning's debriefing with the news about the enemy in the north. He took credit for it—leaving you out of it, thankfully—but in doing so, he made Gaelin look like a complete fool. I think Gaelin is also upset that you felt comfortable enough to even go to Erendrial with this."

"I wasn't comfortable. Not for one second, but my state of comfort was of little concern to me when you all were about to walk into a death trap," I said, pacing throughout the room.

"When did you tell him?" he asked.

"Last night, after dinner," I whispered, feeling embarrassed to say it out loud. "I went to his room."

Levos exhaled, flailing his arms in the air. "I specifically warned you not to be alone with one of them, and then you go willingly into their bed chambers in the dead of night? What am I going to do with you?" He rubbed his brow in frustration. "Did he hurt you in any way?"

"No, he was actually very polite," I admitted.

"Don't start thinking like that. He can control pheromones, remember. He could have screwed you for all we know and you're over here under the impression he was the perfect cavalier."

Shit, I hadn't thought of that.

"I didn't think—"

"No, you didn't, and you need to start. But, in the end, you were right."

An hour later, Levos informed me that the troops had set off to the north. We all waited in anticipation of their return. I hated not knowing what was happening. I'd rather have been on the field with them than here in the safety of the court. I cleaned the same cabinet for thirty minutes as different scenarios of the battle played through my head. It was torture.

The next day was the same. The royals sat on their thrones, safe and unaffected by the battle. I couldn't help but imagine their bodies hung up in the ceiling with ulyrium spears through their hearts. I smiled at the thought, but quickly shook it off, realizing I was taking pleasure in the thought of another's death.

Two hours before dinner the warriors finally made their entrance back into the city. The alfar applauded and cheered as they marched victoriously. Bodies of the fallen were carried through the gate and set aside to be burned and sent to Valhalla. Another stack of covered bodies were brought to the castle, but quickly disappeared without anyone noticing. The creatures that came through the rift, I presumed.

We lined the walls of the throne room as the officers came in to kneel before the king. The dark alfar remained standing. I kept my head down, knowing I would have to face Gaelin soon. The king raised his hands, signaling for them to stand.

"My king, the threat has been eliminated. We have Otar's body, along with some of the slain beasts. Our borders are secure," reported Gaelin.

"And the rift?" asked King Lysanthier.

"Unknown, my king. We are still unable to track the rift's opening."

"Very well. I applaud all of you for your bravery. Tonight, we will feast in celebration. Ambassador Lyklor, you and your forces may stay the night, but I expect you to return home at first light tomorrow morning," said the king.

"Of course," replied Erendrial.

"I commend you on your invaluable instincts, Ambassador Lyklor. Today may have not been a victory if it weren't for you," said the king in a sour voice. I was sure it killed him to give a dark alfar a compliment, but the troops knew who they owed their lives to, or so they thought they did.

"We are all on the same side when it comes to this threat. I hope I have redeemed myself some in your eyes, *king*," said Erendrial sarcastically. The king smiled and nodded. He waved his hand to dismiss the hall.

I rushed to Gaelin's chambers. I ran a hot bath, prepared clean clothes, and had refreshments waiting for him.

Out on the balcony, I watched as the sun set and the

moon rose. I loved the contrast between the stars and the night sky. The way you could create pictures and designs from drawing lines in between the radiant spheres of light. The sound of heavy boots came up behind me. I turned to see Gaelin. His face was long and heavy from the fight. I hesitated, not knowing how he wanted me to react.

"I have food and a bath ready for you," I said softly.

His eyes were softer than the last time we had spoken. His movements calm and steady. He reached out, but I flinched away, remembering our last encounter. Seeing the hurt look on his face, I quickly recovered, stepping towards him.

"I'm sorry about the way I was with you before I left. I had no reason to react that way. Especially because you were right about everything. I was just angry about Lyklor," he said.

"I know, and I'm sorry I had to go to him, but it was worth it if you came back to me in one piece. And here you are." I smiled, reaching for him.

He wrapped his arms around me, inhaling my scent. He smelled of copper blood, sweat, and dirt. He pulled away, looking into my eyes as I spoke.

"No more fighting, okay," I said. "Let's just be here, with each other."

"I'd like that very much." He leaned down and kissed me softly.

"Now go take a bath. You stink," I said playfully. I plastered a smile on my face until he was in the other room, then relaxed, proud of my performance. I looked back into the stars, wondering if Lilian was looking at the same sky. I missed her so much. I missed her songs, her laugh, her golden-brown hair. I missed knowing she was safe.

Dinner was full of excitement and laughter from the alfar. The food was abundant. The wine poured freely and the alfar were extra handsy with the servants. After the meal was over, I moved to the linen pantry to retrieve more towels and rags. I entered the dark room, setting my candlestick on the shelf.

"It's not smart to have such a predictable schedule, Gen," said a voice behind me.

I turned around, reaching for a broomstick near the corner. I swung it at the dark figure, but he caught the broom with ease, pulling my body into his with a single jerking motion. In the flicker of candlelight, I saw swirling silver eyes peering back at me with a familiar devious smile. I relaxed, pulling away from him.

"Dammit Erendrial, what do you want, and why in the hell are you in a linen closet?"

He started laughing, stepping into the light. "Well, I am glad to see you are no longer trembling at the thought of being alone with me. I think we've made excellent progress in the past week."

"I still find you terrifying as hell, but I am too tired to care at this point." I turned back, reaching for the linens I needed.

"Your information was good. We could use that gift of yours back in the dark court. Interested in making a move?" he said, closing in behind me.

I turned around slowly. I hadn't even thought that he would want to use me for his own court. Crap, I had to get better at this if I was going to survive. If I did go with him, I would have access to Lily. But how would we get out? There had to be an easier way.

"Let's not start a war between the light and dark over little old me," I said.

He smiled, his eyes roaming over my face as if searching for something, but I didn't know what. "Don't worry, I just wanted to formally say thank you, and goodbye. I expect you'll still be under Gaelin during our send-off tomorrow morning."

I rolled my eyes and grunted at the thought.

"What? Gaelin not satisfying you properly?"

"Don't start, Erendrial," I said as he laughed at me. "Gods, why do you do that?"

"What?"

"You're constantly getting under my skin. Is it some type of manipulative maneuver or something? Are you trying to feel me out for weaknesses, or test my restraint?"

He shrugged. "Maybe. Mostly I enjoy watching the steam come out of your ears. You're very easy to unravel. Probably should work on that too. I can make you a list of all your downfalls before I leave. Call it a thank you."

I shook my head, hiding a smile.

"Can I ask you a question, and you answer me truthfully?" I asked.

"You can ask. The answer depends on the question."

I paused, holding the towels close to my chest. "Have

you used that pheromone manipulation on me before? Have you taken away some part of my memory that I'll never be able to get back?"

He looked to the wall for a moment, then back at me. "No, Genevieve, I have never used my powers on you. All your memories are intact, I promise," he said softly.

"Your promises can't be trusted," I pointed out.

He laughed, moving closer towards me. I backed up until my body was against the shelf. He reached out slowly to my face, trailing his fingers against my cheek. Even though I knew he was a dark alfar, there was something warm and comforting about his touch.

He breathed out slowly and the scent of warm whisky and oranges filled the air. My body relaxed so much that my arms let go of the linens and my legs collapsed underneath me. He caught me, bracing my body against his as he pulled me back up to a standing position. I shook my head, trying to clear my thoughts. He smiled at me, leaning into my ear.

"That was only a remnant of what my power feels like. But don't worry, half-breed...you will never experience it again," he said softly, his lips brushing against my earlobe. He pulled away and took another look at me before reaching for the door. "May I give you some unsolicited advice?"

"If I say no, would it matter?" I replied, still dazed by his power.

He chuckled. "The greatest power comes from surviving the darkest of nights... Goodbye, Genevieve."

As the door shut, I fell to the floor from the effects of his power. My whole body lit up. His scent was still in my nostrils, and I swore I could still feel his fingers on my face. The sensation was eerie, yet also comforting in a way. I shook off the feeling, reminding myself that he was the enemy. Or at least Gaelin's enemy. He served a purpose, but he was not to be trusted by any means.

CHAPTER 19

I woke early the next morning, unable to stay in bed a minute longer. Gaelin was still sound asleep next to me, exhausted from the past few days. I dressed quietly, making sure not to wake him, and headed down to the castle entrance. Crowds of people were standing back against the walls awaiting the dark alfar's departure.

I fell in line with the rest of the humans, trying to blend in. A few moments passed before Erendrial and the other dark alfar exited the castle into the plaza. He took in a deep breath and turned his head slowly in my direction as if he could smell me. He nodded at me without a smile and continued towards the royals for his send-off. They bowed to one another politely.

The royals walked casually back to the castle's front doors as the dark alfar stood in the clearing. They all raised some type of whistle to their mouths, creating a series of different loud pitches. Together, they created an alluring symphony of echoes. Shrieks roared high in the sky, and we all turned our eyes up. Ragamor appeared in the clouds, circling the castle like a swarm of locusts.

Only a few touched down at a time, allowing the dark alfar to board them before taking off into the sky. Their beautiful scales shimmered in the sunlight as their massive wings pushed them powerfully off the ground. Erendrial was the last to mount his exquisite ragamor. He nodded to the royals one last time before he took flight, shooting up so fast it knocked a few of the light alfar to the ground. The alfar and humans alike watched in awe of the creatures.

The enemy was gone, yet somehow, I felt more alone than I had experienced since arriving to court. I made my way back into the castle before the crowd, finding busy work to occupy myself with until I had to return to Gaelin's room. He was up, standing at the railing of the balcony, looking at the kingdom. I joined him, taking in the beautiful landscape.

"I think we deserve a bit of a distraction, don't you?" he said without looking at me.

"What do you have in mind?" I asked.

He took my hand and headed out of the room. Everyone gawked at us as we passed by, heading through the halls still hand in hand.

"Gaelin, you'll get in trouble."

"If I am to be their king, then they will have to get used to the sight of us together," he said, smiling back at me.

I returned the smile, following him down to the stables. He mounted a horse and offered his hand to me, pulling me up behind him. We took off, leaving the court, the politics, and the laws behind us.

I held onto his waist tightly as the horse ran at full speed. We rode for a long while before Gaelin finally stopped at a natural spring that fed into a massive lake. He dismounted and reached for my waist. I slid gently down beside him, as he kept his arm wrapped around me. We stood for a moment, looking at the crystal-clear water. You could see straight through to the bottom of the lake.

I smiled, taking in the beauty of the fae world. We didn't have anything like this back home. All our bodies of water were dark and murky. I was even hesitant to eat the fish that was caught from our lakes. This was like something out of a dream. I felt his fingers brush a piece of loose hair from my face.

"Do you like it?" he asked, peering down at me with a smile.

"It's magnificent."

He slowly took my headband off, revealing my ears. I went to cover them with my hands, but he stopped me. "It's just you and me here. You can be yourself," he said softly.

I smiled up at him, running my hand along his arm. He sat on the grassy hill, pulling me down to lean against him between his legs. He wrapped his arms around me, pulling me in closer to his body as we watched the water ripple. "Watch closely," he whispered.

I sat back, eagerly waiting for something to happen. As moments passed, I watched as the water began to rise in the middle of the lake. Horses burst through the surface, galloping across in a herd. Made entirely of water, the majestic creatures slid over the lake as if they were skating. The sunlight bounced around their translucent bodies, creating rainbows that danced across the surface.

"Come on," Gaelin said, taking me by the hand, leading me to the edge of the water. He held out his hand toward the water horses, making ticking noises with his tongue. One of them looked at us and slowly trotted over to him. The horse allowed Gaelin to touch its snout. "Go on, touch him," he said to me.

I held out my hand cautiously, allowing the creature to make the first move. It looked identical to a real horse. Its mane feathered around its strong shoulders. Even the small hairs around its mouth and on its eyelashes were visible, but the creature was completely made of water. It walked towards me, moving its jaw from side to side as it chewed on something.

The skin of the water horse was cold and smooth like velvet. I touched the side of its mouth, feeling its strong jaw rotating under the skin. I looked into its watery blue eyes, searching for a soul. It knocked my face with its nose, snorting a powerful burst of water toward me before turning to walk away. I laughed, now completely drenched from the creature's affection. Gaelin smiled, moving my wet hair from my face.

"What are they?" I asked.

"Kelpie. They're water spirits bound to the lakes and rivers of this land. They are shapeshifters but tend to favor the horse form."

"I've heard of them, but our legends say that they draw people to the lake and then drown them."

He laughed. "Humans think everything out here is dangerous, don't they?"

"Can you blame them?"

"Kelpie can take the physical form of a human, but their hooves usually remain visible. They've always been gentle creatures, but I've never angered one, so I don't know what they'd do to retaliate if someone harmed them."

We sat down next to each other by the edge of the water. "So did you need a break from court?" I asked.

He nodded, looking over the water. "I was groomed to be king from a young age, but I never wanted it. I thought that King Lysanthier would find a better candidate for his daughter, but here I am, months away from marrying a female I can't stand the sight of."

"She's beautiful. Any man would be lucky to call her his wife," I said.

"Beauty doesn't mean the same here as it does in The Frey. All alfar are beautiful. We are vain in the worst possible ways. Outward beauty means very little when it comes to being physically attracted to someone," he explained.

"If the alfar are so vain, why do they lay with humans? We are so flawed and frankly ugly in comparison."

He laughed, shaking his head as he glanced at me sideways. "You are not ugly, nor flawed. Besides the physical enjoyment human bodies offer us, I think we take some sense of joy in what humans get to experience in their lives. We live for so long that things like love, happiness, satisfaction, even complacency tends to mean little. A human life is brief, but in that time, they experience all of these intense emotions and feelings. In the span of sixty years, they fall in and out of love. They experience sorrow, pain, yet still find a way to see the joy and happiness in life. They bear children, raise those children, and become grandparents. In a way, I think we envy the simplicity of their lives."

"I couldn't imagine living for a thousand years," I said.

"You might want to. The fact that you heal quickly is a good indicator that you will live the same life span as a normal alfar."

Another possibility I hadn't thought of.

"What are we going to do about that? Won't people notice ten years down the road when I don't age?" I asked.

"We will cross that bridge when we come to it. For now, I just want to be with you," he said, kissing my hand. "Tell me about Lilian."

I smiled at the sound of her name. "She's wonderful. She's sixteen. I met her three years ago when her family died and left her orphaned. She somehow completed our little family. I didn't know what it felt like to be compelled to die for another until her. But she awoke something inside of me. I think she's the first person I've ever really loved.

"She is kind and caring. She is always thinking of those around her first. She has beautiful hazel eyes with brown hair that turns to gold when the sun hits it. Little freckles cover the bridge of her nose and under her eyes. Her presence can light up any room. The sheer sight of her smile can lift your spirit. She's truly something special," I said. A sense of loss welled up inside me.

"You'll see her again. We will find a way, I promise," he said, wrapping an arm around me.

"Erendrial said something to me. He said that a dark alfar had taken her as his lover. Do you think he was just messing with me, or could he be right?" I asked, feeling sick to my stomach.

"I can't answer that. If she is the light that you say, the dark alfar would be attracted to her. They tend to seek out the good, destroying it in their obsession. But Lilian offers them something the court lacks, so hopefully, that will keep her alive until we can get her out."

"And then what? Bring her back here to be raped by the light alfar?" I pulled away.

"Hopefully by then I will be able to protect her, and you. I'm trying, Genevieve."

I looked at him, sighing my frustration away. "I know you are. I just can't stomach the thought of her being hurt in any way." I took his hand in mine, squeezing it tightly. "When is your wedding supposed to happen?"

He dropped his head. "Two months from now after the autumn equinox."

"How long does it usually take for an alfar to conceive?"

"Each one varies. I will be expected to spend three nights a month with her, but once she has conceived, I will not have to touch her again."

"Is one heir really enough?" I asked.

"It will have to be because that's all she's getting from me."

I saw the distress on his face. I had never thought of our roles being reversed. "You're being forced to be with her, against your will," I said.

He closed his eyes. "Yes." A moment went by before he unraveled his fingers from mine. "Is that the way you feel when I want you?" I was taken back by the question.

Surprised that he would even ask, I rubbed my hand down his arm for comfort. "You've never forced me. I've always been with you willingly. You have always shown me kindness and you've been tender during our times together. I would never compare the two," I said, hoping that was enough.

"If you had a choice, would you leave?" He asked.

I turned my eyes away from him, not wanting him to see my face. "I'm scared, Gaelin. This whole place scares me. As beautiful and magical as all of this is, everything here wants to kill me. I'm powerless in a world full of things that see me as nothing more than a lamb."

"That day in the marketplace," he said quietly, "I should have turned you away. I said yes to you for my own selfish reason. I was taken with you, and I knew this was the group that the king would allow me to choose from. I placed you in this position for my own selfish gain. I could have never imagined feeling for you then what I do now. I'm sorry."

"If you wouldn't have taken me that day, I would have found another way in. You were the safest option and I appreciate all you've done for me since." I took his face in my hands, drawing my fingers along his soft cheek bone.

"I know this is an act, Gen. I've felt you slipping away ever since our first conversation about your position. When we're together, you don't smell the same. I feel like I am taking you against your will and I don't want that. I never have. What can I do to fix it?" He asked.

I had never heard such vulnerability from him before. I bowed my head. "I don't know. A lot has happened in the past few weeks. I think I just need time to wrap my head around all of this. But your trust and respect are a good start. And more days like this, where it is just the two of us," I said, smiling at him for reassurance.

He nodded, looking back out to the lake. "I can do that," he replied.

I stood and started to take off my clothes. He looked up at me curiously.

"What are you doing?" He asked.

"The kelpie don't bite, right? I'm going swimming. Care to join?" I said, trying to raise his spirits.

He smiled, standing as he took off his clothes. I ran into the cold crisp water, submerging myself under the placid skin of the lake. He followed, diving into the deep pool. We both pulled up, smiling from the sensation.

I swam over to him, wrapping my arms around his neck, pulling him in close. His breath quickened. I kissed him on his cheek gently as we floated in the clear peaceful water.

∼

Gaelin was true to his word. The next few weeks were better than I had expected. He lavished me with flowers, jewelry, baked goods, and books. He insisted that I stop doing my chores for the time being and just enjoy life. I didn't protest. I read so many books over the next few weeks, getting lost in the worlds of each story.

Levos introduced me to Madison. I watched as he lit up in her presence. If I had to guess, he was in love with her, and she was in love with him. There was nothing fake between them. She wasn't forcing herself to smile as I sometimes did with Gaelin. She didn't cringe at his touch or find excuses not to kiss him. Their relationship was genuine, which meant the pain that they both felt when she was beaten or taken to bed by another alfar was that much more severe. My heart broke for my friend.

Talks of the royal wedding began to spread through the court as the time approached. I cringed at the thought of Gaelin being tied to that she-devil for the rest of his life. Regardless of my romantic feelings towards him, he was my friend and I cared about his happiness.

There were no more trips to the dark court or unexpected visitors. The kingdom was quiet for the first time since I arrived. New batches of human workers continued to trickle in each month. I tried to help them where I could, but my resources were limited. All I could do was pray. Pray to whatever god took mercy on us and hope for a better future for us all.

CHAPTER 20

Our peace ended just four weeks before Gaelin and Princess Daealla's wedding. The rift opened on a clearing on top of a hill near the wheat fields. A dozen unknown monsters and beasts came pouring out, terrorizing anything they came across. I was never permitted out of the kingdom limits, so I was unable to see what they looked like firsthand, but from what Levos and Gaelin told me they came in all shapes and sizes.

Some were scaled, while others were full of hair. One of the creatures they recently killed had skin that burned anything that it touched like acid. They were all-powerful creatures, capable of posing a real threat to the alfar. Though the warriors were successful in killing some, many of the creatures escaped into the thick woods.

Their theory about Otar was wrong, and the alfar hated nothing more than being wrong. The king was more tense than usual. Beating and torturing humans for the simplest mishaps. Gaelin made sure that I wasn't around the king more than was expected, but it didn't save me from his wrath.

One night at dinner, I spilled a drop of wine on the tablecloth near his goblet. Without warning he stood up and struck me across the face, sending me to the floor. Gaelin shot to his feet, his body tensed, ready to attack. The king looked at him, his own posture begging for a fight.

"Is there something you wish to say, Lord Atros?" The king asked.

"That was uncalled for," Gaelin replied in a bitter and hasty tone.

"I am the king; she is my property. I can do whatever I wish to her, no matter your opinion."

"Your Highness, I think the stresses of the rift have been weighing on your judgment lately. Maybe if you would allow me to relieve some of your responsibilities—"

"How dare you question my judgment!" The king yelled. The room fell silent as every alfar turned their attention to the king and Gaelin. I had never heard Lysanthier raise his voice. He was always so fluid and poised.

"That was not my intention, Your Grace. I just wish to be of service—" Gaelin started to say before the king cut him off again.

"Do not play games with me, Lord Atros. I know what this little outburst is really about, and you are out of line. You will have your time to be king, but it is not now." The king looked back towards me as I picked up the broken pieces of the pitcher. "Maybe you can be of use to me, Lord

Atros. Your mistress seems to bring you great comfort. Maybe she could do the same for me."

I froze, looking through my hair at the table. Gaelin went stiff.

"She is my concubine, Your Grace. You have your own. You can have whomever else you want in the kingdom," said Gaelin.

"You're correct, and I want her," the king said, sitting.

The queen didn't even blink. Daealla looked amused as she sipped her wine, watching me through her long eyelashes.

"Your Grace, please," said Gaelin.

The king slammed his hands on the table. "That is enough from you tonight. Guards, please take Gaelin's mistress to my chambers. Also, escort Gaelin to his own chambers and make sure he stays there until the morning."

The guards approached, yanking me up from the floor. I looked at Gaelin, still not being able to process all that had just happened. Gaelin fought the guards, spewing threats at them, but it was no use. I was dragged down the hall to the king's bedchambers and thrown inside.

The room was larger than any other I had seen. It was beautifully decorated with art and instruments as Daealla's room had been. I stood to my feet, still in disbelief. Gaelin had done what I asked. He had fought for me and yet somehow, it only made things worse. I wrapped my arms around myself, shaking from the thought of the king on top of me. I curled myself into a corner, wishing to disappear.

An hour of torturous waiting passed before the king

finally entered. He looked around the room until he found me huddled on the floor. He was tall and lean like most alfar. His golden hair with traces of bronze fell long against his back. His face was thin with prominent cheekbones. His skin was as white as parchment yet flawless.

"Have you eaten?" he asked, snapping his fingers at one of the servants near the door. She disappeared, closing us inside.

"No, Your Grace," I said hesitantly.

He took off his jacket before sitting in a chair in front of a round table. He gestured to the seat in front of him. "Come, sit with me," he said softly.

Someone knocked on the door, then in came the servant with a tray of food and wine. I got to my feet and slid my shaking body into the chair. The king filled my plate with fresh fruits and salted meat. He even poured wine for me.

He sat back, watching me from across the table. "Eat," he demanded.

I took the fork and slowly brought the food to my mouth. He watched intently as I chewed the food. I finished what was on my plate without a word, washing it down with the wine he had poured for me. I sat straight, dreading what came next.

"Gaelin has become quite fond of you. What is your secret?" he asked, studying me slowly.

"I fulfill my duties, Your Grace. Nothing more," I said nervously.

"Did you have much experience in bed before you came

to my court? Is that why he is fond of you? For your natural talents?" he asked.

I swallowed hard, uncomfortable with the conversation topic. "Lord Atros was my first and is my only, Your Grace."

The king chuckled, leaning in closer to me. "Is that so? Very interesting," he said, standing from his chair. He walked behind me. I felt his cold finger move my hair from my bare shoulder. I shivered at the contact. He traced his fingers along the neckline of my dress until he got to my breasts. He stopped, gently sliding his finger under the fabric just a bit. I cringed, feeling sick.

He took my arm in his hand, slowly pulling me from the chair. He began to unfasten my dress from the back as streams of tears fell silently down my face. My dress fell to the floor. He remained behind me, his cold fingers tracing my scars on my lower back before he circled around to face me. He then traced his house sigil on my chest.

His hand made its way up to my face, taking my chin, lifting my eyes to his. His eyes were cold and unfeeling. They were more frightening than Erendrial's had been. He held my gaze as his cold hands cupped my breasts. He watched as the discomfort and fear flickered across my expressions. He smiled, apparently satisfied with my reaction.

Then, my world was turned upside down. *It was only flesh*, I told myself. I didn't focus on the pain or the feeling. I focused on the things that made me happy. I focused on Lilian. On Levos. On the beauty of the world outside of this cell. I focused on the kelpie and how radiant the creatures were.

I focused on getting out of here. How I was going to escape. Maybe I would lure a ragamor here and then take off into the sky, leaving this world behind. Or maybe I would just offer myself up to the fairies and let them end my pathetic existence. I thought of how I wanted to drive a ulyrium dagger through the king's neck. Then his daughter would be next. The thought of stabbing him repeatedly made my lips curl into a cruel, unnatural smile.

Finally, the motion stopped as he pulled away, moving to the bathroom to clean himself. I pushed off the bed, grabbing my dress from the floor and sliding it on my disgusting body. I sat on the edge of the bed waiting for him to return. He strolled out of the bathroom with a smile on his face as he looked at me tauntingly.

"Not the liveliest I've had, but not bad. You may go back to Gaelin now, mistress," he said, moving throughout the room.

I took my leave down the hall. I felt so numb and so disgusting. I couldn't make a clear thought form in my head. Everything was hazy and clustered. I looked up, realizing I was nowhere Gaelin's room, but I was near Levos's.

The halls were quiet as I made my way to his door. *Please let him be alone*, I thought. I knocked on the door twice, still shaking from the encounter with the king. He came to the door in a pair of night pants and a loose shirt. I peeked around his form to make sure he was alone. The coast was clear. He looked down at me with a saddened expression.

"I didn't know where else to go," I said as the tears fell.

He pulled me into the room as I collapsed on the floor.

He caught me in his arms on the way down and just held me as I cried out in pain and terror. He rocked me gently, brushing back my hair and making small shushing noises in my ear.

I took a bath, scrubbing my skin until it was red and raw. I couldn't even look at myself in the mirror. The sight disgusted me. My body didn't feel like my own. I thought of all the human women out there that had to deal with this daily. My heart broke for them, not knowing how they got up each day and continued on. They were stronger than I was. I dressed in one of Madison's dresses she kept in Levos's room.

When I came out of the room, he was waiting for me in a chair. He stood up, not knowing what to say. I looked around his room, taking note of the piles of books and maps that littered his living space. His bed wasn't as big as Gaelin's, but it was still nicely adorned.

"Would...would it be okay if I stay here tonight? I can't go back to Gaelin, not yet," I confessed.

He stepped towards me, taking my arms in his hands. "Of course, anything you need." His presence was comforting. I didn't fear his touch. I trusted him. "Take the bed, I'll sleep on the floor tonight."

"Are you sure?"

"Absolutely," he said, leading me to his bed. He tucked me in before taking a blanket and pillow to the floor. The lights went out in the room, leaving me in complete darkness. I closed my eyes, unable to stop sobbing. *It's just flesh. Get yourself together, Gen. It's over, you survived*, I told myself, but it did little to calm my body's reaction.

I exhaled slowly, trying to calm myself. Behind my eyes, images of that all-too-familiar black imprint flickered across my mind. I stopped, trying to push the memory away. Once I knew who that mark belonged to, I had refused to let myself go there, but tonight I might. Just one more time. I relaxed, watching the replays of my visions from the past. I followed the lines of the marking. I memorized the patterns, the thickness of the design. Then, my mind flickered to his smile. The way his cheeks fell into dimples on either side of his mouth. I listened as the laugh that I had yet to hear flooded through my body, easing me into an unsettling sleep.

I WOKE BEFORE LEVOS DID. I QUIETLY LEFT HIS room, unsure of what I was going to say to Gaelin. The court was barely awake at this hour which I was thankful for. I didn't know if I could bear the looks and whispers of the alfar females.

I got to Gaelin's door. The guards were no longer stationed at the entrance. I pushed open the door, closing it quietly behind me. The bed was empty, unslept in. I looked around the room and found Gaelin on the balcony, leaning against one of the pillars. He turned his head and saw me. He walked towards me. I kept my arms around myself, unable to make eye contact with him.

He slowly reached for me, pulling my body into him.

My head met his chest as the tears began to spill from me again. My whole body shook as he tightened his grip. He placed his head on mine.

"I'm so sorry. I'm so sorry," he whispered as I cried in his chest.

I gripped the loose fabric of his shirt in anger. This wasn't his fault. *You can't blame him. He tried to help you*, I thought. He pulled away, looking at my face, searching for any bruising or markings. His hand traced my headband that still covered my ears. "Did he–"

"No. He didn't take too much interest in my face," I said, wiping my tears with my wrist.

"I'm so sorry. I don't know what else to say," he admitted.

"There's nothing you can say. I just want to sleep if that's okay?" I asked.

"Of course. Do you want to bathe?"

"I already did. I went to Levos's room first after he let me go." I felt Gaelin's body go stiff "I wasn't ready to see you, Gaelin. I needed a minute to just be by myself."

"I'm not mad. I just want to be there for you now. Whatever you need."

"I just need to sleep," I said, crawling into the bed. I pulled the covers up to my face, not wanting to talk anymore. I heard him shuffle around the room nervously until he finally left. I watched the balcony as the sun rose into the sky, signaling the start of another day.

The next few days were a haze. I fell in and out of sleep. When I woke, sometimes I would see Gaelin by my bedside. Other times I would see Levos. I ate whenever I could stomach it, but other than that I just slept. When I finally was able to snap myself out of it, three days had passed. I bathed and cleaned the room, thinking back to all the human girls who had to deal with this day in and day out. I wanted to kill the alfar. Every one of them.

I changed the sheets on the bed, then collected the laundry and made my way to the door. I opened it to see Levos standing in front, preparing to knock. His face lit up at the sight of me. He stepped aside and let me pass, then followed as I walked to the laundry room.

"I'm fine, Levos. No need to be weird," I finally said.

"I'm just glad to see you out of bed. You had us worried there for a moment."

"I just needed time to process, but I am better now. What's done is done. There's no changing it. It happens all the time."

He pulled my arm back, stopping me along a quiet hall. "Just because it happens a lot around here doesn't make your situation any less traumatic or wrong. What happened to you wasn't right. You didn't deserve that." He paused, rubbing my face caringly. "Madison offered an ear if you need to talk," he said with pain in his voice.

I smiled at him. "Thank you, but I am fine. I'd rather just forget all together." I looked to the floor. "How is he?"

"Pretty torn up about it. He is beating himself up about not being able to protect you. He feels it's his fault. He thinks it never would have happened if he wouldn't have reacted the way he did at dinner." I shrugged, feeling slightly bad for Gaelin.

"It would have happened eventually. I'll talk to him." I turned to walk away but stopped. I looked back at Levos, standing defeated in front of the wall. "Thank you for being there for me that night. I don't know what I would have done without you. You're a good friend, Levos."

He smiled at me and nodded before walking away.

No one said a word to me that day, which I was thankful for. I didn't dare go to dinner. Instead, I volunteered for dish duty which kept me out of the throne room. That night I went to Gaelin's chambers, expecting him to already be there, but he wasn't. I got ready for bed and waited for him but ended up falling asleep. Around one in the morning, I was woken by the creak of the couch. I looked up to see Gaelin's massive body curled onto the small seat.

"What are you doing?" I asked, sitting up from the bed.

His head popped up before he fully sat up to look at me. "I've been sleeping here the past few nights. I didn't think you'd want to share the bed."

I exhaled, pulling his side of the sheets back. "Come on," I whispered.

He walked slowly to the bed and crawled in.

I scooted down under the covers, looking him in the eyes. "It wasn't your fault. You did what you could."

"Did he...hurt you? More than the act?" he asked.

I furrowed my brow, not wanting to remember a

moment of it. "No. It was quick and unfeeling. I'd rather not talk about it though."

"Of course," he said. He reached slowly for my hand, tracing my fingers with his. "I've thought of so many ways to kill him since that moment."

I laughed at him, but he looked at me with a serious expression. "Oh, you're serious. Well, please don't do that. I'd rather you not go to Valhalla and leave me here to fend for myself. I'd prefer us just to move on. Let's just both be careful from now on so this doesn't happen again."

"I'll do whatever you ask."

"But Gaelin... it may be a while before I can be... physical again. If you need to take someone else, I will understand," I said, feeling sick at the thought of ever being with a male again.

"I understand. And there will be no need for another. I will wait, as long as you need."

I smiled at him before closing my eyes. I willed the darkness to take my thoughts and dreams from me. I just wanted to sleep tonight. I didn't want to see or feel anything. All I wanted to do was sleep.

CHAPTER 21

Creatures continued to pour from the rift over the next few weeks. A battalion went out every morning and when they returned in the evening, another was sent to continue their work. The kingdom was on high alert. No one was allowed beyond the city borders to prevent any civilian casualties.

Gaelin was preoccupied with the continual threats, which I was thankful for. It prevented any real alone time between us. Though we slept in the same bed, I was not ready to venture deeper. Levos and Madison became my constants. I continued to help the human servants anyway I could, though I never felt like I was doing enough.

The king continued to display unusual behavior that made everyone begin to question his judgment. A few of the humans even began to call him the Mad King. He would have random unprovoked outbursts during meals. He would strike anyone who was near him. He even beat his chambermaid so badly she was bedridden for a week.

He took me whenever Gaelin failed to kill or capture the creatures they were hunting. This sent Gaelin into a downward spiral. He would stay out in the woods long after his infantry had returned home. He was barely eating or sleeping, afraid for my well-being.

Every time the king took me against my will, a little part of me died. I didn't know how much a person could give until there was nothing left, but I was afraid I was about to find out. When I would return to Gaelin's room, he would just look at me as if I was a different person. I guess, in a way, I was.

We fell into the routine of ignoring what was happening to me. Gaelin would always ask if I needed anything from him, but this kind of torture was the type that I had to keep to myself. If I confided in him about my experiences, I was afraid he would break. It was better that I handled this on my own. Avoidance worked most days, but when the reality of my situation would come crashing into focus, I found myself huddling in a corner, screaming, and crying as I lost control.

Levos's room became my haven. When I was about to have a breakdown, I would hide out there, knowing no one would bother me or come looking for me. Levos would hold me until the tremors stopped, but I knew my pain was wearing on my friend. He had to be there for both Madison and me when one of us was taken against our wishes.

The day before the wedding, Gaelin was a mess. He wouldn't talk, eat, sleep, or even look at me. Levos did his best to be there for his cousin, but he already had a lot on his plate with everyone's lives being in disarray. Regardless of what was going on in my life, Gaelin was my friend. He was even willing to rewrite the laws of the alfar to protect me. I had to be there for him.

"Do you want to go for a ride to clear your head before dinner?" I asked Gaelin.

He sat on the ledge of the balcony in his room, looking over the kingdom. "If I leave now, I may never come back."

"Let's try and think of this from a positive perspective, okay? Just humor me."

He looked at me as I approached and smiled softly. "I'll bite."

"You marrying Daealla could be very good for everyone involved. You will eventually become king, having more power than anyone in the kingdom. You can change things, just like we've talked about. You can put Daealla in her place. You can cut communication with the dark alfar and restore your kingdom to the purity you seek."

"But how long?" he asked, looking out over the horizon.

"What?"

"How long will it take for me to get enough power to prevent us from living in the hell that we are currently in? How long will King Lysanthier live? How many times will I have to lay with Daealla to conceive an heir? How long will it take to change the laws so you are safe, and we can be together?" he whispered, already sounding defeated.

"It doesn't matter how long, as long as you get there in the end," I said.

"But it does matter." He turned his head to me. "Living like this is breaking both of us. What if by the time I am given the power, there is nothing left of either of us to save?"

I went to him, taking his hand in mine. *Be positive*, I thought. *Be strong*. "You doubt my strength, Gaelin. I'm a bit offended by it," I said with a smile.

He laughed softly, squeezing my hand. "You're stronger than anyone I've ever met. I don't know how you deal with everything and then still have the strength to sit here trying to find the positive in all of this." He looked at me longingly. He leaned into my touch, closing his eyes to savor the contact he hadn't had from me in weeks. "I love you," he whispered.

"And that is the greatest gift you could ever give me," I said, trying to sound sincere. It was the truth. Without his love, I didn't know where I would be right now. I could be dead or tossed around by the whole alfar court. His love didn't protect me completely, but it did offer a shield of sorts.

He made a graceful gesture toward a vine that was wrapped around the banister. A beautiful red flower bloomed from the base. He plucked it and gently placed it behind my ear. He touched my face softly, slowly circling his thumb around my lips.

I couldn't give him what he needed, but I could at least give him something. I wrapped my arms around his waist, pulling him close. I buried my face in his shirt, taking in his scent. His arms were large and firm as they took my small, frail body against his own. He inhaled my scent from my head, and relaxed. We stayed in that position for at least an hour, not saying another word.

That night at dinner, I was assigned to the royals' table, as I had been ever since the king had taken me the first time. As I reached from behind the king to fill his goblet with wine, his hand slid up my dress to my thigh. I pulled away, but he caught my arm, pulling me to his lap.

The light alfar were discreet about their sexual affairs. It was one of the things that set them and the dark alfar apart. The king no longer seemed to care about what was expected of him or that he had an audience. He dragged his cold, disgusting fingers down my neck until he reached my neckline. He slid his hand under it, watching as I squirmed with discomfort and protest. Gaelin's hands were tightened into fists as he tried not to watch. The king looked at him and laughed, amused by the pain he was causing.

"Lord Atros? What will your mistress be doing tomorrow evening when you are consummating your marriage to my daughter? I think I might keep her company in your stead," he said, turning his attention back to me. He finally let go of me. I didn't waste a second. I rushed back to the wall, feeling disgusting and embarrassed by his behavior. Felicity, the human girl whose brother I had helped, grasped my hand as I took my position by her. I squeezed hard, trying to steady my breaths.

"Are you not grateful to have the honor of being united

with my beautiful daughter, Lord Atros?" asked the king. Gaelin just sat there without a word. Lysanthier's body language went tense as his temper rose. "Or would you prefer I allowed you to marry your human mistress?"

Gaelin's eyes snapped up to meet the kings in anger and hatred.

"Well?" said the king. "Answer me!" he yelled, slamming his fists on the table.

"It is an honor to serve the light court," replied Gaelin.

"That is not what I asked. Would you prefer to marry the human whore?" Lysanthier roared. The room went silent, watching their recurring nightly entertainment. Gaelin swallowed, trying to keep calm. "You would, wouldn't you. You'd prefer that worthless piece of scum over my daughter." The king stood, pulling the tablecloth from the surface, smashing all the dishes and trays to the floor. No one moved.

"We'll see if you prefer her when I am through having my way with her," he said, turning away from his wife, daughter, and Gaelin. He marched to the wall, taking my arm, pulling me to him. Felicity held on until the last moment. He pulled me out of the throne room to his private chambers. I was crying before my foot stepped across the threshold.

The next morning, I went to the washroom downstairs in the servants' quarters. When I entered, there were five girls preparing themselves for the wedding ceremony. They all looked at me as I entered the room. Their eyes scanned me from head to toe, stopping at the bruises and blood now dried on my skin. Last night was the worst it had even been.

I didn't know what to say or do. We just stood across from one another in silence. One of the girls began to fill the tub with water. Two of them approached me slowly, taking me by the arm, leading me to the water. They undressed me, taking note of the wounds that hadn't healed on my body.

One reached for my headband, removing it from my ears. They all stopped, staring in surprise at my secret. I didn't even look up. I didn't care. They poured the water across my body, cleaning me gently without a single word. They gathered clean clothes and helped me dress, hiding the evidence of the night before. They brushed my hair back into a braid, placing a new headscarf around my ears. My eye was no longer swollen shut, but you could still see the bruising around the soft tissue.

"Thank you," I whispered.

"You've been through enough," a young girl whispered. Before kissing my cheek.

"Your secret is safe with us, do not fear," another girl approached, kissing my temple.

"For what you've done, for our people." *Kiss.*

"For the boy you took the lashings for." *Kiss.*

"To remember your strength." *Kiss.*

A single tear escaped my eye. I walked back to the main hall, trying to gather the courage to act like I was unfazed about what I had endured the previous night. I couldn't let Gaelin see me like this. Not today.

I went into the throne room, trying to find work to do. The servants in the hall looked at me for a few moments as I took a seat at a table and began polishing the fine porcelain dishes. None of them said a word as they returned to their duties. I stayed there, finding small things to busy myself with until the ceremony began.

That evening, the high houses of the light alfar filled the throne room. The humans took their places along the walls. The room was filled with fresh flowers, candles, and beautiful sculptures created just for the occasion. The king and queen stood at the front of the room on the platform, waiting for their daughter and Gaelin to enter.

The musicians began to play as the alfar stood, honoring their future king and queen. Gaelin and Daealla entered the room, elegant and luxurious as ever. This was the first time I had seen Gaelin in anything besides his warrior's uniform. His suit was a soft cream color, his jacket long, like the one Erendrial wore. Gold stitching covered the cream fabric. His hair was loose around his shoulders and back. His face was solemn.

Daealla wore a beautiful satin white dress. It fell off her shoulders and hugged her waist, accenting her perfect form. The long train trailed behind them both as they ascended the aisle. Her long hair fell straight down her back. A crown of crystal-clear diamonds sat on top of her head. She did not smile.

They walked arm in arm towards the king and queen.

Once they ascended the platform, Gaelin looked back at the wall to me. His face didn't show signs of emotions. He just stared. I forced a smile and nodded, trying to break the uncomfortable moment. His attention turned back to Daealla.

The ceremony was beautiful. The king and queen watched as a Nordic priest conducted the vows. Gaelin and Daealla knelt before each other, wrapping their hands in a white silk ribbon, representing the eternity of their union. After the religious aspect of the ceremony was over, they both signed a blood contract, cementing their union. Each had to sign their name in their own blood. They then took each other's hand, uniting their wounds so their blood could be mixed between one another.

After the ceremony, the alfar celebrated. We worked the room, filling wine glasses and tending to their needs. Gaelin didn't look at me during dinner. He nodded at the high houses that offered their congratulations to him and his new bride, without a glint of emotion. *He had broken*, I thought. I was sure I'd be the first to shatter, but I was wrong...it had been him.

I looked at the king as he flirted and laughed with anyone who came close. My stomach began to turn at the very sight of him. If I had to endure his touch one more time, I might offer myself to the fairies willingly. At least I would be certain that the pain of their torture would eventually end.

Levos appeared behind me as I collected the dirty plates from a table. I acted like he wasn't there, but he continued to follow me. I made my way back to the servant's hall, emptying my hands. He pulled me aside, out of earshot of the others. I pulled away from him, feeling my skin begin to burn. Even his touch now affected me in the most unsettling way. He looked at me curiously as he slowly lowered his arm.

"What do you want?" I asked.

"I hadn't seen you since last night. Are you okay? Why didn't you come to my room?" he asked.

"I'm here, aren't I?"

"That doesn't mean anything. Some of the servants told Madison that you were pretty beat up this morning. Where did you go after? Back to Gaelin's room?"

I shook my head, not making eye contact. "I stayed in the linen closet on the main floor until morning. Then I went to the servant's washroom and cleaned up before helping with the preparations."

"Why didn't you come to me? I would have helped you. You know that."

"You have enough to deal with. With Madison going through the same thing and Gaelin cracking, I have to learn how to take care of myself."

"I will always have room for you. You aren't in this alone."

"But I am, Levos! I'm the only one that can fix me."

He looked at me with pain in his eyes. He touched my face softly. It took every ounce of restraint not to flinch away. "You won't have to worry about the king tonight," he said heavily.

"That's not what he said yesterday."

"Gaelin has made sure of it."

I looked at him, trying to figure out what they had done. "What do you mean?"

"Gaelin had an elixir made. I slipped it into the king's wine when I went to congratulate them. It will knock him out in a few hours. He won't be able to hurt you. At least for one night."

I dropped my head, feeling pain in my heart for Gaelin. "How was he today?"

"Worried about you mostly. He will do what he has to do in order to accomplish the long game, but he's changing, and not for the best."

"I know," I said heavily. "Can you tell him thank you for me? I doubt I'll be able to get near him tonight."

Levos nodded. He turned away from me reluctantly, exiting the servant's hall. I made my way back out the throne room, feeling lighter, knowing I wasn't going to have to share the psychopath's bed tonight, but Gaelin was now going to have to face a similar situation.

After dinner, I went to Gaelin's room. It felt weird being there without him. I bathed again and got ready for bed. I laid my head on the pillow, looking out at the stars, my safe place. If I could only find a way out of this. Or find a way to kill the king. That would expedite Gaelin's path to the throne. Oh, how I would revel in watching the bastard die. The more gruesome, the better.

I would be happy to watch the fairies filet him into an angel. Or maybe one of the beasts from the rift rip him apart. I wanted his torture to be painful. I wanted his death to be public and violent. I wanted him to watch as everything was taken from him: his power, his family, his life. I wanted him to suffer, all while knowing I was the one responsible for his downfall.

CHAPTER 22

Flashes of darkness rolled through my head that night. Blood, pain, and death crept in every vision. Finally, the pain stopped as my eyes focused on a creature I had seen before...Otar. This time, he wasn't sitting on the throne in the light court, watching the royals swing from the chandeliers. He was dead, lying on a wooden table in a dark basement. His body had been cut open; his organs removed.

His black, leathery skin was now gray. His yellow eyes were shut, and his lips lazily hung open, revealing his mouthful of sharp teeth. I saw myself approach him. I felt the fear and uncertainty as I hovered over his lifeless body. I placed the candle down on the table next to him, then picked up a hollow point needle and black ink.

I flipped my left wrist over and began to carve a sigil into my flesh. A circle with an inverted triangle in the middle, with a black dot at the bottom point. A line arched from the bottom left side of the circle, up and through the triangle before ending at the bottom right side of the frame. The wound healed, but the black mark remained on my flesh. I took a knife and slit my palm, placing the dripping stream of blood over Otar's lips. The blood pooled in his mouth until finally spilling down the sides of his cheeks.

I took the candle, stepped back from the table, and lit Otar's body on fire. I watched the flames devour his corpse. My mind flashed to another scene. Otar was now alive, bound by iron shackles. He was talking to me, telling me everything I wanted to know. He did everything I commanded of him, as if I controlled him. Then I saw a dagger made of white apophyllite crystal. Otar feared the dagger.

My mind spun around and around before I finally opened my eyes to the empty room. I sat straight up, panting and sweating from the vision. I got out of bed and staggered to the balcony, welcoming the cool air. Why was I having this vision? Why was I seeing this? Otar was dead. Gaelin had killed him. I slid down the pillar, trying to wrap my head around what I had just seen.

The next morning, Gaelin was nowhere to be found. I waited for him to come back to the room, but it had been two hours after breakfast, and he was still absent. I took off, filling my time with meaningless chores as I thought about my vision. During lunch, I ran into Madison and Levos on a terrace enjoying the peace and quiet. I tried to duck away without being noticed, but Madison caught me before I could escape and beckoned me over to them.

"Did you two have fun at the wedding?" I asked, trying to be polite.

"Not so much at the wedding, but afterward I did," said Madison. She glanced over at Levos who bashfully smiled, dropping his eyes from hers.

"Did you sleep well?" Levos asked me.

"Better than most nights. Thank you for that," I said, taking his hand in mine.

"You should have stuck around. The king fell asleep at the table. The guards had to carry him back to his bed. The queen was so humiliated. It was priceless," added Madison.

"The talk about his mental state is starting to catch traction. The court thinks he is losing his mind," said Levos.

"He is, believe me. He mumbles to himself, and he can't seem to control his temper. Has he always been like this?" I asked.

"No, not at all. For the most part, the alfar are even tempered. They're able to control themselves and their emotions. You saw the way he was when the dark court was here. Ambassador Lyklor was pushing each one of his buttons, but he didn't flinch. Now, everything sets him off," said Levos.

"In the past, even the humans he's taken never have mentioned him being aggressive. Cold maybe, but not physically abusive," said Madison.

"Well, that has definitely changed. I am living proof of that," I said, taking a bite of a date.

They both looked at each other before dropping their heads uncomfortably. "Sorry," I whispered.

Madison took my hand this time. "Don't ever apologize for that. We're here for you. Whatever you need," she said kindly.

I smiled, shifting awkwardly. One of the other servants came rushing in, signaling for Madison to follow her. Madison exhaled, getting to her feet. She bent down and gave Levos a small kiss. He looked at her tenderly, pinching her chin in between his fingers. She smiled before following the servant out of the room.

"Looks like things are good with you two," I said, happy for my friend.

"They are. Gaelin told me last night he is going to make me a lord, which will allow me to take a mistress. Madison will never be forced to sleep with anyone she doesn't want ever again," I smiled, knowing what this meant to him.

"That's amazing. He's going to make a great king," I said heavily. "Have you seen him?"

He shook his head, looking out into the fields below us. "He didn't come back to his room last night?"

"No, nor this morning. At dinner last night he was so cold and distant."

"He's putting on his armor, Gen. He needs to appear unwavering now that he is to be king."

I nodded, understanding the logic. A few moments went by as we sat in peace. I hit him in the boot playfully. "I know you have another lady to dote over now, but would it be too much for me to ask you for a gift?"

He smiled, leaning in towards me. "What do you want now?"

"Hey now, I don't ask for a lot?"

"Out with it."

"A dagger, made of apophyllite crystal."

He sat up straight, frowning. "What in Odin's name do you want a dagger made of apophyllite for?"

"I think it's pretty and I want to be armed when I go out in the fields to pick herbs. I've almost been eaten out there a couple of times already."

"You've what? What haven't you told me?" he said in surprise.

"Not important. Can you have it made or not?"

"Yes but promise me it isn't going to end up in the king's chest. I would really hate to have to watch you get beheaded. I like your head just where it is."

I laughed, enjoying the image of me standing over the king's bloodied body. "I'm not stupid. I know that apophyllite won't kill him, but if it makes you feel better, I promise. How long do you think it will take to get?"

He shrugged. "I can have it for you by dinner. I will have to get it made. Weapons aren't usually made out of crystal, unless it's ulyrium as you well know, but since I'm the cousin of the soon-to-be new king, it shouldn't be a problem."

"Thank you, Levos."

"You're not going to tell me what the dagger really is for, are you?"

I shook my head. "Not now, but I will tell you one day," I said, getting to my feet, leaving him on the terrace alone.

I still didn't know what my premonition meant, but if Otar was somehow going to make another appearance I wanted to be ready for him. I wasn't all too confident the apophyllite dagger would kill him, and I still had no clue what the sigil meant, or why I fed Otar my blood.

I rounded the corner of the main hall and slammed right into the king and two of his advisors. He looked down at me with a haunting smile. I stood still, too afraid to move. I began trembling, trying to will myself to run, but I was planted to the floor.

The king waved his hand and the two alfar left his side. He took a step closer to me, dragging his hand along my arm. His eyes were hungry and dark. He licked his lips before pulling my body into his. My chin began to tremble. He never had taken me during the day. In the daylight, I was safe. The darkness of night was what I had to fear.

"I'm sorry I was unable to fulfill my promise about taking you last night," he whispered, swirling one of my curls around his finger. "I'd like to make it up to you, darling Genevieve." That was the first time he had ever used my name.

"I have my chores to do, Your Grace," I said, hoping to escape.

"Your only job for the next hour is to satisfy your king," he said, pushing me towards his chambers.

I turned, walking slowly to my own living hell. I shuddered as his footsteps followed behind me. I could feel his eyes undressing me with each passing second. I pushed open his door, standing aside until he entered.

I rushed back to Gaelin's room to bathe and change, trembling. Tears no longer came. It was almost as if I had run out of them completely. The alfar looked at me with curiosity as I pushed through them down the hall. I flung the door open, slamming it behind me with more force than I ever had. I stripped my soiled clothes off my body. Blood stained my dress. I filled the bath and submerged myself, demanding the filth of him to burn off me.

I yelled as I scrubbed. I scrubbed, and scrubbed, and scrubbed some more. Then I just sat in the tub, my knees pulled to my chest as I raged. I had to find a way to be rid of him. I had no expectation of surviving this life. I knew what my fate held. I was going to die in this place, used and beaten. If I was going to die, then I would at least rid the world of King Lysanthier on my way out.

I thought back to my vision. Otar. I controlled him. He had to do whatever I told him. Was he, my key? Could I raise him from the dead and command him to kill King Lysanthier? I knew that the apophyllite dagger would possibly kill him. I knew iron restrained him. This could work. I could do it. I could raise Otar and control him to do my bidding. If I was wrong, and he came back without a leash, he would kill me. Somehow, that gave me a haunting sense of comfort.

I got out of the tub, wrapping the towel around my body. I had to find out where they were keeping Otar's body. I had to get to him. Tonight. Tonight, after the king had me, again, I would find Otar and raise him to kill the bastard. I opened the door to the bathroom to find Gaelin sitting on the edge of the bed, holding my soiled dress. I stopped, not knowing what to say or do. He hung his head, gripping the dress so hard his knuckles were white.

"The elixir didn't work?" He asked in a low voice.

I stepped forward, going to the armoire to get a clean dress. "It protected me last night. Just not this afternoon," I said hesitantly.

He threw the dress, standing up from the bed in anger. I dressed and composed myself before speaking to him again. I had to be strong. I had to put a mask on and act like I wasn't affected by what had just happened thirty minutes prior. I had to use Gaelin to find where Otar's body was being held. He sat on the couch, looking at the bookshelf in front of him blankly. I took a seat next to him, not knowing if he wanted my touch.

"Do you need anything from me?" he asked coldly.

"Only for you to be here with me now," I said softly.

He nodded, not looking at me. I reached for him, but he moved his hand before I could make contact. He had never shunned away from my touch before. I felt a sting of pain dart through my heart. I was losing him, and I didn't know how to fix it.

I held my head in shame. "Do you not want me, because he's had me?"

His head snapped to me. His eyes were full of hate and pain. He studied me for a moment. I tried to control my face and appear whole, but I knew he could see through my mask. "I want to save you from him. I hate what he does to you, but that doesn't reflect poorly on you."

"I'm sorry," I whispered.

"What for?"

"All of this," I said, feeling guilty. For what? I had no clue.

"How is any of this your fault? You didn't ask for this. This is his fault. This is my fault. This is everyone's fault except yours," he said, raising his voice. His sorrow and pain, now turning to rage.

I stopped, remembering what he had to endure only a few hours ago. He was forced to perform with another against his will. He calmed himself, bringing his hands to his lap.

"Do you want to talk about it?" I asked.

He chuckled. "Yes, let's share stories about our forced sexual encounters. That's exactly what I want to do. Talk about how I fucked another alfar with the female I love."

I hung my head, not knowing how to deal with him. I had never experienced this side of Gaelin before. I nervously fumbled with my hands, trying to think of something.

He exhaled, shaking his head. "I'm sorry, you don't deserve to be talked to that way. I'm just...wounded is all."

"It's okay. You have every right to be angry about all of this."

"Yes, but not at you." He took my hand, finally turning to look at me. "Did he hurt you badly?"

"Not the worst he's done. Most of the bruises are gone already. Just a little sore," I said, trying to sound somewhat reassuring. "How are you after last night?"

"She insisted we do it more than once. I couldn't even...I

couldn't at first. I'm ashamed to admit I had to think of you to even perform with her. Hopefully, she's pregnant and that will be the last time I have to do that," he said.

"If the thought of me brings you any comfort, don't feel ashamed about it." A few moments passed as we sat, holding each other's hand in silence. "How is the situation with the rift going?" I asked, trying to move the conversation to where I needed it to go.

"Reports of the rift opening around the kingdom are still coming in. We've caught a few of the beasts this past week, but it's hard to keep up with their numbers. The council is considering calling in the dark court again to help get a handle on things. Our pride has prevented the call for help thus far, but we're running out of options."

"This doesn't reflect poorly on you. Once you have a little help cleaning up the masses, it will allow you to prepare and anticipate where the rift will open next so you can get on top of it," I said, running my fingers through his hair.

"Maybe. I just hate asking the dark alfar for anything."

"I know, but they're a means to an end. Nothing more. You have the larger kingdom and more people to protect. Your burden is heavy." I let a few moments pass, trying to make the progression of thought sound natural. "Whatever happened to Otar? Did you ever find anything useful?"

He shook his head. "No, his anatomy is interesting, but we still don't know anything about him. Where he comes from, what he is, or who he was working for."

"So, what happened to his body?"

"He's still here," he answered. I felt my heart leap for joy. I wanted to smile, but I kept my expressions on lockdown.

"Here, in the castle?"

"Yes. We keep him below in one of the labs where the alfar can continue to study him and the other things we catch." Gaelin turned then to look at me. His eyes filling with questioning. "Why are you so interested in the monsters all of the sudden?"

Without hesitation I answered with confidence. I had prepared for this. "Well, if there's a war coming, I want to know what monsters we'll have to face. Is that so hard to believe?"

"No, but with you, I never know where that beautiful head of yours is."

I grinned at him, nudging my shoulder into his. "So is the place where you keep their bodies under the servant's quarters?"

"Yes. It's not a secret. Most of the alfar don't want to be bothered by the things we catch. They'd rather act like everything is normal and their way of life isn't at risk."

I nodded, letting the subject drop before he got much more suspicious of my questions. Tonight, I would find the labs and find Otar. I would raise him, and I would have my revenge.

CHAPTER 23

I was able to snap Gaelin out of his depression only for a moment before it was time for us to attend dinner. As soon as we entered the hall, the king's gaze locked onto me, and I felt Gaelin's small ounce of happiness dissipate into thin air. He glanced at me from the side before taking his seat next to his wife. I moved to the wall, taking a pitcher of wine.

That night, the king took me again. I was still sore and bruised from this afternoon's encounter with him, but my mind went into survival mode, focusing on anything besides what was happening to my body. This time I focused on Erendrial's imprint. I thought of the black marking and compared it to the one I would soon be giving myself.

He had told me that his marking appeared magically. When the dark alfar took a wife that the imprint would appear on them as well. There was no hollow needle or ink involved. I wondered if the mark I would have to make on my own skin would hurt. Hell, I didn't care. I would probably die because of this crazy plan I had concocted, but it would be worth it to watch the life fade out of the king's eyes—to watch his blood saturate his perfectly white robe. It was worth any price.

The king kept me around a little longer than normal that night. He continued to call me darling Genevieve. Genevieve darling. Darling Gen. I hated the sound of my name on his lips. I wanted to rip his tongue out with my fingers and make him choke on it.

Finally, he released me. I went to the linen closet where I had stored a bag that contained the hollow point needle, the black ink, the iron chains, and the apophyllite dagger Levos had given me before dinner. I wasn't as beaten this time around, which made it easier for me to move throughout the halls. I made my way down the castle, past the main hall, past the servant's level, and into the basement. It took me an hour of roaming before I found the place they were keeping the creatures.

The whole area smelled of blood and decaying flesh. The lab was underground, which allowed no natural light or fresh air to enter the space. They must have dug into the mountain to create this place. The walls were made of natural stone and felt damp to the touch. The only light was the candle I had with me, which didn't provide much comfort.

I peeked through the bars into the first room. A small, child-sized creature lay dead on a wooden table. Its chest was cut in two, held apart by two hooks. The thing had no skin on its bones. Only raw muscles and tendons were visible. It didn't have the face of a human either. It had two large black bug-like eyes that protruded from its head. Three holes where a nose should have been and a large slit for a mouth that stretched from ear to ear. I looked away, feeling sick just by the sight of the thing.

The next room that I peeked into had a winged creature displayed on the wall. It had a long beak for a snout, six arms, and five red eyes on its forehead. I continued, seeing creatures of all different forms, dissected for study to understand their origin better. Knowing these things were lurking out in the woods made my skin crawl. Gaelin was right to feel overwhelmed. Not only was he facing an unknown enemy, but there was no known way of stopping them from coming.

I opened a door to the room that contained Otar's body. Taking a deep breath, I stepped inside, shutting the door behind me. I used my candle to light the sticks around the room, illuminating the space and Otar's corpse. I moved in closer, looking at the thing that would deliver me from hell.

He was uglier than the images I had seen in my head. His skin was wrinkly and black like oil. His nose was long and beaked like a bird. He had thin, wrinkly lips and long fingers with shiny black talons. His body was long and gangly, thin, and sickly looking. He had no hair anywhere that I saw. A brand was burned in the left side of his chest, in the shape of a rune I had seen in one of Levos's books. I didn't know what it meant or stood for, but I made a mental note to look into it.

One last time, I weighed the options of what I was about to do. This was a creature from an unknown world. I didn't know what it was capable of, or if this would work. It could kill me in a second, kill Levos and Madison. I stepped back, hesitant to continue. I breathed in, feeling my chest rise and fall. My insides cramped from the pain I had just endured under the king. *No, this was worth it*. It was worth any risk.

I took a deep breath, placing the candle down next to me as I remembered doing in my vision. I took the hollow point needle and dipped it into the ink and began to mark my left wrist. It stung as blood dripped from my skin, but it was bearable. When the imprint resembled the sigil I saw in my vision, I stopped and waited for it to heal. The ink remained. I smiled.

I slit my right palm, holding it over the creature's mouth. I wrapped the iron chains around his neck, wrists, and ankles, anchoring them to the wall of the lab room. Once I was certain he wasn't getting away, I pulled the apophyllite dagger from the bag and picked up the candle. I took a deep breath and let the candle fall onto Otar's body. The skin of the creature caught like oil, spreading a devouring his entire form. I stepped back against the wall, shielding myself from the flames.

The fire spread, turning his skin to black ash. His form was still visible, but he was charred to a crisp. I sat against the wall, waiting to see if he would be reborn like my vision had shown me. After forty minutes of waiting, his hand moved, shaking off the old ash to reveal smooth, shining, new black skin. I stood to my feet, holding the dagger in my right hand, readying myself for anything.

Otar sat up, shaking from side to side like a dog. His eyes were a brighter shade of yellow than I recalled. His teeth were white as ivory. The talons at the end of his fingers retracted in and out as if he were flexing a muscle. He took a deep breath, tilting his head to the ceiling. He slowly brought his head down, closing his eyes as he began to purr.

"And who do I owe the thanks for this new body?" he said in a deep, hellish voice. He snapped his head to the side in a predatory motion towards me. His eyes expanded as he assessed his savior.

"My name is Genevieve Autumn. I resurrected you," I said in a shaky tone.

"Obviously," he said, looking his hands over. He shook the chains, realizing he was trapped. "And how did you know how to raise me, little one? I'm not from your world and no one knows my kind's secrets."

I swallowed hard. "That isn't important. I want to make a deal with you," I said, trying to get to the point.

"And why would I make a deal with something as stupid and fragile as one of you?"

"Get off the table and bow!" I said assertively.

He did as I demanded, his chains rattling with each movement. Taking a knee in front of me, he looked up at me as if he wanted to shred my skin from my muscles.

"Fall face down on the ground!" I demanded.

Again, he followed my exact command. I exhaled,

hoping this wasn't an act and he was truly under my command.

"You may get to your feet," I said, softer.

"Seems like you know most of my secrets, *meat suit*," he said, still glaring at me.

"I don't want to harm you. I only want you to complete what you came here to do."

"And how do you know what I came here to do?"

I stood silent, not daring to give away my secret.

He ticked his tongue, shaking his head slowly. "Very secretive, meat suit."

"I want you to kill King Lysanthier, then his wife and daughter. Can you do this or not?"

Otar's eyes gleamed and he smiled widely. "I am listening."

"Tomorrow night, after the plates from the first course are cleared, I want you to enter the throne room unseen. Until then, you may stay hidden in the castle. You are not to harm, kill, steal, or be seen by anyone or thing until then. Stay in the castle and do not contact anyone outside by any means," I said firmly.

"Attention to detail, I like," he snapped.

"As the second course is being served, you will approach King Lysanthier from behind his chair and kill him in the most brutal way you are capable of. You will then move to his wife and then his daughter. After that, you may kill whatever other alfar in the throne room you desire. There are two alfar you are not allowed to harm: Gaelin Atros and Levos Atros. I will mark them both with my blood, so you are aware of who they are. You are not allowed to harm any human and you are not allowed to harm me. After you have had your fill of alfar flesh, you will flee and not return unless I call upon you," I finished.

He laughed, tapping his long nails on the table. "Anything else?"

"No one is to know that I am the one who resurrected you. This stays between you and me."

"Deal," he said, walking towards me. He stopped as the chain holding him to the wall went taunt. He reached out his hand, touching my face with his skinny fingers. With his talons retracted, his skin felt like fresh leather. "You are either very brave or very stupid, little one," he said, smiling.

"Tell me about your kind, and do not lie," I demanded. I sat against the wall, facing him.

"As you wish," he said, taking a seat in front of me. "You know the fallen Christian angel?"

"Lucifer," I responded.

"Yes. Well, his demons are the most similar thing you know of that can be related to my kind. I come from a plane of ash and fire. My home is dead, devoured by my kind. We go to other worlds, planes, and realms searching for life to snuff out. We do not mate. We do not breed. There will never be more of us. What you see is what there is."

"And your bond to me? How does that work?"

"I have never been bound to anyone because, as I said, no one knows our secret...which still makes me question who you are." He waited, searching my face. "I am bonded to your life. If you die, I die. You may command me as you wish. If you die, I can be revived by another, as you did to me just now."

"And what can permanently kill your kind?" I asked.

His face fell, his eyes squinted into small slits of anger. "An apophyllite crystal to the heart," he said, forcing the words from his lips. He scoffed, spitting to the ground as if speaking the revelation left a foul taste in his mouth.

I pulled the dagger out from my side, holding it in my lap.

His eyes widened and his teeth began to grind together. "How did you—"

"I don't want to use this on you. I don't want to kill you. My fight is not with you, and you have done me no harm, but if you are lying in any way or try to hurt those who I love, I will not hesitate to use this on you. Are we clear?" I asked.

He nodded, tilting his head. "Out of curiosity, why do you want me to kill your people?"

"They aren't my people," I said between my teeth.

"Not completely true," he said, pointing to his ears.

I rolled my eyes, taking the headband from my ears. "How did you know?"

"I can smell you. It's a delightful smell by the way. Makes my mouth water." He smiled and licked his lips.

"You are not to tell anyone about my mixed blood either," I said firmly.

"Well, you are no fun," he hissed, folding his arms across his chest as if he was a toddler throwing a tantrum.

"I am allowing you to kill as many light alfar as you wish. How is that not fun?" I said, reveling at the thought.

He laughed, stretching his arms in the air. "You're quite wicked. I like you, meat suit. Now, can we please remove the iron? It burns, and I'd rather not mark up my new body just yet."

I was hesitant to even get close to him, but I had to for this to work. I held the apophyllite dagger in my hand as I removed the iron chains. He was small, only coming up to my chest. He continued to smile and purr as his sniffed me and moaned anytime I got too close.

"Do as I have asked," I said nervously.

He moved so fast I didn't see where he had gone. I turned around, searching for him, but he was nowhere to be found. Suddenly, a cold hand knocked into me, and I dropped the apophyllite dagger. It fell to the floor as Otar slammed me into the wall. His yellow eyes seemed brighter than before. He slowly leaned his face into mine. His long tongue extended out, licking ever so slowly from my jaw to my eye. He pulled away, flashing those sharp teeth.

"Delicious," he whispered in a deep, hunting voice while drawing the word out. "I will do as I am ordered with pleasure," he said.

I blinked and he was gone without a trace. I rushed to the dagger to arm myself, but he didn't reappear. I was shaking with fear. I quickly gathered my supplies and left the room, turning to check behind me every few steps.

I made my way back to Gaelin's room and entered quietly,

making sure not to disturb him. I hid the bag in the armoire and went to the bathroom to bathe. Sitting in the warm water, I traced the black raised skin of the imprint on my wrist. I smiled at it, knowing this was a marking I would always be proud to wear.

I crawled into bed, still nervous about the shadows in the room. Either Otar was truthful, and my visions had been correct, or I had just freed something else that wanted to kill me. Either way, my suffering would soon be over. Gaelin shifted slowly in the bed and turned towards me. His eyes opened heavily to look up at me. I smiled at him.

"I'm okay," I whispered.

He exhaled, reaching for me. I allowed him to wrap his arms around my waist even though the sensation made me want to run for the hills.

"We're going to get through this in one piece. It will get better. I promise," I whispered, settling down into the bed.

CHAPTER 24

The next morning, I woke up refreshed and rejuvenated. Truth be told, I was a little relieved Otar had not found me and killed me in my sleep. I guess what he told me about our lives being linked was true. If I died, so would he. I checked my wrist, making sure the imprint was still there. I traced my finger around the black design. Gaelin was still sound asleep. I leaned over and kissed him on the head. "Your suffering ends today," I whispered softly.

I got out of bed and dressed, making sure to choose a dress that hid my favorite new adornment. I strapped the apophyllite dagger to my thigh, just in case. I went to the main hall and gathered breakfast for Gaelin, bringing it back just as he was waking. I sat the tray on the bed with a smile on my face. He looked at me apprehensively; I hadn't brought him breakfast in bed since before the battle with Otar had started.

"Are you okay?" he asked wearily.

"Just trying to get back to a sense of normalcy," I responded.

"You don't have to do this."

"I wanted to. Find the smallest moments of happiness. That's what I tell myself. Seeing you happy makes me happy."

He smiled at me, picking up his fork and digging in. I didn't know how he and I would change after tonight, but anything was better than our current situation.

I watched him dress in his uniform. He kept turning to me as if surprised I was still in the room. I smiled at him each time and he laughed uncomfortably, no doubt uncertain of my behavior. Once he was finished, I pricked my finger with a pin from my hair and made my way over to him. I kissed him softly on the lips, pulling back with a smile on my face.

"To start your day off on the right footing," I said softly.

"Waking up to you each day does that for me," he said, wrapping his arms around my waist. He pulled me into his body, moving his head down slowly to take another kiss. I used the opportunity to press my bleeding thumb in the back of his collar, hiding the crimson stain in the thick folds of the fabric. Then I moved to the back of his hairline, pressing my bloodied thumbprint there as well.

I left Gaelin's room in search of Levos. He was in the kitchen with Madison as she prepared lunch for the alfar.

"Well don't you look chipper this morning," he said, looking me up and down. "I haven't seen you this bouncy in months."

"I'm trying to look on the positive side of things. Look to the future, not dwelling on the present," I said.

"That's the spirit," said Madison, moving the raw dough to the oven.

"Can I steal him away for a bit?" I asked Madison.

"Please do. I can't get any work done around here with him hovering over me."

Levos rolled his eyes, plopping down from the counter, pulling Madison in for a kiss. "Soon, you won't have a choice but to endure my hovering, mistress," he said playfully.

She laughed, hitting him in the chest. "Get out of here," she said.

It was still odd to me that the title of 'mistress' could hold any type of sentimental meaning for a woman, but I guess in her situation, it would mean she would be able to be with the male she loved. Levos followed me out of the kitchen and into the city.

"Why are you so happy?" he asked, not taking his eyes off me.

"I just have a feeling we are all about to get everything we want a lot sooner," I replied.

He laughed, stopping in front of me. "What have you done, sweet Genevieve? Does it have something to do with that dagger I had made for you?"

I shook my head. "How is a dagger going to get us everything we want?" I asked, stepping in front of him.

"Did you have another vision?"

I shrugged. "Maybe..."

"Oh, come on. Do tell. Don't leave me in the dark here."

"I can't. I don't want to jinx it. If it is true, you will know soon enough."

"I hate secrets."

"Yeah well, I am full of them, so get used to it."

"You aren't lying there," he laughed, pulling in front of me again. His face was softer, more focused. "Just tell me you aren't in danger."

"No, Levos, I am not," I said, unsure if I had just lied to him.

He smiled. "Okay then, I can wait for my surprise a little longer, I suppose." He started walking ahead of me.

I pulled the pin from my hair and pricked my finger. "Levos," I called.

He turned around.

I rushed into his arms, hugging him tightly. I marked his clothing with my blood in the same places I had Gaelin's then marked my print behind his hairline, out of sight. "You are truly the best friend I could have ever asked for." I pulled away, looking into his eyes. "Out of everyone here, I am most grateful that I met you."

He smiled shyly, yet question and concern filled his eyes. "Why do I feel like this is a sendoff or a goodbye? Gen, you are starting to worry me. What's wrong?"

"Nothing, Levos. Everything is okay. I just... I want you to know how much you mean to me," I said, pulling out of his grip.

"Well, don't let Gaelin hear you say that. He would string me up and gut me for taking your affection away from him."

"I like him too, but what you and I have...it's different."

He smiled, nodding at me in thanks. "I feel the same way." He kissed me on the head as we continued through the streets of the city.

Dinner had begun. It was almost time. I was so close to getting everything I had dreamed of for the past few months. I was nervous and terrified, yet excited with anticipation. I wondered how Otar would kill him. Would he rip out his heart? Tear him to shreds? Rip the artery in his neck with his teeth and then laugh as the blood splattered on his wife and daughter? I didn't care. As long as it got done.

Otar was roaming around here somewhere. He would have smelled my blood on Gaelin and Levos by now, so they were safe. Everyone else wouldn't be so lucky. I smiled, imagining the mess that would have to be cleaned up.

First course was almost over; time to move. I walked out of Gaelin's chambers, heading for the throne room. The alfar would be seated in one room, lined up perfectly for Otar to slaughter. I would enter the room and stand directly in front of the royal table, taking the best seat in the house. I would look at the royals, daring them to hurt me. Just as the thought crossed their minds, Otar would attack. I laughed.

I got to the doors of the throne room. The servants began to move through the aisles, preparing to clear the alfar's plates. One minute until Otar entered the room. Two minutes until the king would be dead. I stood off to the side, counting down the seconds until I would step in front of the table to watch him take his last breath. My heart was racing, and my hands were trembling.

I took a pitcher of wine. Time seemed to slow as my senses became hyper aware of everything that surrounded me. I wove in and out of the alfar as they feasted. They didn't look up. Why would they? I was just another pig roaming their halls. Nothing more than something to spit on and use. Little did they know this pig would be responsible for the death of their king and potentially their entire court.

I made it to the main aisle and headed for the royal table, stopping ten feet from the platform. A line of servants spilled from behind me, carrying the second course of this evening's meal. I raised my eyes slowly. The king's gaze met mine. He grimaced at me, but I didn't care. I smiled.

Before the king could reprimand me, Otar appeared behind his chair as instructed. His black glistening body caught the light of the candles as razor-sharp horns appeared down his spine. Two additional arms and hands emerged on either side, creating thirty razored talons poised to strike.

Otar dug his nails into the king's chest, tearing him to shreds. Blood splattered everywhere as the screaming and yelling began. Otar buried his sharp teeth into the king's neck, pulling out his artery. A ulyrium blade appeared in one hand as he stabbed the king over and over again. For Otar's final touch, he shoved one of his hands through the king's chest, ripping his heart out and tossing it to the ground in front of me. The king slumped across the table as Otar finally released his mutilated body. I couldn't help but smile as small tears of relief rolled down my cheeks.

The guards emerged from every angle, working to obtain Otar, but he was too fast. He disappeared in an instant, then reappeared behind the queen, stabbing her in the heart three times before evaporating into thin air again. The guards surrounded Princess Daealla, making it impossible for Otar to get to her. He appeared briefly behind me, only for a split second as if to ask for his next marching order.

"The others," I said.

He nodded, disappearing again. The high lords and ladies couldn't move fast enough. Magic began to erupt throughout the room, but Otar was too fast, and the members of the high houses had been too complacent. They had allowed Gaelin and his warriors to do their fighting for them. Now, they were weak and out of practice, unable to think tactically.

Otar spun around the room, ripping, tearing, and stabbing as many as he could. Blood pooled on the polished stone floor. Body parts littered the tables. Beautifully crafted alfar heads were flung to my feet. I once thought the sight of a severed head would send me hunching over in sickness, but now I just stared, watching as my demon did my bidding.

Something hard and full of momentum slammed into me. I looked up, realizing Gaelin had picked me up and was hauling me away from my symphony. I glanced at the throne room one last time, memorizing the sight of the king's dead body. Dozens of guards filled the room and closed the doors behind them, locking Otar inside with them. A part of me hoped he survived; the other hoped he would parish with his victims. I didn't know which feeling was stronger, but I was thankful to him, nonetheless.

Gaelin carried me to his room, slamming the door and locking it behind us. I turned around to see Levos and Madison also on the edge of the bed. I snapped out of my blood rage and exhaled in relief that my friends were okay. Madison was trembling, clinging to Levos tightly.

"What in the hell was that?" asked Levos.

Gaelin was breathing heavily as he turned around to face us. He checked me over, making sure I was okay. *Oh yeah*, I thought. *I am supposed to be panicked and scared.* I let my face fall to the floor as I took a seat on the edge of the bed and wrapped my arms around myself, as if I was in shock.

"Otar," Gaelin muttered.

"I thought you killed the bastard. How is he alive?" asked Levos.

"I don't know. His body was missing this morning. I've had men out looking for him and I doubled the guard around the palace, but apparently, he never left. He was inside the entire time," answered Gaelin.

"Why would he stay? I thought you said he was smart. Wouldn't it have been the wiser choice to go and regroup with his armies?" asked Levos.

"I don't know. None of this makes sense," said Gaelin. He paced the room, his face stressed, his body tense from the shock.

"The king is dead," muttered Madison. "Which means you're our new king."

Gaelin looked to her, then to Levos, then to me. "I'm going to go check on the throne room to see if they've captured him yet. You all stay here until I come back. Do not open the door for anyone or anything," instructed Gaelin.

We all nodded. I rushed to him, taking his arm before he could leave.

"Please be careful," I whispered, kissing his cheek softly.

He nodded and then left.

I sank into the couch, waiting to hear if my reaper had been killed. Levos settled Madison into Gaelin's bed before coming and sitting next to me. He didn't look at me.

"This was your vision?" He asked, quiet enough that Madison couldn't overhear.

"What if it was?" I said without an ounce of remorse.

He shook his head. "Not all those alfar were evil like him, Gen. They didn't deserve to die like that."

"Their sacrifice was worth the reward," I said coldly, turning to look at him.

He looked at me with disappointment for the first time. "I know he hurt you, but those alfar—"

"What? Were they nice, civil, merciful even? Does it not please you that some of those alfar who lay dead in that hall right now were the same males who took Madison against her will? Who spat on her? Who beat her? Who looked down upon you? Do you not feel the slightest feeling of satisfaction from their deaths?"

"Who am I to condemn them?"

I crossed my arms and huffed. "You sound like a Christian. Do you realize that?"

"Revenge isn't worth the cost of even one innocent life," he whispered.

"That is where your opinion and mine differ. To me, it was worth all of them," I said coldly, getting up from the couch and moving to the balcony.

Gaelin returned an hour later. We surrounded him for an update.

"The king and queen are dead. Princess...Queen Daealla has survived. We have captured Otar and are holding him for questioning," said Gaelin.

"How many others were lost?" asked Levos.

"Fifty-eight light alfar," replied Gaelin.

"And humans?" asked Madison.

I held my breath.

"None. Not a single one."

I exhaled, fighting a smile. I felt Levos's eyes on me, but I didn't acknowledge his judgment.

"It is safe for you to return to your room. Stay together tonight, just in case." Gaelin said to Levos and Madison. They nodded, taking their leave.

Gaelin collapsed on the bed, looking exhausted and overwhelmed. I went to him, wrapping my arm around his shoulder, trying to provide him with comfort. I kissed his head, running my hand through his smooth white hair.

"I am glad you're okay," I said.

He turned to me, pulling my head to his. "For a moment there, I thought I was going to lose you."

"What do you mean?" I asked.

"There was a moment when I looked up and saw Otar

standing next to you. I thought he was going to tear you to shreds like the others, but he just vanished."

I swallowed, praying he didn't connect the dots.

"It must be your human blood."

"What?"

"Your human blood. He must not kill humans or something along those parameters. It is almost improbable that he didn't kill a single human. Something must prevent him from doing so. I don't know yet, but I will find out. I am just thankful you are okay. I couldn't get to you fast enough. You were just standing there in the middle of it all, not moving. Are you okay? It must have been traumatic to see all of that."

I smiled at him, nodding my head. "I'm okay. I will be okay, I mean," I said, trying to seem casual yet a bit stirred up. "I guess this means you're king now."

He smiled and nodded. "I guess so. It happened faster than I expected, but what's done is done. Too bad Daealla survived," he said.

I chuckled, leaning my head on his shoulders. "Yeah, sorry about that."

"Well, at least one of our problems is taken care of. You'll never be with anyone you don't want again. I promise you that," he said, kissing me on the head.

"Thank you," I whispered, feeling a weight lift off my chest. I was free from King Lysanthier. Truly free.

"I mean it. Even if you don't want to be with me. I won't force you, Gen. You will never be forced again. As long as I live, I promise you that."

I looked up, feeling truly grateful to him. I kissed his lips softly, pulling away with my eyes still locked onto his. "Just give me time, okay. Let's see where the future leads us."

He nodded, leaning his head back onto mine. We sat in the comfort of each other's presence, knowing our future was now changed forever thanks to Otar. Thanks to me.

CHAPTER 25

I slept better than I had ever slept in my entire life that night. When I woke, Gaelin was already gone, interrogating Otar I presumed. I stretched across the bed, enjoying the freedom I had earned. I picked up the small star pendant Gaelin had given me and admired its beauty before kissing it. Freedom was mine. I wasn't handed it. I didn't have to beg for it. A weak, half-breed like me had went out and conquered it. And to my surprise, I was still alive.

I was prepared to die if needed, but the fates had other plans for me apparently. Now, I just had to figure out how to cope with the horror that had been my life for the past few months. I didn't know if I was ever going to be able to enjoy a male's touch again without thinking of King Lysanthier. But that didn't matter now. I could turn my focus back to my mission. Lily.

I went to the bathroom and washed. I stood in front of the mirror for a long while, staring at myself. The first step was being able to look myself in the eye and not be disgusted by the sight. He used and abused me, but that didn't define me. I traced his house's sigil that was branded in my skin. This wasn't a reminder of the pain, but a symbol of my accomplishments. I would overcome this. I had to.

I got dressed and headed down the hall. I walked into the throne room, hesitating with every step. The room was spotless. Unless I had witnessed the event with my own eyes, I wouldn't have known there had been a massacre here the night before. I looked up at the king's empty throne and smiled. He may have been light alfar, but there was nothing good about him. His heart was as black as the dark magic that ran through the dark alfar's veins.

I smiled, remembering his body being ripped to shreds. I stood tall at that moment, relishing one last time in my victory. I turned around and walked out of the throne room, leaving King Lysanthier behind me. I helped with the laundry and in the kitchen, smiling the entire time. The alfar were still recovering and needier than normal. I complied, not making a fuss.

Now that Gaelin was king, I had to make sure I was on my best behavior. I wanted his reign to be an easy one. I didn't want him worrying about me. Sooner or later, he would conceive an heir and then he would fight for my freedom as he promised.

Levos avoided me the rest of the day. I knew he was still mad about my opinions on the events of last night. Gods, what he would have thought of me if he knew the whole truth. He didn't understand. He couldn't. He had never been raped. Yes, watching those you love around you going through it was one thing, but he never had to experience being used in such a foul way. Having something so private and intimate taken from you. Having to suffer the abuse of a tyrant. Levos would eventually forgive me. He just needed time.

I went to clean up before dinner, filthy from the flour I had been using to make bread. I made my way to the throne room with a smile plastered on my face. Crowds of alfar and humans huddled around the doors waiting to be let in. I frowned at the sight, wondering what all the fuss was about. Eventually, we all were allowed in. Queen Daealla and King Atros were seated on the royal thrones.

I made my way back to the wall. There were no trays of food, no wine. I looked at Felicity, asking what was going on with my eyes. She leaned in close, making sure not to attract any unwanted attention.

"The queen demanded that we not serve anyone. Everyone here was in attendance at dinner last night. She believes someone helped the creature kill the others. She's out for blood and she isn't going to stop until she gets it," she whispered.

My heart dropped. I tugged on my sleeve, covering Otar's sigil. I didn't know how dangerous Daealla was. I was too busy fending off her father to worry about her. I knew she was vengeful and reckless, but to what extent, I had no clue.

The doors of the hall closed us in as the last alfar took his seat. The queen stood, Gaelin seated at her side. Her face showed no sign of remorse or fear, only determination. The room went silent. She looked across the crowd of people, noting each of their faces. She snapped her fingers with a single fluent motion.

Two guards came in from behind her, dragging Otar in iron chains. I had to focus on controlling my breathing and facial expressions. I kept my head down, not making eye contact with anyone. The alfar sat stoically silent. I heard the chains rattle as they threw Otar's body in front of the court.

"This is the creature who has taken so much from us," began Daealla. "This creature was slain by my husband over a month ago, yet somehow it kneels before you now, still reeking of our race's blood. In past months, traitors have been discovered among us. Alfar who we believed to be friends turned foe. This creature lay dead under the keep of our kingdom only two days ago. Yesterday, its body went missing and last night it tore through our court like a storm.

"The creature was cut open. Organs were removed. Flesh was taken, yet he sits here... whole. How can this be? He rose from the dead, just like the Christian god has been acclaimed to do. Are you the Christian Jew known as Yahweh?" she asked Otar.

He snickered on the floor, shaking his head from side to side. "Stupid queen," he said, spitting at her feet.

The guard hit him across the face, causing black blood to seep from his mouth.

"I believe someone," she continued, "in this court has betrayed us. They have turned their backs on our race and helped this creature wreak havoc over our houses and over our kingdom, and I will not stop until that person is brought to light." She stepped down in front of Otar, looking at him as if fire could blaze from her eyes. "Who assisted you?" she demanded.

"I didn't tell your pretty king, why am I going to tell you?" he laughed.

She pulled out an iron knife and slashed across his face. He turned his head slowly and licked at the blood with delight.

"You will tell me who helped you or I will torture you slowly for the rest of your immortal life," she said through her teeth. She had a temper, that was for sure. She wasn't calm, cool, and collected like her father had been, before he began to go mad.

"What makes you think that is a punishment? Torture is foreplay, my dear," he said, snapping his teeth at her with a low growl.

She hit him across the face again. "Was it a human or an alfar?" She demanded. "Answer me!" she yelled.

He shrugged. "Human, alfar, maybe both. I don't remember. It was dark and he, she, it, didn't stick around to chat," he said mockingly.

I smiled only for a brief second, reminding myself of the fire I was toying with.

She went to strike him again, but a cold mist came over the hall. Shivers went down my spine as I looked up to see what was happening.

Black fog swept through the room in an instant. The guards pulled Otar back to the platform as others appeared from the sides of the throne and surrounded Queen Daealla. The court began to look at each other frantically. Out of the black mist formed bodies. They appeared into focus one after another. Twelve dark alfar warriors stood in a circle. Erendrial Lyklor appeared last. He did enjoy grand entrances.

Erendrial stepped forward, his long black jacket perfectly pressed. His hands were folded behind his back as that wicked smile stretched across his face. He gave a half bow.

"Queen Daealla, King Atros, first let me say congratulations on the wedding ceremony. Though I am a bit hurt I was not invited." He looked directly at Gaelin. "I thought we had developed a mutual respect the last time I visited."

"How dare you enter this court unannounced. How did you mist through our runes?" demanded Queen Daealla.

"We disarmed them the last time we were here," Erendrial said, winking at her.

"How dare you," she snarled.

"Yes, yes, bad dark alfar, I know," he said mockingly. "Now, please let me continue to extend our condolences on the sudden and unexpected death of your mother and father. What a terrible way to go," he said, looking at Otar. "Our friend here doesn't like to stay dead apparently."

Otar smiled at him.

"What do you want, Ambassador Lyklor?" asked Gaelin.

"My king and our court would like to guarantee we start this new regime on the right foot," continued Erendrial.

"And what have you come to offer?" snapped the queen.

"Actually, I have come to propose a peaceful trade."

Daealla shrieked in amusement. "Of course, you have. Gods forbid you come to offer something without anything in return," she said.

Erendrial shrugged. "What can I say? I'm a businessman at heart." He held her gaze.

"What do you want?" she asked.

"We will get to that, but first, let me tell you what I can offer you. I can give you the key to finding the alfar or human who assisted our friend here in the attack on your court," said Erendrial.

My hands began to quiver. *Shit, shit, shit.*

The queen's face went blank as she mulled over the offer.

"For what in return?" Gaelin finally asked.

Erendrial tilted his head, scrunching his face together. "Unfortunately, I can't reveal that yet, but I promise you, *queen*, what we take you will not miss. It is a small price to pay for discovering the traitor in your court, I assure you," he said with certainty.

Queen Daealla looked down at the floor as she thought. Gaelin leaned over and whispered harshly, no doubt trying to talk her out of the deal. Whatever the dark court wanted it couldn't be good. It would hurt the light court in the long run. You couldn't trust a dark alfar, especially Erendrial. Even I knew that.

The queen flung her hand up to Gaelin, whispering something aggressively in his direction. She calmed herself before turning back to Erendrial. She looked at Otar and then nodded at Erendrial. "You have a deal," she said.

Erendrial smiled widely in satisfaction. That same smile I had seen so many times in my visions. "Excellent, onto business then. The accessory to our friend Otar here will have a sigil marked in black on their left wrist. It is an upside-down triangle with an arch going through it, encased in a circle," he said cheerfully.

I began trembling. How could he know? It made no sense. Otar said no one knew about his secrets. I held my left wrist tightly with my right hand as I began to shake. *Get yourself together, Gen. You knew death was an option, now face your fate with dignity.*

"Guards, check each other first and then begin to search the room," demanded Queen Daealla. The guards did as they were told. Ten minutes into the search, they finally began to search the humans. This was it. My end. A guard stood in front of me, grabbing my left wrist with aggression. I brought my eyes up to his and held my head high. He pulled back my sleeve to reveal my sigil.

The guard grabbed me by the neck, carrying me through the rows of tables before throwing me down to the floor in between Daealla, Gaelin, and Erendrial. Gaelin's face went white as the guard held up my wrist to reveal the imprint. Queen Daealla's eyes widened so intensely, I thought they were going to pop from her head. Erendrial folded his arms across his chest, bringing a hand to his mouth as he laughed.

"Well, this is delightfully delicious," Erendrial said behind me.

I glanced at Otar. He looked back with those yellow eyes,

still smiling as if this was all entertainment for him and his life wasn't on the line here either.

"Stupid queen," Otar laughed, looking at me and then back at her, egging her to strike him again.

"You? How?" Daealla yelled. "How did you resurrect the creature? Answer me!"

I stood up, head high, not backing down. I'll be damned if I was going to go out bowing to this bitch. "Not as dumb as you thought, am I?" I replied.

Gaelin moved in between us, trying to defuse the situation. "Queen Daealla, Ambassador Lyklor could be lying. He is known for it," said Gaelin.

"Oh, I assure you this is no lie, though I couldn't have seen this coming no matter how hard I looked," said Erendrial.

"You have no power, so sit down and shut up, king," spat the queen.

Gaelin turned to me, eyes full of fear and worry. I gave him a reassuring smile.

"It's okay. It was worth it," I whispered to him. The guards stepped in front of us, ushering Gaelin back to his seat next to Daealla.

"How, *human*?" Daealla asked me again.

"Just kill me and be done with it. I am not going to tell you a thing," I said, without an ounce of fear in my voice.

She gasped in shock at my disrespect. She looked at Otar and then at me. "You will tell me how you resurrected this thing and how to kill it or I will butcher you where you stand," she demanded.

I looked at Otar again. His face went blank, knowing I had the information that could send him to a permanent grave. His life for mine; what a deal. It wasn't worth it. Living only to be tortured for the rest of my life. I'd rather die. I held my head up high again.

"No," I said.

"No, you don't know how to kill it or no, you won't give me the information I seek?"

"No, I won't give you what you seek. Your father deserved what he got. In my opinion, his suffering ended far too quickly."

The whole court gasped in rage.

Otar started laughing, slapping his hands on his legs. "Wicked, wicked, one," Otar screeched.

The guard hit him to shut him up.

"You stupid girl. You would throw away your life so this thing could live?" Daealla asked.

"I refuse to be kept prisoner by you any longer. And yes, if sacrificing my life and refusing you the key to killing Otar makes you this unhappy, then it is well worth it." I smiled at her, flashing my teeth in a wicked grin I hoped made Otar proud. Little did she know, Otar's life was attached to mine.

She held her head high. "Very well. Guards, kill the human," she said without feeling.

Gaelin jumped from his seat but was restrained by three guards that stood near him. Four guards approached me swiftly, swords drawn, ready to remove my head from my shoulders. I closed my eyes, welcoming the cold edge of the blade.

"Leenia," I heard Erendrial say calmly from behind me. Suddenly, an explosion of force and wind ripped through the room as something heavy smashed into the distance. I opened my eyes to see the four guards slammed up against the exterior walls, held there by nothing. I turned around and looked back at the alfar Erendrial had called to. She was tall and thin. Her black hair was cropped into a neat bob that ended at her shoulders. Her black leather was tight on her body. She was covered in daggers, swords, and an ax at her waist. Her entrancing red eyes glowed as she held out her hands towards the guards, her stance effortless. She smiled and dropped her hands, sending the four guards to the floor unconscious.

Erendrial began to move towards the thrones, hands casually folded behind his back. He looked directly at Daealla and smirked as he tilted his head to the side. "Yeah, about that," he said, stepping in front of me. The circle of dark alfar encased me, leaving Erendrial on the outside to combat Queen Daealla's wrath.

CHAPTER 26

"You are out of line, Ambassador Lyklor," snapped Queen Daealla. "How dare you assault my guards in my own court and interfere with matters that are none of your concern."

"In any other situation," Erendrial began, "I would allow you to kill whatever human offended you, but you can't kill this one."

"Who are you to tell me what I can and can't do? We made a deal. Take whatever you want and leave the girl to me," she yelled.

He put his hands out to the side and shrugged. "Yeah, see, this is where this whole thing gets a little hairy. The girl you want to kill is actually the thing I came for," he said.

My mouth dropped. What could he want with me? Was it because of my visions? Did he want to use me to get the upper hand on the light court?

"You are not taking her anywhere!" yelled Gaelin.

Erendrial began to laugh. "Would you rather I leave her here so your wife can gut her? Dear Gaelin, weigh your options. In this case, I am her savior in a sense. Something you have clearly failed at time and time again."

"You are not taking her. She is responsible for the death of our king and countless other lives. She will face the consequences of her actions and die for her betrayal," said the queen.

Erendrial exhaled in annoyance. "I really hate to repeat myself, but since you're new to all of this, I will," he stopped, exhaling in annoyance as he shifted his weight from one side to another. "We made a bargain. I revealed the traitor, and you will allow me to take what my king desires. It is unfortunate for you that the traitor and the thing that I came to retrieve are one and the same, but that is not my problem."

"The bargain is broken. It is clearly stated in our laws that if a human is found guilty of an attack or the death of one of our own, they will be sentenced to death. Our law negates anything you or your king wants. Justice must be paid. She is my subject, which makes her mine to do whatever I wish with," Daealla yelled in frustration.

"Oh, wow. This is a very busy and embarrassing first day for you," Erendrial said sarcastically. "But I am afraid you are wrong again. First, let me make myself explicitly clear on one thing... *you will not lay a hand on her*. Second, you've been fooled sweetheart, she isn't human, therefore, she is *not* your property. Thirdly, and probably the most important correction to that little speech of yours...she isn't your subject. She is King Drezmore's. She belongs to the dark court, which means her protection falls under my jurisdiction."

I stumbled back, shocked at what I was hearing. I shook my head. No, this couldn't be. *What the hell? What in the actual hell?*

The court gasped again as they began to talk amongst themselves, trying to figure out what was going on. I looked at Gaelin, not knowing what to do. He looked at Erendrial and then at me, shaking his head in complete shock. The court quieted as the queen looked from Erendrial to me.

"What is she?" Daealla asked.

Erendrial smiled, turning to walk back to me. He stood in front of me, locking his swirling silver eyes onto mine, reaching for my headband. I shook my head, desperate for him to stop. He winked at me and then took the headband off. He pushed my hair back around my ears, revealing the inadequate points. The whole court roared in rage, demanding I be slaughtered on the spot.

I didn't understand any of this. The dark alfar had the same laws when it came to half-breeds. They were to be put down to keep the races pure. Why would he out me? Did he just want to take me back to the dark court as a sick joke and have his king kill me there? I dropped my eyes to the floor, thinking of all the horrible ways they would punish and torture me back at his court. It was a fate worse than death. I had done this. I had let Erendrial see who I really was. I knew it was going to come back and bite me in the ass. The crowd was yelling and screaming for my head.

Erendrial lifted my chin with his fingers, taking my eyes with his.

"Head held high, remember. You will never bow again," he said, nodding at me. He took my arm gently, bringing me to the front of his guarded circle. He looked around, waiting for the crowd to quiet down, still holding onto my arm.

Finally, the room fell into silence.

"We have the same law in regard to things like her. She is to be put down immediately," said Queen Daealla.

Erendrial let go of my arm, stepping back to look at me with a smile on his face. "May I present, for the first time, Princess Genevieve Drezmore, sole heir to the Kingdom of Doonak," Erendrial said proudly.

I felt like the wind had just been knocked out of me. The light alfar went crazy, yelling, and flailing like children. The twelve dark alfar warriors bowed to one knee, still in their circle formation. Erendrial bowed, smiling as he looked upon me from under his eyelashes.

I shook my head, not understanding. Was this some type of joke? I looked at Gaelin trying to find the words, but there were none. No, my father couldn't be King Drezmore. I was not the heir to the court of horrors. This wasn't happening.

"Silence!" yelled the queen.

The dark alfar stood to attention as did Erendrial.

"What game are you playing? She cannot ascend to the dark throne. She is a half-breed. She should never have been permitted to take a single breath."

"I don't have to answer any of your questions, *queen*. All you need to know is that she is the daughter of King

Drezmore. He has claimed her as his own and declared her heir to his throne, which negates any law you wish to enforce upon her," said Erendrial.

Queen Daealla's temper was at its peak. "Guards!" she yelled.

Two rows of guards marched into the throne room from the hall. They surrounded the dark alfar, ready to attack when given the signal. The dark alfar warriors readied their weapons, crouching down into attack position.

Erendrial watched as they circled us. He laughed, placing me behind him gently.

"She is not going anywhere," snarled Daealla. "I do not care who she is or what your king has deemed her. She will pay for her deception with her life."

"I love that you think taking her life is even an option. I am going to have to agree with our friend here," Erendrial said, tilting his head to Otar, "stupid queen." He paused, waiting for the insult to take root. His methods were masterful. "I promise you that if you attack our princess here and now, you will be ending your own life in the process. She will survive and then her father will turn over every last stone of this palace, not resting until every light alfar is sent to Valhalla. You forget who you are dealing with," he said, baring his teeth as he walked slowly towards her. His patience appeared to be wearing thin.

He raised one hand slightly, twisting it ever so slowly. The queen doubled over in pain, gasping for air. Veins bulged from her neck and forehead as I watched her wither in agony and discomfort. Otar spat laughter louder than any other sound in the throne room, throwing himself to the ground and rolling from side to side like a dog. The guards approached, but were frozen in place, unable to move a second later. Two dark alfar, twins, spread their arms on either side of the circle, keeping the guards stationary. Erendrial dropped his hand, allowing the queen to breathe freely. She held her chest in pain. The light alfar from the high families rose to their feet, moving behind the queen in a defensive position.

Queen Daealla rose, waiting for all her subjects to join her side. The dark alfar were heavily outnumbered, but somehow, I'd bet they'd be the last ones standing. She looked down at Erendrial. She was reckless, but she wasn't stupid. She would die if this thing took a turn for the worse. She had just come into her power; she didn't want her reign to end like this. She stood tall, looking from me to Erendrial once more.

"Take her and leave," she said in a hoarse voice.

Erendrial smiled, clapping his hands together in satisfaction. "Excellent. I am glad you saw the error of your ways and agreed to uphold our bargain after all. Very wise for such a stupid queen," said Erendrial, taking my arm to escort me back into the circle. I stopped him, looking back at Otar. He followed my eyes and exhaled in frustration but nodded. "Our princess would like to take Otar with us. Consider this an apology for trying to kill her majesty."

The queen grumbled, nodding to the guard. Otar walked towards us. I went to meet him, but Erendrial stopped me.

"It's okay. He won't hurt me," I said to him. I walked over to Otar. "The keys," I demanded to the guard. He threw them on the floor. I released the cuffs on Otar and looked at him. "Thank you for what you did."

"I had no choice in the matter, though I did enjoy it thoroughly. I'm curious though, why did you not give away my secret?" asked Otar.

"Just because I know your secret doesn't mean it's mine to give away."

He smiled at me, genuinely for the first time.

"Would you consider coming with me?" I asked.

"I don't have a choice," he said.

"Well, I am giving you one now," I replied.

He tilted his head to the side. "I guess your wicked mind is better than the other prison I was in. I will come with you, wicked princess," he said, smiling at me.

"Thank you, but you can't kill anyone unless I give you permission. Or hurt anyone," I added.

"Where did the wicked girl go who dreamed of me tearing out the king's throat?" He laughed, moving behind me.

I never spoke to anyone about the methods in which I envisioned the king dying. Was he in my head? Could he read my mind? I stood up, staring down the queen. My gaze turned to Gaelin. I wanted more than anything to talk to him in private one last time, but I knew there wasn't time. I turned away from my shining knight.

Erendrial led Otar and I into the protective circle. I looked around at the dark alfar that had bowed a knee to me.

I still didn't believe this was happening. This had to be some sick joke.

"Oh," said Erendrial, turning back to face the queen one more time. "One more thing," he said with a bitter tone. He snapped his fingers in the air, twisting his wrist in a quick motion.

An arrow shot from one of his warriors, landing on Daealla's chest, on the right side, below her collar bone. She gasped as the alfar around her took a step towards us. She pulled the sizzling marker from her chest, revealing a ulyrium stamp at the end of the arrow. Her skin was branded with a crescent moon that held a nine-pointed star inside the outline. I touched my necklace.

"The Drezmore sigil. I thought it only fitting, since you thought it was okay to brand our princess with yours."

"I didn't know she was your princess," she snarled under her breath.

"Well, now you will never forget, will you?" said Erendrial.

I smiled, taking a moment of happiness out of her pain.

Erendrial turned towards me, reaching for my arms. I stepped away, still scared of him. He laughed. "Princess," he whispered tenderly, "you have nothing to fear. I am going to mist you out of the castle. You may feel a bit dizzy, but it will pass. I just need for you to hold on, so I don't drop you in the middle of the light guard."

"Otar, follow us, please," I said before Erendrial wrapped his arms around me. I reached around his broad frame, unable to clasp my hands together. I slowly placed the side of my cheek on his chest, smelling the faint scent of oranges and whiskey. His grip tightened as I closed my eyes, readying myself for anything.

I felt the air around me thin as my body felt like it was being pulled apart at every seam. I gritted my teeth at the feeling, holding onto him for dear life. In another moment we were outside in a field beyond the light court's borders. I felt dizzy and sick, letting go of him and falling to the ground. He laughed at me, walking towards me to offer a hand. Everything was spinning. He caught my arm, pulling me to my feet.

"Deep breaths; it will pass," he instructed.

I pulled away from him, readying myself for the other shoe to drop. "What joke is this? What are you going to do with me?" I asked.

He shook his head, closing the distance between us. "This isn't a joke, Genevieve. You are the princess and heir to the Kingdom of Doonak."

"Why leave me in there then? Why let them use me like they did?" I demanded.

"Your father will explain all of that to you when we arrive at the dark court."

"No, tell me now or I will have Otar kill me. I refuse to leave one court only to be tortured and abuse in another," I snapped.

He looked at me curiously. "You control the creature?"

"Yes."

"How?" he asked.

"Tell me what I want to know!" The other alfar acted like they weren't listening as they misted in from the palace.

Erendrial exhaled. "Your father has been unable to produce an heir with the queen, or any other alfar female, for that matter. He is at the end of his lifespan and did not know of your existence. Once you crossed the border a few months back, you were revealed to our seer, and she was able to see your true lineage. She told your father of this, yet he was hesitant to believe it. He's been desperate for an heir for centuries and because you are a half-breed, he was wary of how the other alfar would react.

"He needed to make sure that you were who the seer said, so he used the Otar attack as an excuse to send me to court to see if you were who we thought." He paused, looking at me in silence for a few moments. "Your eyes are a dead give-away. I've never seen another alfar's eyes that color except for your father. Then, when you revealed your gift to me before the battle, I was certain you were who the seer said. When King Lysanthier," I winced at the name, "had your hand smashed, I took a sample of your blood and sent it back to the dark court to get tested. It was a match to the kings. You are his daughter."

"Again, you just left me there," I said, angered at the events that happened with King Lysanthier after the dark court left the first time. If they would have taken me then, I would have been able to avoid the hell I had yet to figure out how to escape.

"We had to. If we were to pull you from the court at that moment, King Lysanthier wouldn't have allowed it.

Especially knowing he had King Drezmore's heir in his possession. We had to get rid of him so Daealla would take the throne. Though she is quite the beauty, she is new to all of this. I had no right in taking you just now. I lied to her to make her believe we had the upper hand."

"So, what was the plan?"

"The plan was to wait until the king died of what looked like natural causes."

"I could have been stuck there for centuries!" I yelled in anger.

He laughed. "No, princess. We accelerated that timeline. Before we left the light court, I had a warrior of mine curse the king with madness. One of the many gifts we possess. He would have slowly appeared to be losing his mind. Eventually, the sickness would have taken over, leaving him brain dead. He would have died in his sleep, and no one would have been the wiser about it. Though, I liked your flair for the dramatic much better. I'm going to have to watch out for you. I think I've found my match."

I folded my arms over my chest, trying to block out the images of the king on top of me. Erendrial looked at me concerningly.

"He went mad and became a psychopath because of you?" I asked.

"Yes. When Daealla took the throne, we planned to sweep in and claim you. We were quite surprised when we heard of the Otar attack."

"Is that how you knew about the sigil, connecting us? Because of your seer?"

"Yes. Her gift is very similar to yours. I think you two are going to get along splendidly. During the time we had to wait for the light king to go mad, your father worked to eliminate the law about half-breeds being sentenced to death. Once he did that, he announced your claim to the throne. I must warn you; you have an uncle and three cousins who were not thrilled to learn of your existence, but we can deal with that at a later time. Now, we should get you to your father," he said, walking away.

"Thank you," I said before he got too far. "For saving my life... again."

He stopped, turning back to me. "I think I am up by one with the whole life-saving game." He smiled back at me.

"I can tell Otar to kill you and then stop him right before he delivers the final blow. Then we'd be even," I said, trying to comfort myself with humor.

He laughed at me. "Evil little thing, aren't you."

I shrugged. "I don't like losing," I admitted.

"Another thing you and your father have in common." He brought a whistle-shaped instrument to his lips that I recognized from his last departure. Seven ragamors descended from the sky, slamming into the ground around us. Otar flashed in next to me, causing me to jump. He looked at the beasts with disgust.

"I am not riding one of those things, wicked one," he grumbled deep in his throat.

I laughed. "Meat suit, wicked one. Can't you just use my name?" I asked.

"No," he spat shortly.

I shook my head. "Just follow us to the dark court. We'll discuss your living arrangements once I figure out all this mess."

He nodded, disappearing into thin air.

"Come on, princess. It's time for your first flying lesson," Erendrial said, walking towards one of the ragamor.

I followed, moving around the creature to examine its fascinating form. I followed the shifting colors of its armored hide, remembering the scales of the only other ragamor I had encountered back in the lavender field. I walked to the front of the creature, looking on its face. I smiled, realizing it was the same ragamor. The beast nuzzled my neck, just as it had the first time we met. I laughed, taking its face in my hands.

"Well, hello again," I said.

"Again?" asked Erendrial.

"We've met before. The day you first arrived at the light court for the battle," I said.

Erendrial smiled, looking at the ragamor, patting her on the neck. "Eeri old girl, are you cheating on me? After all these decades," he said playfully to her.

She made a low grunt reaching her neck to the sky. She slowly lowered her body. Erendrial climbed on her back, reaching his hand out to me. I hesitated for so many reasons. One, I didn't trust him. There was a darkness about him that told everything inside of me to run. Two, he was escorting me to the court of horrors and torture where I would have to witness humans being brutalized even more than what I had experienced at the light court. Three, I was about to ride a dragon creature. I didn't like heights. The list went on and on.

"Princess, we're losing daylight," he said, reaching down for me.

I took a deep breath, extending my hand to him. His strong grip pulled me to Eeri's back. I sat in front of him, between his legs. I shivered at the feeling of a man this close to me. I shifted uncomfortably, trying to get away from him. I felt his body still behind me.

"Are you going to be okay?" he asked bluntly.

"Yeah, I just don't like physical contact is all." Not a lie, but not the complete truth.

"Could have fooled me. The last time I saw you, you were practically naked in Gaelin's chambers."

"Shut up, you don't know what you're talking about," I snapped.

He laughed, taking a knife, and slitting a gash in each of his palms. "I'm sorry to make you uncomfortable, but I am going to have to lean over you to get us home. I need to fly Eeri here and I also need to make sure you don't fall from the sky to your death. Your father would have my skin peeled off if I let that happen."

A shiver ran up my spin as he leaned against my back, sliding both bloodied hands into small slits in the back of Eeri's scales at the base of her neck.

"What?" I asked in surprise and curiosity.

"It's how we control them. Our blood bonds with them, allowing me to tell her where to go and how to fly. Don't worry, you will learn." He leaned forward, tucking me underneath him. "If it makes the trip a little more bearable, I have a certain human waiting for you as soon as we arrive. I thought she'd make your homecoming a little easier."

"Lily," I said as a smile stretched across my face.

Eeri shot into the sky with a force I had never experienced before in my life. The wind was ripped from my lungs, and I fought to breath. Erendrial's body smashed down on top of me, keeping me from sliding off the smooth scales. Eeri eased up as we soared into the clouds, traveling towards the sunset on the horizon. Her wings stretched out, creating a beautiful kite-like effect.

As she steadied out on top of the clouds, Erendrial eased up on my back, keeping his hands in the slits hidden beneath her scales. I peered out into the pink and orange sunset. The sky was tranquil and peaceful. The only sound I heard was Eeri's wings flapping slightly as she navigated the wind. I smiled, touching my star pendant with my fingers. I inhaled, taking in the clear air.

"Freedom."

ABOUT THE AUTHOR

Jessica Ann Disciacca, an Italian American from Kansas City, Missouri, holds a Master's in Educational Leadership from Northwest Missouri State University (2023). Graduating in 2015 from Park University with a diverse Bachelor's degree, she now pursues a career in educational administration while teaching.

    Beyond her professional life, Jessica is an avid artist and writer, finding solace in family moments. Her lifelong passion for literature and storytelling led her to debut as an author with "Awakening the Dark Throne."

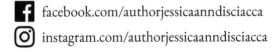

facebook.com/authorjessicaanndisciacca
instagram.com/authorjessicaanndisciacca

Acknowledgments

To my dear friend Kara, whom without, this book wouldn't be possible. I know no matter what life throws at me, you will always be there, ready to give me the most honest advice. I admire you in so many ways.

To my husband Joe, for supporting me through this journey and encouraging me to never give up. Thank you for supporting me through endless hours of editing, reading, and writing.

To my daughters, Aurora and Freya. You two are my guiding stars in the darkest of nights. Everything I do is for you two.

- Jessica Ann Disciacca

Printed in the USA
CPSIA information can be obtained
at www.ICGtesting.com
CBHW082129130724
11461CB00022B/524